A Call to Sarah

Helen Iles

A catalogue record for this book is available from the National Library of Australia

Copyright © 2024 Helen Iles
All rights reserved.
ISBN-13: 978-1-923174-35-1

Linellen Press
265 Boomerang Road
Oldbury, Western Australia
www.linellenpress.com.au

Dedication

To my family, for all your patience and support
while I fed my imagination.
My love to you all always.

Contents

Dedication iii
Contents v
Prelude 1
In Jessie's Hand 6
Chapter One 1
Chapter Two 12
Chapter Three 16
Chapter Four 25
Chapter Five 29
Chapter Six 37
Chapter Seven 44
Chapter Eight 54
Chapter Nine 60
Chapter Ten 72
Chapter Eleven 92
Chapter Twelve 110
Chapter Thirteen 128
Chapter Fourteen 136
Chapter Fifteen 151
Chapter Sixteen 164
Chapter Seventeen 167
Chapter Eighteen 203
Chapter Nineteen 219
Epilogue 224

Prelude

The decrepit sign on the gate read WHISTLING GUMS and looked as old as the gate itself, the wire holding it on now flimsy with rust and as red as the metal gate frame that held it. The gate itself no longer swung on the gatepost, having long ago fused with age to its hinges, so Jessie was forced to climb over. Nothing would stop her intrusion onto the property this day, not even the spiky nettles that tangled about on either side of the narrow path on the barrier's other side. The nettles snagged at her jeans as she climbed, the long tendrils seeming to grab her each time she carefully prised them off, annoying her no end as it was some time before she could freely continue her trek into the valley. Looking back with suspicion, she truly believed those vines had tried to bar her way.

Had that daunting feeling washed over her a short time earlier, she might have listened and gone no further. She might have listened to the gate and remembered the events of the past. But she hadn't: she'd forced aside those disturbing feelings, those stinging thorns, and pushed on, desperate to see the old farmhouse at the end of the path. She had seen it before, a long time ago, and again in photographs in her mother's family album. Now she just had to see it again. Surprisingly though, she felt guilty, for her mother had always warned her never to go there. But, like any inquisitive child, when those words had prodded her fiercely as she'd straddle the gate, she'd ignored them.

Her mother was gone now, her last gasping words uttered in absolute anguish: "The farm is yours, child, but you must never go there!"

"What's the point then?" she'd shot back at her, irrespective of her mother's flagging will to live. "What is the point if I can never go there!"

"*Never!* Do you hear me? *NEVER!* ..." They had been her final words.

Whistling Gums, the ancestral home, had been in the family for more generations than Jessica could remember. Her mother had never revisited the place since Jesse's father died there, and often Jesse had wondered why. She had even asked her mother the reason, but it was a subject her mother refused to talk about, and, like any normal, growing child, Jesse had eventually lost interest, and its absence in conversation had swept it from her mind.

Now she trod the narrow path down through the thick belt of trees that ringed the property, heading purposefully down into the valley where she knew the cottage stood. Alone, according to photographs she'd seen, it sat along the righthand fork, slightly on the rise of the hill.

Chilled by the spirits of that thick, wide strip of foreboding timber, Jesse finally stepped into sunlight and looked down onto the vast, pastured clearing thick with wild grass. And there below, on the downward slope to the valley, was the briar-covered shack. A compulsion to go forward dragged her on, and she didn't fight it. In fact, her heart pounded fiercely with excitement.

That no one had been on the place in God knew how long didn't bother her, and she pondered deeply over what her mother had found so disturbing to refuse every request she'd made to go there. It had to be more than her brother John's untimely demise, for it had been a lifetime of excuses she'd endured. "I just want to walk about the farm," she'd often said;

that would have been enough. "What harm can come from wandering along the boundaries just to see the extent of the property?" – the property she now owned.

She'd already done that – partway at least – albeit from the outer fence line. The fences looked in such a sad state of repair she wondered if she could ever afford to replace them.

After just over an hour of walking back and forth along the wire barrier, always finding herself drawn back to the rusted front gate, the voice niggling inside her head had become too strong to resist. So she'd ignored her mother's warning and climbed over.

Now, as she stood looking down over the rustic little house that could barely have contained a few small rooms, the voice came again – many voices this time, and they were singing in beautiful harmony.

"Come, Sarah ... come ... come."

The soothing melody drifted around her on the wind, and she obeyed, completely entranced with the glorious, lilting tune of words that cushioned her footfalls on the long-untrodden path to the valley. As the cottage loomed larger, her heart leapt with anticipation of seeing where her mother's life had begun – because she sadly missed her so, even though their arguments over the past year had cleaved an irreparable rift between them. The conflict tore at the very heart of her being, for she had no one else in her life ... Well, she had Ryan, and their dear son Jade, of course, but she and that little boy were the last of the Sanderson clan – the last living members of William Kenton Fintish Sanderson's bloodline. Somehow, she felt it was him calling her forward, *his* voice singing deeper and more resonant than the rest. It was him she obeyed the most.

And then she was there, the cottage standing before her, so badly battered by the elements and suffering its dismal neglect; she knew she would be the one to repair the damage time had vented on it. Inside her head, he told her she had to. And, as she stood boldly before the warped, misshapen door, she nodded amiably, not the slightest concern for what Ryan might say of her plans: Ryan would not pose a problem – he would not be allowed to.

"Come in, Sarah," the voice came again, its beautiful tone deep and stirring, making her heart beat faster.

She pushed open the barrier, surprised that it moved with minimum resistance after all these years, and entered the cottage; she scanned the room in all directions, hoping to locate that vibrant sound and the man to whom it belonged. She knew he would be charming, a handsome man with steel grey eyes and a harsh profile that told of a hard life, yet he had an underlying warmth he could bestow if one was so generous as to please him.

She could not see him in that gloomy room, the sun barely penetrating the density of bracken on the eastern wall. She wondered if perhaps he was concealed by the gossamer greyness of the chamber, or was he deliberately standing in the shadows, making her seek him out? She would not be drawn into his trap.

The meekest of smiles formed in Jesse's eyes and on her lips, and a quiver of excitement rose from deep in her core. She trembled nervously.

"Sailor?" It was her voice this time, she noted … *yet not my voice*. She could feel his nearness, his warmth radiating.

"Jessie, leave this place! Leave *NOW!!*"

The harsh words hissed in her ear, their urgency snapping the strange aura from about her. It broke through the many chanting voices until she recognised that one voice in particular. Then she wanted to cry. "Mother? ..."

"Leave this place ...!" the words ordered again. "Go! Run, child. Run for your life!"

Her mother sounded so frightened, her words barely a hiss, and Jessie grew afraid at their utterance.

"MARTHA!" It was his voice again, angry now, and she heard her mother whimper like a scolded child.

Turning, Jessie ran. She fled the tiny cottage on the side of the hill, turning back only once as if in urgent need to find him. She heard his lonesome wail calling her back, and, as she felt the urge to do just that, a sudden wall of air blew through her, and she bolted away again up the hill, not daring to stop until she'd exited the trees and scaled the gate like a quivering, frightened gazelle. Only then did she turn, her lungs burning for air, her side tearing deeply with stitch.

Inside the fence line, the treetops started swaying in the breezeless afternoon, a gentle whistling coming from their leaves, and she heard him call again.

He called her 'Sarah'.

In Jessie's Hand

What does life hold for Jessie Kendall?
Born one day, yet has no belonging
Now to her teens she has come grown,
Yet still without a soul she's sighing.

Time will heal that dreadful longing,
Time will come to make a stand
Never fear, soul's time is coming
And I hold Jessie's soul in my hand.

by Jessica Kendall
13 years old.
18/12/76

Chapter One

7th November, 1991

Dusk had fallen by the time Jessie pulled into her Mosman driveway and stepped from the car. She stood a moment watching the golden glow of evening draping itself over the radiant rose blooms surrounding the sprawling two-storey house, then swept her gaze over the beautiful old home that had been in the family since before she was born, since even before her brother John was born. He would have been thirty-nine next birthday had he not died a year ago. Even though he was a good ten years her senior, she missed him terribly.

The neighbourhood, which skirted Port Jackson, was an old one that had, in its time, been the elite suburb for Sydney's wealthy. The house looked much like others on the city's perimeter yet had weathered well over the years and was still considered prime real estate. For that reason, she and Ryan had moved into her mother's house and put their own home up for rent. Her mother's home was by far the larger of the two, and, though old-fashioned in many respects, it suited their purpose: they had ample room for themselves, their young son, and their regular guest Leesa when she came down from Brisbane University. Leesa was down now, the small, green, hired Fiat in the driveway next to Ryan's station wagon indicating she was in. Jessie felt a sudden urge to go inside and hear how her day had been.

Leaving dusk behind her, she climbed the six curved steps to the wide porch and went inside. Through the large French doors in the foyer, she immediately noted Ryan in the lounge room sitting cross-legged on the floor, playing with Jade, their son mirroring his father's image of blond hair and bright blue eyes. They pushed about the allotment of new toys Leesa repeatedly spoilt Jade with, but Jessie didn't mind. Leesa had no children of her own, and Jessie often wondered who gained more pleasure from those impromptu gifts – her wee blue-eyed baby boy, her bigger blue-eyed babe, or Leesa for hunting the stores to buy them.

Ryan looked up as she entered, his jaw setting as he shot a look her way. "Where the hell have you been all day?" he demanded, putting Jade aside with a colourful block to keep him amused. He stood and went forward. "I've been worried sick! ... thought you'd had an accident or something!"

Jessie shrugged. She was home now, so it was obvious she hadn't. She looked back at him with what she hoped was surprise, but didn't answer. She was, after all, later than she'd said she'd be.

"So? Where have you been all this time?! You're three hours late!"

"I got waylaid,' she said bluntly. "Got held up ... and the traffic was simply awful, bottled up all the way out of town."

"Not for three hours it wasn't, Jesse! Now, where were you?!"

She heaved a sigh, but knew his worry. She hadn't been herself since her mother's death – another reason why he'd agreed to move back into the family home – he worried about her mental state. *I'm alright though,* she nodded inwardly. *And the moments of depression are getting less ... I just miss Mother so much ... and I don't burst into tears at the drop of a hat as often.* She was just glad they didn't know how close she had sometimes wanted to be to her mother.

Those unpremeditated breakdowns had caused Ryan to take a leave of absence from his government job – for medical reasons, he'd told them – Jessie's, not his – but he hadn't told them that. She was alright, of course, but Ryan worried so.

Sometimes Jessie wondered if he could even begin to fathom what she was going through: his own family were so close and supportive. Hers, in the last few years, had sadly drifted apart, been torn apart by arguments since Jade's birth, even more so since John's death. And just when she had needed her mother the most, the woman had turned away and built a strong wall around herself, and that had hurt deeply. John was gone: tragically killed when lightning struck the farm gate as he climbed over almost a year ago. And now, her mother was gone too.

Jessie didn't think she would ever recover from John's death. Oh, she and her mother had tried to pull together for a long while after the tragic day; they had stayed close and had almost gotten along. Then the arguments started again, and her mother had slipped into non-sensibility, her mind wandering first, followed by the shrinking of her slender upright frame. By the time Jessie had noticed, it had been too late. Her mother had simply withered away and left her behind.

Oh, why hadn't I noticed earlier? she often grilled herself. *Had I been too deep in my own grief over John … over our senseless arguments?* Tears filled her eyes, and she swallowed hard. *If only I had noticed sooner …*

Ryan's arms wrapped around her. "Jesse," he said. "Oh, Jesse, what am I to do with you?"

Her head fell against his shoulder, and she shrugged. "I just needed to drive," she admitted sullenly, her throat tightening. "So I did. I found myself on the Great Western Highway and just kept going."

His arms increased their pressure, and he drew her closer, his concern deepening. She didn't want it to. He'd already suffered too much on her account, and besides, she really did feel much better today. The drive had done wonders ... getting back to nature and all. She looked up at him, the tears now gone. "And Ryan ..."

He looked down at her.

"... I feel fine. It really did me the world of good."

Yet, even though her tone had cheered, he frowned deeply.

"Honestly, I don't know why, but I feel great. I really feel great! I stopped at this little road-house down near Lake Oberon, and sat for about an hour, had a cup of coffee and then drove on back. And I feel great! I really do." His face warmed to the keenness in her eyes, to the brightness of her voice. "I'm sorry if I worried you."

His hug tightened further, strong, warm and loving. "Just ring me next time, will you?!" She nodded. Then he released his hold, his anger fully dissipated.

Leesa stood in the doorway, watching them, her expression warm, the tea towel in her hand, and the divine smell coming from the kitchen a clear indication she had taken over Jessie's duties and prepared the evening meal. Jessie looked forward to it – Leesa was a good cook, something Jessie envied her for.

Returning to Jade, Ryan flattened his length on the floor and lifted Jade onto his stomach, while Jessie followed Leesa down the hall to the kitchen. She needed to talk.

"And how was *your* day?" she asked Leesa.

"Fine," Leesa said tautly, heading for and pouring two cups of coffee from the percolator before turning back to her. "And yours?" Her brown eyes held the challenge to tell all.

How can she always tell I have a secret? Jess wondered. Indeed, Leesa could always pick it, right back to when they were incorrigible, giggling teenagers. *Or is it so obvious that something's up, and if so, how come Ryan couldn't see it?* She thanked God he hadn't.

Moving to the window, she peered out to the yard, not interested in anything out there; she just needed to move closer to her friend. "I went to the farm today," she whispered.

Leesa's jaw dropped. Wiping her hands on the towel, she turned to face her, her expression tightening.

"Don't panic! I just wandered about for an hour then came on back. It's a beautiful place, Leesa. So beautiful."

"Why didn't you tell Ryan that's what you did?"

Jess shrugged. "I don't want to worry him further: and he was happy enough with what I told him."

"And?" Leesa delved further.

"And what? I went there ... I walked around for a while then drove on back. What else is there?"

Leesa shrugged this time. An anti-climax. "Tea will be ready soon," she said.

"I'll call Ryan." But as she turned to leave, her gaze drifted back out the window to the tall gum trees in the yard swaying in the evening breeze. "Sarah's such a nice name, isn't it?" she said, musing over it as she left the room.

As she reached the doorway, she stopped and frowned. *Why did I just say that? I don't even like the name Sarah.* Indeed, all the Sarahs she'd ever known had been harsh, selfish, compassionless people. Her lips pursed and she shook her head, trying to shake the thought away. It didn't matter. She felt too good at the moment to let anything matter anymore.

Absently, she turned to the calendar on the wall between the overhead cupboards. Lifting the pages, she took the pen that hung like a felon from its noose and circled the thirteenth of December. She didn't know why.

That night they ate in the dining room, which they usually did when Leesa visited. Otherwise, it was an unbearable crush at the corner nook in the kitchen where Ryan and Jessie usually ate to be close to Jade in the high chair on the lino tiles. The pleasant evening was further enhanced when Jade downed his supper without the usual raucous ordeal then almost immediately fell asleep in his chair, the three unaware for a while until his silence alerted them. Ryan carried him upstairs and tucked him in, returning a short while later to announce that 'the babe was down for the count!' Jessie sensed Ryan had deliberately worn Jade out during the day and told Ryan and Leesa to take a break while she took care of the dishes. She did so alone, whistling as she scraped and stacked, sudsed and dried.

Ryan and Leesa withdrew to the lounge room. Jessie could hear their muffled exchanges across the distance and smiled: it was great they got along so well, which was not always the case in most marriages. They, however, had never suffered the jealousy wrangle between boyfriend and girlfriends and sharing of time during their courting. Ryan had been marvellous, accepting Leesa from the beginning and treating her as if she were Jessie's sister. And it wasn't just tolerance; Jessie knew that. He genuinely felt affection for Leesa, and Leesa for him. They were pals from way back – three men in a tub, only it wasn't the butcher, the baker, the candlestick-maker – they were the architect, the stenographer, and the 'Tree-maker', as Ryan often called Leesa, which was better than him mispronouncing genealogist with gynaecologist.

Right now, though, Ryan was on leave; Jessie's skills had been overtaken by motherhood; and Leesa? ... Well, Leesa seemed able to do whatever Leesa wanted to do. Right now, she was working out of Brisbane University but had taken some time off to work on a thesis of some sort, something way over Jessie's head, and Leesa knew not to bother saying too much about it. Jessie had been baffled when, straight from high school, Leesa had opted to study Sociology and the origins of family life. She was still surprised Leesa was so hooked on it, though she remembered her mother had often sat and listened to Leesa prattle on about her work, that she'd become fascinated by the various methods one could trace one's history. Her mother had even delved into her family roots for a while but then dropped off onto other things, as she usually did. With Leesa frequently away, having won grants to continue her research and studies, her mother had eventually stopped delving and talking about the family history.

And Jessie? Well, after high school, she'd secured an excellent job in the city; was promoted to 'top floor', and met Ryan. A year and a bit later, they married, and a year after that, they made Martha Kendall ecstatic by announcing Jade's impending arrival.

So here they were now, a happy little family – albeit with Leesa back and Mother gone – sharing a quiet evening at home. Leesa and Ryan had their heads together in conversation when Jessie came through with the coffees. They looked up as she entered and dropped their discussion. Leesa's attention returned to her book until her cup was empty, then she closed it and said goodnight, leaving Jessie and Ryan to their own time.

"Going to bed with Dear Diary?" Jessie teased as Leesa headed for the stairs.

"Naturally," came the theatrical retort. Leesa gave her short black hair a good tousle for bedtime comfort as she climbed the stairs. "Can't miss Dear Diary now, can we?"

Leesa's journals dated back to before Jessie met her – for her memoirs when she became famous, Leesa had always joked, and like a good friend, Jessie had let it go. She knew that sometimes she even featured in the entries.

Leesa padded up the stairs and was gone, and Ryan and Jesse were alone, one of those rare nights when Jade had been a good boy, and the phone hadn't rung to disturb their peace. Jessie folded her long legs up on the lounge, sighed as Ryan's arm slipped around her shoulders, and snuggled in.

"You do seem so much happier," he noted, looking fondly down at her.

"Oh, I am," she sighed again, meeting his blue eyes with honesty. "Today, I'm sure is the turning point, Ryan. Today I feel alive again."

He kissed the top of her head and said no more, though Jessie sensed the tension that had invariably accompanied him of late had suddenly gone.

That night, late into the darkest hours, Jessie lay awake, staring at the ceiling. Her thoughts dwelt on the day and why she hadn't told Ryan where she'd gone – she usually told Ryan everything. Keeping secrets was just something they didn't do.

By the first grey of dawn, and still without sleep, she stood at the end of Jade's cot, staring down at the sleeping babe who was now her whole life.

"It was beautiful," she whispered to him, "and I must take you there, my beautiful boy. I *will* take you there."

Bubbling with enthusiasm that she hadn't felt in the months since her mother's death, Jessie prepared breakfast with gusto. Today, she'd decided sometime during the night; she would show them all that this, indeed, was the turning point of her depression.

Ryan's jaw dropped as he entered the kitchen to be met by the wafting breaths of bacon sizzling, the popping, pungent aroma of coffee on the boil, and a plateful of freshly buttered toast. Leesa stood behind him, her satin dressing gown two parts the way secured about her well-shaped form. Ryan, still barefoot and tousled, signified her doings in the room below had disturbed them both. Jessie caught the astonished glance they cast each other but ignored it. This was, after all, unusual behaviour for her, not being one to eat breakfast, let alone cook it. But life was too glorious to waste it lounging in bed all day.

There were things to do, places to go.

And it was Friday. On Friday, Ryan visited his folks, and Jessie sensed over breakfast her rising spirits further gladdened him, for now, he could go without worry, without burdening her care to Leesa. Of course, all this had supposedly been kept secret. Their quiet conversation the night before would have been organising who would watch her throughout the day to ensure she didn't drift into depression. She hoped they understood it was the most devastating feeling to be one of the last living members of a lineage. It was like she and she alone carried the family into non-existence because mortality pushed itself forward until she couldn't ignore that death was inevitable. And Jessie had felt so incredibly alone. She had no family left. Except Jade.

Ryan, unfortunately, didn't understand what that was like: he still had his mother, father, and brothers; he could still enjoy their kinship and love, their closeness. And today he would do just that. He would drive for an hour down the Federal Highway, then cut back across to Penrose, spend the day on the family farm then drive back again after supper. She, on the other hand, would fill in her hours, preferring not to inflict her doldrums on his folks while still so affected by the thought of family ties. The only link she now had was to Jade. It was him and her now.

"You can leave little man home today," she said as Ryan started to pack the baby bag. "I am fine, really, and I really should make up for lost time and for neglecting him yesterday." She had indeed a lot of time to catch up on, for Ryan had shouldered much of the care of him in her melancholia, that affliction stemming firstly from John's sudden death while she was in hospital giving birth, and her mother's death so recently.

Ryan stared at her for a long moment, as if pondering the sensibility of her suggestion. *Or did he sense it isn't a suggestion? Did I maybe push the point a little too strongly? Well, of course I should have! He's my son too! I have every right to have him with me!*

Her smile convinced Ryan all was well, and he returned it with a warm, reassuring grin that she was indeed truly better.

Kissing him briefly for his understanding, she hurried him along for it was a long drive, and he should spend as much time with his folks as he could. One day, he, too, would be alone.

With Ryan gone, Jessie turned her thoughts to Leesa, her friend's head deeply buried in a pile of Heritage manuals, coloured shields, and coat-of-arms shining boldly out from glossy pages. She'd barely noticed her movement around the room as Jessie hovered, cautiously considering her options for the day. Jade was now up and playing happily on the floor, and she tossed a few more of his toys his way, slipped several more into her bag for later, watched Leesa flip a few more pages back and forth in the book. Leesa scratched her head, jotted a few notes, then pulled another book from the pile and started delving through its pages.

Jessie settled into a chair, watched as Jade became bored with his game, his interest soon waning in most things. Crawling across the room, he pulled himself up to the table and pulled at Leesa's notebook. The movement broke her concentration, and Jessica felt guilty.

"Oh, dear! I'll take him out of your way," she apologised quickly, "... let you get on with your work."

Leesa smiled her thanks and refocused her attention on her book. Such an important thesis – the university hubbub was far too noisy for her concentration, hence her pre-empted visit – only Jesse's problems had got in the way of that study. And now? ... Now that Jessie was well again, Leesa could catch up on lost time.

"I'll go and get out of your way altogether – give you the peace and quiet you deserve," she announced.

Leesa merely nodded.

With Jade strapped safely in the car seat, and with a full day's provisions packed in the boot, Jessie threw Leesa a glowing smile and headed out the door. They were soon on their way down the street and in the flow of traffic heading west out of Sydney.

Chapter Two

The drive seemed to take forever, yet only an hour and a half passed before the signpost to Oberon loomed out of the distance. The road-house cafe at the intersection stood empty as Jessie turned and headed north towards Amberlay and Lowes Mount. A short way up and around behind Mt Bindo, a dirt track branched off to the right, and she took it, following the tyre tracks left from the day before. The road wound up from the valley, forked ahead, and she took the lesser path, carefully guiding her little Ford in and around heavy stumps and boulders at the side of the track. The rusty gate eventually blocked further wheeled progress, and she parked the car in the ruts of yesterday's journey.

For a long while, she sat behind the wheel, staring at the tall grove of timbers nestled within the fence line. She focused on the paint-faded sign hanging loose on the gate, and the faint words scrolled on its surface – WHISTLING GUMS – then back to the trees, for they had whistled to her yesterday. They had spoken to her.

The trees were now silent. Even when she climbed on the gate and leaned over to peer down the path along which she had run the day before, they were silent. Their stillness bothered her. She wanted them to speak: she needed to hear that voice. And she wanted to speak to her mother ... she was so wrong for forbidding her to come here ... so, so very wrong!

With Jade in her arms, the climb over the gate was awkward, the trail down with the weight of him on her hip endless. Still, it was important for them to go forward.

The winding path inclined gently down through the tall belt of gums, their overhead silence depressing. *Why will you not speak to me today? Why have you made my journey fruitless? Has Mother maybe interfered?!* Her jaw tightened at the thought.

In time, she stopped on the southern break of shelter, the cottage below slumbering in the sunlight, embraced by the brier and enhanced by a tangle of wild rose and bracken that almost concealed it. Then down she went, not called this time but compelled to push open that door of her own volition. Somewhere would be what she was looking for. Somewhere would be the reason she'd come back.

The cottage looked doleful in its ruination, the woodwork exposed to the weather suffering, with not the slightest look of dignity as it had appeared in the old, worn photos in her mother's album. Of this, she felt sad. Leaves had piled up around the door, leaves she had not noticed in her haste the day before. She foot-scraped these aside, not wanting them to blow inside and clutter the house with debris. It was such a beautiful house, low-slung, with a quaint low-eaved veranda that extended the full perimeter of the dwelling, though that was hard to fully determine due to the extent of overgrowth. The door was tight this day – very tight – as if it had warped in its framework, and she cursed that her strength was not enough to force it aside. *This isn't fair! I've come so far, and now you won't let me in! Or is it you, Mother? And if so, why are you being so cruel?!*

"Mother, … please," Jessie begged, her arm on the wooden barrier still trying to force it aside. It didn't work. And her mother didn't reply.

Barred entry, she turned, hoisted Jade a little higher on her hip and looked around. Maybe there was another way in. Maybe there was a back door. She walked the perimeter of the house for a look. There were four windows, all grey with the dirt of an age, and a back door, but heavy planks had been nailed across its opening. Her temper rose. She wanted to break them down. Maybe she could find a heavy branch or something to break the seal of timber against timber. A tear slipped from her eye as she looked around for anything that would fit the task, but she wiped it quickly away. *I have come so far ... and for what?! A wasted journey? To be shunned in my own house?!*

"Sailor ... let me in!" she cried, her eyes now filling with tears. "We're home."

The fronds on the bracken beside her started to stir, the leaves on the rose vine fluttered on their stems, and her heart instantly soared. Away up on the hill, the tips of the treetops began a gentle sway, all working in unison, telling her to go forward, yet no words came audibly to her. Her direction took her back to the front of the cottage, back towards the path leading through the trees. The front door now stood ajar as she passed, and she stopped and sighed with relief. "Thank you."

The trees on the slope above were now still again. Everything was still. Not a movement anywhere. Her thoughts steeled.

Why the reluctance to come forward?
Is it Jade's presence here?
Or did my fear yesterday ruin everything?
More to the point, are you angry with me for not obeying you?
Sailor always liked to be obeyed.

"Sarah."

The word was a sigh brushing past her ear, yet it filled her with warmth and excitement, the tone so overwhelmingly caring she knew she was no longer alone. And for that, she cried. The babe in her arms grew suddenly lighter, and her burden had been lifted two-fold.

No other words were spoken – there seemed no need. She was here now; he was here now, and they had much to do. The farm had fallen into such a state of ruin, and the time was right for it to be returned to its former glory, to how it had been in the beginning, to how it should have stayed if fate and time hadn't dealt it such a cruel blow.

Putting Jade down to play on his blanket, Jess set to work removing as much of the debris and overgrowth from the walls as her hands would allow, but it soon became evident more than pure physical strength was needed. She needed tools: saws, pruning shears, a wheelbarrow. She looked around … cleaning rags, paintbrushes, paint, a hammer and nails. And for her vegetable patch that had disappeared under centuries of grass and weeds, pick and hoe and seeds. And she needed more time, for it was now time to leave. The sun was lowering behind the hills in the west and the door to the house had just closed to catch her attention. Her sleeping son, that dream of a child who had played so pleasantly for such a long time, occupied it seemed by the whispers she occasionally heard through her toil, was gently stirring. She must now take him home before the night chill made him ill.

Chapter Three

Just on dark, Jesse parked her small car behind Leesa's in the driveway, the empty space where Ryan usually parked the station wagon indicating she'd done well to return home before him. Leesa met her on the veranda and, by the scowl on her face, Jesse knew she was not impressed with her long absence. Her own smiling face only increased her friend's annoyance.

"Did you have a good day?!" Leesa challenged sharply from the top step, her hands jammed on her hips, making her look more like her mother than a friend.

"Simply marvellous," she smirked, realising Jade on her hip seemed back to his normal weight. Avoiding a confrontation, she sidled past Leesa and went inside, made herself busy tidying and settling her son. Then she headed for the kitchen and the coffee pot.

"You were gone so long," Leesa said from the doorway, "I became so worried I almost rang Ryan to see what I should do."

Jesse turned sharply. "*No!* You mustn't ring Ryan, ever. You mustn't!"

"Oh, don't worry, I didn't," Leesa huffed. "He's got enough to worry about. A day off once in a while isn't really enough."

Jesse didn't comment, and nor did Leesa until it was obvious Jesse wasn't going to.

"Well? Are you going to tell me where you were?"

Jesse shrugged offhandedly. "At the farm."

"Again?" Leesa moved forward to where Jesse stood at the sink, and peered around to view her face. Her friend's expression could only be read as uncontainable pleasure even though the pain of her thorn-torn hands was becoming horribly apparent.

"My God, what have you done to yourself?" she admonished. "Jesus, Ryan will kill me for letting this happen to you!"

Her theatrics annoyed Jesse, and she nudged her aside. "It's only a few cuts. Don't make such an issue over nothing!"

"What do you mean? ... nothing. Your hands are lacerated!"

"They're not! Just pour some disinfectant over them and I'll be all right," Jesse told her. Yet it was obvious now that one or two of the scratches had run a little deep, the blood flowing a little too freely even for her liking. She reached for the First Aid kit in the cupboard, and while Leesa helped by binding her right hand firmly to seal the slices of flesh together, Jesse made her promise not to make a big thing out of it.

"Ryan has enough to worry about, and my afternoon of cleaning up the family farm is nothing for him to worry about. Besides, it gives me something to do with my life."

Ryan arrived home an hour or so later, the headlights of his car swinging brightly through the lounge-room window as he pulled into the drive. Jessie was ready; Leesa was quiet yet agreeable, while Jade had thankfully been a dear and let Leesa bath and feed him. He had then drifted off into a happy, deep slumber, and was now tucked snugly up in bed, silent.

The glass front door opened, and Ryan came in looking a little weary from the long drive. His gold-blond hair looked ruffled from the open car window, that strategy undoubtedly employed to keep him awake. His blue eyes swept the room where Jess and Leesa sat, and he smiled that all appeared well, just two friends sitting in comfortable conversation. Jess had been telling Leesa about her day, about the beautiful, wild white roses that trailed gloriously about the house, and how they could be trained to climb back up a trellis (if there was a trellis), and how she had piled high the bracken ferns after removing them from the northern wall. Leesa had asked her what the house was like, but Jesse couldn't tell her much, for she hadn't really seen it; hadn't even felt the slightest twinge of curiosity to enter through the door and view the gossamer grey of age as she'd done the first day. There seemed no need. The time would be right when the outside was tidy, and besides, she hadn't felt the urge to enter – that strange sensation that had pulled her so strongly only a day ago had now kept her busy outside. She knew too: *He* was outside, not hiding within. But she didn't tell Leesa that.

Ryan plopped himself into one of the single armchairs, between where Jesse sat curled up on the long settee and where Leesa sat rigidly in her mood. He glanced briefly from the stern stare Leesa sent to Jesse, and back again. Then his frown grew as he noticed Jessie's bandaged hand.

"My God, what have you done?" he snapped, rising and changing seats to sit beside her. Leesa rose and left the room, taking with her the empty china cups to replenish their contents.

"Just got some scratches from the rose bushes," Jesse said briefly, slipping in a brief smile to show she wasn't bothered by it.

"Bad?"

She shook her head. "Just scratches, but Leesa didn't want infection to set in, so we're just being careful."

He blew out a deep breath, and Jesse knew he had swallowed her story. Leesa came back and served hot cuppas all round, Jesse slipping up to bed soon after, her own long drive and manual labour nagging at her muscles. She soon found deep sleep; dreamt of walking along the harbour wall, admiring ancient tall ships, the gentle slosh of water slapping against the quay further soothing her conscience. And she dreamt of roses in full bloom, and gum trees swaying in the breeze, the sound alluring to her mind, and she felt wonderfully comfortable, eternally embraced, secure. She woke in Ryan's arms, his gentle breathing stirring her deep within, and she lay very still and pondered over why she loved *this* man so much.

Ryan, indeed, had always been a good provider, and his handsomeness had stirred her heart from the moment they had met; she simply couldn't resist his blond-haired, blue-eyed, mature surfer look, and she certainly knew he loved her. Yet she often wondered what he ever saw in her, a very plain, straw-haired, blue-eyed office girl with a propensity for swimming, sailing, camping, anything that gave her time under an open sky. She felt the sudden need to go camping right then.

Unfortunately, Ryan's surfer looks stopped there. He'd spent his childhood on the family farm; he'd struggled through school to get an education that would enable him to get away from the land altogether. He sure as hell didn't want to go back there. And that was going to be a problem. She could sense they were heading rapidly towards crossroads.

Moving out of his arms, she rose quietly. At six o'clock, she had the urge to be doing something. What she really wanted to do was drive, but she had to be careful – she couldn't just up and go. And she wanted Jade to be with her again, for she sensed he made all the difference.

Ryan looked so peaceful in sleep, so she left him and padded downstairs with an armful of clothing so she could dress without disturbing him – he was always rather jaded the day after a visit to his folks; and was always reluctant to do a great deal, which now seemed such a waste of a good Saturday. Downstairs, she started preparations: a nice cooked breakfast first because it had pleased him so much the previous morning and a scrumptious picnic lunch as a bribe to escape the house. They'd spent so much time at home lately that a picnic would be a relaxing way for Ryan to enjoy the day. And she had the perfect place in mind.

Her whistling must have woken the two sleepy heads upstairs for they entered the kitchen as yesterday, tousle-haired, bleary-eyed, confused, yet the odours lingering in tempting layers about the room stirred their appetites well enough the early hour was ignored. They were on the road by eight o'clock, Leesa deciding to tag along 'to keep an eye on them', she said. Besides that, Jesse and Leesa had had words on the quiet – Leesa, close friend that she was, had asked Jesse if she was having an affair, her 'beaming eyes and bushy tail' a dead giveaway that love was in the air. Naturally, Jesse had jumped down her throat at her stupidity, and now Leesa was tagging along to make amends for her stupid aspersions.

Jesse pooh-poohed the idea of having a snack at Lake Oberon, appealing as it was, for she had a place in mind even more appealing than the lake.

Then Ryan complained bitterly about the narrow track she'd taken from the fork, and worried profusely over his precious paintwork being scratched. He didn't think much of her great idea anymore and had grown hungrier and more tired by the minute. Thankfully the gate appeared in front of them, Jesse becoming suddenly afraid he'd order her to turn around and go back to the lake.

He did as she had the day before – sat and peered over the dashboard; looked critically at the rust-encrusted gate, at the barely readable sign, the fine print reading J. E. RAYBOURNE. Then he turned slowly, his expression unreadable.

"So what's all this about?" he asked drily.

"This is our place," Jesse said. "I thought you might like to see it."

"This is *your* place," he corrected, "and your mother said you were never to come here."

"I know what Mother said, but what's the purpose of having the farm if I can never come here? And what's wrong with having a look at it anyway?"

Ryan's jaw tightened. She had tricked him. "You know what your mother said. I don't know why she said it, but you should take her wishes into account."

"Well, listen to it!" Jesse huffed, stepping out of the car. "Oh, he of the rule not to waste anything. And besides, I've been here before, and nothing's happened. In fact, it's a beautiful old place … I just thought you might like to see it."

Ryan sighed deeply, and Leesa's broad smile congratulated her that her ploy had worked as he opened the car door. Passing Jade over the gate, he climbed over and stood waiting for Jesse to lead the way, the picnic hamper carried between Leesa and Jesse, Jade back on Ryan's hip.

"How far?" he asked, his tone showing a little interest growing.

"About a K." Then she saw him look down at the nettle-strewn track. His eyes followed it briefly forward then back again to the car. Apparently, walking posed less effort than clearing the way for the car or freeing the gate. Jesse didn't mind – she liked the walk; it gave her a feeling of warmth and companionship.

"Come on," she said, leading the way.

Ten minutes later, they exited the trees and stopped where Jesse usually stood on the slope above the cottage, the silence noticeable in its extreme. *Birdlessly quiet.*

Taking a firmer hold on his son, Ryan scanned the treetops then panned down across the valley. "This is eerie," he said, frowning at the absolute absence of sound.

"There's an old oak tree down behind the house," Jesse chirped, ignoring his comment. "It'll make a great place for a picnic."

Leesa had trouble keeping up with her as she trundled off down the hill, Ryan lagging behind. Jesse suspected he deliberately took his time to peruse the land, the cottage, and the thick belt of trees surrounding the valley proper, growing even thicker down in the steepest drop where the brook bubbled by, watering the stands of ancient fruit trees as it did, their harvest now completely ruined by time.

Her own eyes cast a wide arc, desperately searching as she tried to force that sense of feeling she'd had before. She came to stand at the pile of torn bracken left from the day before. Ryan now looked at her; his eyes had missed nothing in his scrutiny.

"You said you'd been here before," he recounted her words. "When?"

"The other day," she replied openly, not in the least concerned with what he thought. He would not be allowed to pose a problem.

"And yesterday," Leesa prated, backing down on her previous agreement.

Jesse flashed her an evil glare. *What the hell is she doing? Scoring Brownie points off Ryan? And whose friend is she anyway?!*

"I thought so," Ryan replied deeply. "Newly pulled weeds, still green, and our rose bushes at home haven't been touched … But these have."

Jesse's expression stayed blank. She didn't care.

Ryan put Jade down on a thick sward of grass, the same place he'd played the day before. The little boy looked keenly around, Jesse's eyes following his but finding nothing.

"What's going on, Jessica? Why all the secrecy?"

"What secrecy?" she defended, huffing at the interminable stillness that dominated the scene – that annoyingly persistent stillness. "And if you want to know what's going on, Ryan, I just needed something to do. I hate being mollycoddled by you. You're stifling me with your care. I just had to get away and do something for myself. I had to get busy.

'So I came here to the farm ... came here to find out why Mother wouldn't let me, and I found it all so terribly run down, almost ruined. That's why she wouldn't let me come here! She was ashamed of how she'd let it become. And I don't care what else she says!"

The words blurted out as tears streamed down her cheeks at the decay that had taken hold everywhere. "It's not fair, Ryan! It's not fair that she let his farm get so run down!"

Ryan's brow creased further at her outburst. "Whose farm?" he asked warily.

A cold chill of fear washed over Jesse. She'd said too much.

She swallowed and hoped the action had gone unnoticed. "Grandfather's, of course! This was grandfather's farm, and his father's before him, and his father's before that! She had no right to let it get in such a state of ruin. She had no right at all!"

Ryan went forward and brushed the tears from her cheeks. He knew her well enough to know how important 'family' was to her in her loneliness. *Hopefully, he knows how important it is that I be allowed to do what has to be done.*

Jade's infant laughter caused them all to turn.

The babe sat giggling, chuckling at the sky, his face beaming with delight ... at nothing. Jesse moved away from Ryan's touch and saw the cottage door now stood ajar.

"I need to put it back to how it was," she told Ryan seriously. "I need to do this for my sanity, or I can never forgive Mother for what she has done." Her ears shut out her mother's crying, shut out her begging to be heard, opened to the warm tones overriding hers, a voice that warmed her inside, that filled her completely. "I need to do this so I can find myself."

Ryan sighed again. "Okay, whatever you want. It'll probably be good therapy for you."

He smiled, and Jesse couldn't help but kiss him for his understanding, yet she flinched as a cold wind swept up across the pastures and blasted a sudden wall of air against the house. Their hair ruffled in its path and the front door slammed fiercely shut. She wouldn't make that mistake a second time.

"Gee, this place is creepy," Leesa said from behind them as she stared at the cottage, then at the valley below where the river wound quietly by in the shadows of the trees. "Have you noticed there's no birds?"

Jesse and Ryan looked at her mockingly. Sometimes she could come up with the most stupid things, yet Jesse noticed Ryan had taken a quick glance skyward.

"Come on, let's have morning tea," she intercepted keenly, "then we can take a nice walk around the property. I haven't seen it all myself yet."

So they laid the blanket out under the gentle spread of the old twisted oak and dotted the blanket's centre with the trays of sandwiches Jesse had made that morning. Thermos coffees were poured, and they sat back in the shade, Ryan and Leesa on one side of the blanket, Jade and Jesse on the other, to keep their distance. The morning whiled away, Leesa breaking the pleasantness by noting there were also no ants, no sounds of crickets or bush life in general, no breeze. Jesse laughed at the triteness of her observation.

The peacefulness was so restful Ryan reneged on the walk around the farm, but Jesse wasn't bothered by it. Leesa's offer to keep him company in his idleness raised an eyebrow, though. They kept Jade with them to save her the burden of hip-carting him around; said she could move faster and be back quicker if she went alone.

"And this is, after all, *your* project," Ryan chided.

Chapter Four

The slope down to the creek was gentler than it looked and Jesse ambled towards the sound of bubbling water, towards the sound Leesa had failed to hear through the silence. There was indeed sound here – sounds of running water cascading over rocks – sounds of whispering voices through the leaves as a gentle wind followed her into the grove. The darkness overwhelmed her. The coolness chilled her skin. The faint fog rising from the ground made her turn on her heel to peer deeper into the surrounding haze.

Shivers ran up her spine and she shuddered. For the first time since coming here, she felt truly afraid, her eyes widening to the ever-rising mist. And then a warmth touched her, a gentle caress of air that heated her skin, and told her she was safe. Then a voice cut through the grove, its vindictive hiss overriding the warm cover of security. It said: "Go away! Leave her alone!"

It wasn't *his* voice, and Jesse turned instantly and ran from the grove, a sharp crack emitting as she raced back into the silence, into the cleared ground above the river. The tips of gum trees tossed wildly above that ominous place below.

"Sailor, I don't like her!" Jesse said, her hands shaking as she looked back the way she'd come.

His touch soothed her nerves, and she knew not to go back in there. She knew that maybe Mother had her reasons after all. Yet she heard not her agreeance to her thoughts.

Looking up, she gulped a breath as Ryan and Leesa came

running down the hill towards her, their startled faces showing their fear.

"What happened? What is it?!" Ryan shouted.

Gulping for air, her hand on her chest, Jesse forced a laugh, that in itself starting her mirth in earnest. *How it must have looked to those who don't know!*

Ryan's strong hands grabbed her, his face pale and drawn. "What is it?! What's so funny?" he demanded.

"You," she chaffed. "I thought you had come up here for a lazy day, and here you two are running about all over the place."

Standing further back, Leesa didn't look at all amused.

"We thought something was wrong," Ryan said deeply, "... seeing you came bolting out of there like a bat out of hell. What was it? What frightened you?"

Jesse chuckled again. "Nothing … nothing frightened me, except my own wild imagination." Her hand remained at her throat at the thought of what had just occurred. "It was very dark in there, but I wanted to see the waterfall so I kept going. Then I thought I heard something, noises behind me. I thought it was you, but when I called, I heard no answer … I got scared. Then there was this loud crash, and I just turned and ran."

Ryan steeled to her words, and his gaze delved deep into the woods.

"It's alright," she gasped another breath. "It was a tree branch falling. That's all it was. I'm fine now. Really."

Ryan wiped his brow and looked down at her. "Well, I don't think you should go back in there. That's a very old grove, and the moisture from the creek has probably rotted a great deal of the timber. Bits could drop off trees at any time, especially if the wind comes up suddenly like it did just then."

She nodded her compliance.

"This place isn't normal," Leesa complained from above them on the slope. "Did you see how the trees just up and blew like that?! Just the trees, nothing else." She shook her head. "I don't like it here … I don't think it's safe."

Her words stirred Ryan's thinking. "Jade! We left Jade!"

Turning, he bolted back up the hill, Leesa dogging his heels, something which Jess had noted was happening far too often of late. She wandered along behind them, not seeing the need for alarm: Jade would always be safe here. *Jade will* always *be safe here*: *Whistling Gums is his home.*

The little boy lay curled up on the blanket, asleep, his peaceful face glorious in its repose, his nature far improved since Jess had first come here – this little boy who had been a bane since his birth, who had worn her ragged, who had made her resent him. But she loved him now … he was an angel, a dear, darling angel. And now he slept beneath the oak named Jarvis …

Her brow creased deeply. *Why did I think that? I know I'm correct but where did that information come from? Maybe Mother told me about it …* She shook her head, confused. *Why would anyone name a tree?*

With Jade so deep in slumber, Ryan offered to take a look at the shack, leaving Leesa behind with her books to watch over him. The open door seemed a proper invitation that everything would be alright to enter.

Once inside, he briefly scanned the four rooms, some still graced with the odd piece of furniture, ancient dry pieces covered in an inch of dust. The carpet of leaves already on the floor made her previous worry seem stupid. Above the three lower rooms ran a long loft with a small ladder-like affair running up to it. The upper room ran half the length of the house, while the lower part was dominated by the expansive parlour-kitchen. What was used as bedrooms came off either end of this main room. The only entries in and out were the front and back doors, and these Ryan said should be replaced, both being too twisted by weather to repair. The glass in the windows would also be fragile, he warned, so treat them with care and they might last till the essentials were renewed, then they too could be replaced.

"I'm amazed they've lasted so long given their age – look at that purple hue across each pane."

Jess's back softened, and her full lips hinted at a smile: the cottage was structurally sound, and with a little bit of attention in a few places and maybe a new tin roof, Ryan had deemed it quite suitable as a comfortable weekender. Her hopes soared for she had plans that included more than just Saturdays and Sundays. Today was just a start!

"No," Ryan bristled, taking hold of her hands as she started to brush away the dust on the cracked wooden table. "You are not doing any more cleaning around here until your hands are healed. And what's more, you are not doing any more here without the proper tools."

He made a list of things she needed to buy as she drove them home – all the things she already had on her own list, she smiled. And, as she drove, her smile widened: Ryan sounded much more enthused about the farm on the drive home than he had when climbing the gate. That too, he'd said, would require attention, noting also that to resurface the inward path would be expensive.

"Don't worry about it … you can leave it as it is. The walk will do me good, and I hate the thought of clearing any of those beautiful, beautiful trees."

"What! Don't tell me you're becoming a Greenie!" He cast her a sideways glance. "As ancient as those trees might be, I'm not about to go lugging truckloads of tin and timber in there by hand!"

In theory, Jess agreed with him but this would cause a major problem. Her jaw set, then she scowled. *Is he really serious about cutting down the trees? Maybe he's also getting too interested in the farm?*

And she wondered, too, at Leesa's incredible silence.

Chapter Five

"I don't want you doing too much up there on your own," Ryan persisted over dinner. "Just do the light tidying jobs around the house, and clean up the cottage ready for when we go up on the weekends. Maybe Leesa will go up with you and keep you company." He looked to Leesa for confirmation and Jess caught her shudder in response.

"The place gives me the creeps," she retorted, to which Ryan raised his eyebrows and strengthened his request at her. She then quickly added, "… but sure, I'll go. I can watch Jade while you work."

"There's really no need to put yourself out!" Jess snapped back, her anger stirred by Ryan's interference. "… And Jade plays perfectly well on his own."

This time Leesa cast the blatant glare, and Jess wondered if her friend knew she was angry with her as well. This protection thing was getting out of hand, and she didn't want, or need, a babysitter any longer. *Maybe the sooner Leesa goes back to Brisbane, the better. She and Ryan are getting far too close in their support system.*

"No, I don't mind," Leesa countered. "I can give you a hand with the heavier stuff."

Jessie's mood darkened that night when she thought of her friend constantly tagging along wherever she went; she wanted the farm to herself. *It is, after all,* my *therapy.*

Ryan lightened that mood later that evening by announcing he had considered returning to work if Jess was sure everything was truly okay. Her cheery mood had given him trust that things were indeed returning to normal – the heavy cloud had suddenly lifted from her spirit.

"I *am* fine, Ryan. I feel alive again, and that haunting fear of death that has hung over me for so long just doesn't seem to matter anymore. I have a purpose now." Indeed, she felt this was her destiny; her life would be important now, the restoration of the farm essential to the rebuilding of the family's heritage … with *his* dreams becoming fully revived.

Several days passed before she could get away again, and it had to be a day when Leesa was available. They drove up to Amberlay in the early morning, having loaded all the equipment she'd gathered in the preceding days into the station wagon – the wheelbarrow not even remotely looking as if it would fit into the boot of her car, nor Leesa's, hence the swap with Ryan. They were under orders to be back before Ryan's return from work, and Leesa had to remind Jesse to slow the speed on the outward journey; the rusty gate, therefore, seemed to take forever to loom ahead of them.

The walk down through the trees this time felt less strenuous for the wheelbarrow carried the tools as well as Jade. The cottage seemed to glow in the distance, the trees a warm comfort around her as she hurried down the hill, squinting in the summer glare to see if the door was open. To her delight, it was, as she'd sensed it would be, for the gums had whispered gently as they'd traversed the gate. Leesa shot her a quizzical look as Jess started whistling as she walked, the urge so powerfully deep inside her she just couldn't resist.

"What is that tune?" she asked as Jess trilled it for the third time in succession, enjoying its bright and lilting rhythm. Jade seemed to enjoy it too for his wee face beamed outward from the barrow.

"It's an old sea shanty," she said jauntily. "Mother used to sing it to us when we were kids, I think. Why?"

"No reason. It's just one I've never heard before."

"This one goes way back from memory. I dare say my grandfather used to sing it to Mother, and probably his father to him."

Leesa shrugged and gave Jade a light tickle under the chin.

As they descended the hill to the cottage, Jess noted Leesa had turned around several times and cast long looks back at the path along which they'd come and that a shudder visibly rocked her shoulders, but she said nothing.

The door was pressed back, wide open, a obvious signal they were welcome. Leaving the barrow and tools outside, Jess picked up Jade and entered the house, a gentle breeze rising up and blowing the leaves around the floor and ejecting some out the door as they did so. Jade's clear blue eyes lifted from watching them dance and sway, and he panned the room with keen interest, chuckling as the leaves swirled magically around them. Jess's heart filled at his mirth and reached a similar yet more silent delight.

"Ooh, it's so pokey ..." The voice came from the doorway and the leaves dropped back to the floor, "... and dusty."

Jess turned, surprised at Leesa's rude observation. The way she saw it, this part of the house was vast and open, a room large enough to comfortably accommodate eating and lounging areas for a small family. "It's lovely," she sighed, contradicting her with enough intent Leesa didn't dare argue, which was something they'd been doing much of late, she realised. "And the dust can be cleared. What do you expect after twenty-five years of being vacant? ... the Ritz?!"

"No, but I do find it odd that no one has used it in all that time. Why was it never rented out? What is it that your mother had against this place?"

Jess turned on her. "What makes you think she had anything against it?"

"Well, she never came here, did she!"

"No. Not since I was a child."

"And when she did, it was with John ... and he died," Leesa reminded her pointedly.

"I know, and she never came again. Personally, I think she blamed the farm for both Grandpa's and John's death."

Leesa's eyes narrowed slightly. "But that's ridiculous!"

"Isn't it just."

Jess eased a breath out at Leesa's conclusion and looked at her more amicably. Her friend gave her a warm smile in return and Jess knew their friendship was indeed solid, all thoughts of Leesa and Ryan drifting away, all thoughts of her interference subsiding.

"Come on," she said cheerily, "let's get this place into shape then ... and there's a hell of a lot to do, I might say."

Working on through the morning, they cleaned, dusted, swept, and moved all the furniture that had been left by her grandparents into the end bedroom, that too which Leesa thought was 'pokey', yet which Jess envisaged as beautifully adorned with a double bed and chintz curtains on the windows, in white to brighten the dark-wooden boards of the walls. When all the leaves were discarded out the door, the room emptied of all encumbrances, Leesa suggested they start their project in the upper room – clean that first to save having to re-dust the ground floor. Jess left her to climb the ladder, preferring to stay with Jade below where a cooling breeze now wafted around her feet.

Carefully scaling the rickety ladder, Leesa disappeared into the distant recesses of the upstairs loft. "There's a lot of boxes and things up here," she shouted down. "Shall I bring them down?"

"What are they?"

Jess frowned. Her mother had removed all personal belongings from her house, keeping what she wanted in her bedroom cupboard and storing the rest in the roof cavity, where she hoarded most of the junk she refused to throw away. So, what was *left*?

"Just old papers by the look of it," came the reply. "Hang on ... hey, there's a lot of other stuff in here. You might want to have a look through these. They look family-related. Old certificates and pictures ... journals ... all sorts of stuff."

Jess's nose wrinkled at the thought. "Leave them there ... I'll go through them later."

Working through till past noon, they took a break; walked back to the car and spread a picnic lunch across the bonnet. Leesa dominated the conversation by waffling on about her work and that time-consuming thesis which was finally coming to an end. She looked forward to the summer break, and was well overdue for a long rest, one involving the odd weekend with her and Ryan at the farm "... if, of course, I'm still welcome," she'd added as an afterthought.

How can I say she isn't when she's always joined us on our outings? Then her eyebrow raised furtively. "I thought you said this place gives you the creeps?"

"It does," Leesa quipped back, "but you know me: I like being scared out of my wits. It's good for the circulation." She chomped heartily into another sandwich and smiled.

"Well, as long as your vivid imagination and racy heartbeat don't affect Ryan, I don't mind. Three sets of hands are better than two."

They packed away the hamper and headed back down to their work, Leesa reminding Jess that they could only afford to spend another two hours or Ryan would beat them home. Leesa's attention again drifted up to the trees, then across the valley to the grove from which Jess had scampered several days before.

"What was down there?" she asked, her eyes narrowing.

"I told you ... nothing. I got frightened by my own imagination."

"Well, you did it good and proper. You were ghostly white."

"I don't think I've ever run so fast in my life," Jess admitted. "And I won't ever go in there again."

"Look ... what's over there?" She pointed along the left fork of the track.

"I don't know. I haven't been along there before."

"Let's go then. I feel like exploring," she said, sparking Jesse's interest.

Taking Jade from her, Leesa hoisted him over her hip and tramped off down the other path. With a quick glance down the valley to the waiting cottage, Jess reluctantly followed. She needn't have worried though: the path soon petered out in a clearing atop the hill – ended nowhere – the only object of mild interest was an oak tree of the same species as Jarvis; that name coming instantly back to taunt her. Even so, this tree's solitary stance saddened her in its exile.

"This is *her* tree," Jesse muttered softly, admiring its superb growth.

Leesa looked only mildly surprised, maybe even a little glum at there being nothing else. "That's really odd that two American oaks have thrived so long, so far apart and not been overtaken or choked out by natural bushland."

Jess shrugged. That same thought had crossed her mind. However, it was less important than her need to return to the cottage. Time was running out and she still had so much to do.

"You really should have brought those boxes home," Leesa said on the trip home, her previous silence obviously on the contents of the upper room chests.

"There's enough of that stuff in Mother's ceiling already without adding more to it," Jess retorted.

"But it could be important family history. Don't you know how hard it is to come across the details of your origins? … and yours could be sitting up there in either of those places, going to ruin, to be forever lost to time."

"So?"

"So, why don't you save it?" Leesa looked at her in astonishment. "Don't you want to know where you came from?"

"I know where I came from." Glancing back at her, but not really wanting to take her eyes from the winding mountain road for a second, Jess verified the query on her friend's face. "My mother was Martha Kendall, nee Raybourne. Her father was Bertram Kendall. Her grandfather was Alistair Kendall, who married …."

"No … go back to your mother's side," Leesa deftly turned the conversation.

"My grandfather was John William Raybourne, my grandmother Elizabeth … Elizabeth Rose, I think …" Jess paused a moment, trying to remember who was next on the Tree she had seen in her mother's folio.

"Go on," her friend prompted, her interest obviously rising in her friend's past.

"I'm trying to remember," Jess told her. "I know I've seen it written."

"Where? Where was it written?" Leesa turned in her seat.

"Mother had a big old scrapbook she used to keep. It had things in it like old birth certificates, marriage certificates, a copy of the family tree."

"She got all those when she was tracing the family back," Leesa told her frankly. "She went back about seven generations if I remember rightly."

Jess shrugged – it didn't really interest her.

"You'll be sorry later in life," Leesa said. "People should know where they came from. Most of us originate from convicts, you know."

"You might have, but I didn't," Jess laughed, teasing her just a little. Leesa had traced her own heritage back, only to find her grand-dam of the 18th century had been a murderess, having killed a soldier in an English Inn to prevent him from taking liberties with her daughter: she had been sentenced to death, but that had later been amended to transportation to a penal colony.

"Don't you want to know?" Leesa pushed again.

"Not particularly. I just can't see the point in chasing up ghosts to find out their indiscretions in life."

"What about the farm then? Wouldn't you like to know when it came into the family, and how?"

"I already know that," Jess said, her annoyance growing at Leesa's badgering. "It's one of the few farms in the area dating back to the first colony. Of course, it's not as big as it used to be. Bits of it were sold off over the years to cover debts and such. But it's big enough as it is, I feel."

"Well, how was the farm purchased? Was your first ancestor over here rich, or was it a land grant for services? Or maybe even stolen from the Aborigines! It could be a sacred site, you know."

"Don't be ridiculous!" Jess flashed her an unamused glare.

"Well? You don't know, do you?"

"And I don't care."

"Well, I think you should." Leesa cocked her head and pursed her lips. "You'll be sorry later."

Jess didn't answer her that time, just let the matter drop, and concentrated on the steep meandering road ahead, but her friend's words stirred her into thinking that maybe she should know just how and where the rest of His farm had gone.

Chapter Six

"So, how was your day?" Ryan asked when he arrived home, and smiled when Leesa told him it was pleasant but uneventful.

"You know, I was thinking today, Jess, we should try to make the farm financially profitable, at least enough to cover the rapidly rising fuel costs of your running back and forward. A few sheep would be viable; they won't cost much to buy and pretty much look after themselves."

Jess resisted arguing over such a minor detail, but said, "The fences are in a rather sad state for stock, especially sheep." *Logic should deter his interest.*

"We can do something about the boundary fence. It will be well worth our while to spend the weekend up there, put in two good full days, then it won't be so necessary for you to go so often."

Jess's back tightened. *Not go there so often!* Her jaw clenched but she quelled the urge to object to his line of thinking. *Now is not the time.*

And so, early on Saturday morning, with the 'wagon loaded with camping cookware, clothing, bedding and tools, they headed west, Ryan driving this time. He missed the turn-off at Oberon and had to reverse back, then at Amberlay missed the track that wended down to the farm gate. Leesa enjoyed his failed attempt at navigating and conjured jokes about the wayward traveller, which Ryan took good-heartedly: Jess just wanted him to hurry, for they were wasting precious time.

The wheelbarrow came in handy again to transport all their gear, plus Jade, down the path to what Leesa now called 'their country estate'. They walked with a low sun promising warmth and long working hours, a slightly cooler breeze travelling up the valley to meet them as they exited the trees. The cottage below looked quaint, inviting and cosy, while Jarvis stood alone on the slope above it, unusually still in the breathy wind. Jess felt a little sad that he should be so resistant for he had grown so splendidly. He should have let his limbs spread and bend as the gums around them had. His continued unwillingness to speak touched her heart and, as if to pacify him, she put Jade on the blanket beneath his sheltering arms, quelling that loneliness.

"You can't leave him here, Jess. It's too far from the shack," Ryan said. "What if he wanders off while we're working."

"He's fine here. He's in our sight and never makes any attempt to leave the blanket. In fact, he's perfectly happy here. It's cool and shady, well within our reach, yet far enough away for him not to be underfoot or at risk of getting hurt."

The little boy's gurgling chuckle as the breeze tickled playfully about him convinced Ryan Jess was right.

By the end of the morning, the cottage had been transformed to a livable condition, their camping equipment had been set up in a corner for cooking, some old kerosene lamps Ryan had snaffled from somewhere had been hung in strategic places around the lower room, with two more placed upstairs in the open loft where Leesa had begged her room to be.

"You'd better not fall out of bed," Ryan warned her. "It's a long drop."

He had inflated and tossed the double bed air mattress in a corner of the bedroom while Jade's mattress, surrounded by assorted chests of drawers to keep him contained, had been set up in the closest side room.

Jessie stood scanning the cottage, its subtle warmth touching her deeply as she thought of her mother playing in that very room while her grandparents sat around the open fire in the main room. On that fire they planned to do some of the cooking, as well as keep themselves warm during the cold mountain nights. Even Ryan thought that sounded cosy.

Lunch first, however, which was a light meal of awkwardly made sandwiches, lap-made for lack of working surface, but edible in their hunger. Leesa offered to clear away and prepare a better kitchen for the night meal while Ryan and Jess went to inspect the perimeter fences. With Jade down for a nap, Jess hoping to accustom him to his strange bed before nightfall, she was surprised he 'crashed' immediately, and so was Ryan

"Must be the fresh country air – it's good for the soul," Jess dropped a strong hope that Ryan would see why they had to move here.

The property covered fifteen hundred acres, much of the land now overgrown with tall grass and timber, the bordering scrub sneaking through the fence lines in an attempt to overtake the pasture. The boundary fences were straight and level from corner to corner on opposite sides, each gracing high-level hill tops while the other two dropped steeply down into the point of the valley then rose steeply up the other side. A wide gap in posts traversed the creek at its base. Here their progress slowed, the rocky incline difficult to scale.

Dejected by the condition of the fence, especially where branches had crashed down on them, Ryan trudged ahead of Jessica, shaking his head. He crossed the creek on a series of exposed stepping stones, reached dry ground on the other side and stopped to give her a hand across the last two rocks, which he had found rather slippery. Reaching out, his hand clasped hers, the pressure just increasing with his pull when the slight breeze suddenly gusted down the valley. The gravelly ground under Ryan's feet started to slide precariously away.

Quickly releasing his grip, he flailed his arms to save himself, but too late: he landed with a thud on the seat of his jeans, his sneakers and socks now washed by the cold running stream. Cursing profusely, whether at his ungainly decline and the resulting pain, or at her uncontrollable laughter, Jess couldn't tell, and nor could she help him. He regained his feet, checked the ground carefully for further loose spots and, warning her to be careful, trudged soggy-footed up to the top of the rise.

Jess followed till they came one by one to the top of the hill. It overlooked the valley from the other side, the cottage now completely obliterated by the vast belt of trees within the ragged fence line. Ryan emptied the water from his shoes and, returning to his list, recommenced counting fence posts that needed replacing, his steps pacing out the rough distance for the purchase of wire. Totally engrossed, he failed to see the cloud of dust and the approaching vehicle coming along the track towards them until Jess tapped him on the shoulder.

The dust-streaked utility crawled to a halt and stopped beside them, and a gent, looking about as old as her grandfather would have been had he still been alive, poked his head out the open window. His face, which looked like well-worn leather, hadn't seen a razor in many weeks and had a generous profusion of silver-grey hair bordering it. The eyes almost matched the day's sky, eyes that squinted as a lazy waft of smoke from his rather scantily rolled cigarette burned across them.

"Gidday," he said, blinking, his tone cheery even though his eyes treated them with suspicion. "Can I help you folks?"

Jess presumed he was a little concerned at them being on his side of the fence and, letting Ryan be the dominant family member, stood back meekly while he went forward.

"Good day," Ryan responded, hating to sound like a bumpkin just because he'd been raised in the bush. "My name is Ryan Robinson." He offered his hand in friendship. "… This is my wife, Jessica."

The man squinted again. "Jessica Kendall?"

Jess nodded, her surprise obvious.

He reached out and shook Ryan's hand. "We'd heard the farm had passed over again. Can say I'm surprised that you folks are actually visiting the place though."

"Actually, we're working out what it's going to cost to fix these fences," Ryan said, casting an eye down the length of the line.

"Oh, I wouldn't worry about it," the man suggested flippantly, his lips wrinkling upward in negation. "My stock won't wander onto your place."

"No, you don't understand," Ryan countered. "We're going to put sheep on here."

"Well, that's different then. You'd better make sure they're damn good fences then," he quipped with amusement, "'cos they're not gonna to want to stay there neither."

He caught Ryan's eyebrows dip in confusion. "The place is haunted, son. Nothing dares go on there. Haven't you noticed it yet?"

Ryan straightened defensively. "No …" He glanced back down across *Whistling Gums* as if assessing the farm in one clean sweep. "No," he repeated more determinedly, "I haven't noticed a thing. And besides that, I don't believe in ghosts."

The old man laughed. "You will, son. You will." He winked. "They all know about it, you know." He cast an accusing grey eye Jessica's way. "Family secret it is."

Jess laughed, a short snorting sound at his absurd notion and looked away. "Someone must have misinformed you," she cut back at him. "I've never heard anything like that before."

Catching her look of concern, Ryan took her hand. "Ghosts are a figment of the imagination, Mr ..." He suddenly realised the man had not introduced himself, and halted mid-speech.

"Carter ... Syd Carter," the man nodded. "And no offence, son, but I'll continue to listen to the stock. They refuse to set foot on your place even though it's ear-high in tucker, and that includes when pickings are slim on my place. And I heared a lot a stories over the years about what's gone on inside that fence line, and I don't intend to put nothin' to fate."

"Unfortunately, people will talk, Mr Carter. And everybody loves ghost stories."

"Well, do me a favour, son," the old man became serious, "keep a close eye out. My wife, Annie, she's done a lot of research on this neck of the woods, followin' up history of settlin' folk and such; she's found out a lot of stuff about your place there, heard a lot of tales about the goings on on that piece of land – some she got from her great-grans who lived in these parts in that time. Those stories last a long time for nothing to be true of 'em."

He read Ryan's deepening expression; read the stern glare from Jess. "Well, I wish you folks well. If you need anything, our track comes off the main road about three mile up from your'n."

Ryan nodded his thanks, half-heartedly waved goodbye as the ute slowly picked up speed and continued along the fence line they had just travelled. "Silly old coot," Jess heard him mutter, that head shaking habit of his making her feel easier inside.

What a lot of nonsense people believe in! And what right do they have dragging Whistling Gums into their repertoire of weird happenings?! She swept her gaze over the farmland, over and through the trees that enhanced and protected the acreage within. How could anyone believe that such a glorious plot of earth could hold such preposterous foolishness as harbouring ghosts. She chuckled at the thought of it, Ryan's widening grin telling her he agreed and she tightened her grip over his.

"And don't you dare go telling any scary stories around that open fire tonight," she warned him, a severe finger backing up her words. "I'll never forgive you if you do."

His glinting eyes gave his wordless reply … that it would be a long while before the spook stories would die down.

Chapter Seven

Leesa had filled her time well in their absence, tidying more of the garden outside, sweeping more of the age-gathered rubble from inside to join it; she had even moved several pieces of furniture back into the main room to facilitate comfort. She now sat on the edge of a dusted wicker chair, leaning forward, when they entered the cottage, her interest firmly fixed to Jade who was now up and playing in a cleared corner of the room. Astonished, she looked up slowly, her frown showing her quandary.

"He's been playing there like that for over an hour," she said darkly. "Playing and laughing …"

The little boy, oblivious to their presence in the room, continued his game, the soft round ball spinning beneath his hand delighting his mind, tempting his infantile mirth to issue in deep, belly-rooted gurgles. His blue eyes danced with wonder, then blinked again before another of those gleeful sounds emitted.

Ryan looked at the scene with pleasure. "Hey, don't knock it!" he chided. "Accept the good with the bad. And personally, I like the good." He went forward and lifted his son from the floor.

Removed from his game, the little boy's face straightened, the happiness changing to utter disappointment – *if a babe of this age could feel disappointed,* Jess noted – then it turned to absolute remorse. Then the crying started, the screwed-up face and glistening eyes preceding woeful sobs of sadness. Ryan shook his head and frowned; jostled him on his hip to affect a mood change. But there was no chance. Hurt, he handed Jade to Jess, and looked further hurt when the sobbing slowly subsided. Then he went silent, his expression tensing when Jess put their son back in the corner. Jade wasn't the same there though, and he didn't return to his game as she'd hoped; he just sat and gazed about as if looking for something.

"I think you frightened him," she consoled Ryan. "He wasn't aware we were here until you picked him up."

"We were here long enough! And I spoke to you for God's sake!"

"He wasn't aware … too deep in play …"

Leesa looked candidly from Jess to Ryan and back again. "He was totally oblivious to me being here too," she interrupted. "I even called him, but he didn't hear me."

Ryan started to panic. "Do you think there might be something wrong with him? I've heard of some of those diseases that start to appear like that. Autism is one. You don't think there could be something developing with him, do you?"

Jess laughed at his foolishness. "Of course not! Look, he's listening to us now, isn't he?"

Indeed, Jade now stared straight at them, his grief completely forgotten. "Hello, baby," she cooed.

His smile told of his attention.

"See!"

Ryan muttered something about being thankful and sighed, but didn't attempt to pick him up again. Instead, he wandered out to collect firewood for the night's warmth, which would definitely be appreciated in the rising chill of the approaching evening. They ate and cleared away, sponge-bathed Jade – water being a rare commodity unless someone wanted to walk down to the creek and refill the bucket (the rain tanks having rusted away in the dry years), but no one did. Weary from work, they sat in silence for much of the time staring into the yellow-gold flames, relishing the warm red glow radiating outward until Ryan's words chilled Jess's skin.

"This place is haunted, you know," he told Leesa seriously. "Our next-door neighbour told us today ... said the ghosts are family secrets."

Leesa looked up quickly, a shudder visibly running over her as she took Ryan into her vision. "Really?!"

"Yeah. He told us not to worry about fixing the fences because his stock refuses to come over here." Then he smiled. "And thank God for that!"

"For what?" Jess snapped, greatly annoyed at him for bringing the matter up at all.

"That either our ghosts are going to save us a heap of money ... or he happens to have very snobbish sheep."

She thumped him on the leg – the first of the ghost jokes had started.

"Do you think they'll help?" he questioned after a long pause, his chin dimpling with deliberation.

"Who help what?"

"The ghosts. Do you think they'll help clean up this mess? I mean, they must have made it, so I feel they can jolly well give a hand. Many hands make light work and all that."

Jess placed a well-aimed fist in his chest, rose, and said if he wanted to be silly, he could sit up alone. She headed for her sleeping bag, hearing Leesa comment again about no birds, no ants, not even a spider in the house; she'd have thought there would have been at least a plague of spiders.

"Will you two shut up and go to bed?!" Jess snapped again.

Their whispers continued a while longer, then Jess heard her friend scale the ladder to the loft, and Ryan dimmed the kerosine lamp on the wall and climbed into the bed roll next to hers. The light from the glowing fire and the lamps from the upper room cast enough light that Jess could see the look on Ryan's face as he rolled on his side and gazed lovingly down at her. The fire had apparently provided just the right setting for his thoughts to be aroused. She shook her head in answer, flicked a quick glance at the upper room and smiled at his disappointment; she was sure the fire couldn't die quick enough for him, and Leesa's friendship was stretched to the limit as the loft lights continued to blaze well into the night. Of that, Jess was thankful.

Soon they fell asleep.

Hours later though something disturbed her. Her rapid blinking failed to produce clear vision in the moon-hazed blackness. She felt the coldness immediately, the fire having burned itself into nothing. Rolling over, she realised just what had woken her: Ryan's bed roll was much closer to hers than before. He was pressed up against her back as if seeking other warmth now the fire had died. And it didn't take long for her to fathom that his thoughts were back on just how warm he wanted to get. His hand slowly unzipped the length of her sleeping bag, entered and glided around her waist, encouraging her to move a little closer. His lips claimed hers, stifling any protest she might have made while his fingers fumbled to lift the tracksuit top she had chosen to wear as pyjamas.

Hearing a gentle murmur outside the house, she tried to pull away. She wanted to tell Ryan to be careful, to stop his nonsense for they weren't alone. But he wasn't going to allow any words to escape until he'd aroused her enough that she didn't care. She couldn't let that happen. This was not the place!

Struggling to break away from his possessive mouth, she sensed the force doubling as it blew up the valley, as it swept down around the trees and developed into a solid wall of wind that whipped the ground and tossed the treetops in a rising storm. Ryan hoisted himself over her, pinning her down. Jess sensed his amusement in her reluctance for it made the game more challenging. Only she wasn't playing.

Then a solid body of air hit the side of the cottage with incredible determination. It swirled viciously around the tiny structure till it rocked the cottage on its feeble foundations. The walls shuddered violently. Iron on the roof rattled fiercely, creating an awful din inside, dropping an accumulation of dirt and dust from the inner straw-thatching down onto them. Ryan's lips left hers and Jess presumed he had looked upward, but he made no other motion to move. Another roaring blast hit the walls, the southern side this time. Windows cracked throughout the house, a spine-chilling tinkling warning of the breaks, a sharp brittle crinkling coming from every pane of glass. Then, with a loud crash, moon-glistened shards exploded inwards, showering the room with luminescent silver splinters. Jess felt Ryan fall over her, heard herself scream, heard Ryan curse loudly. Then Leesa's shouts rent the air. "What is it? My God, what is it?!"

"It's alright," Ryan shouted back at her, barely audible over the racket above and around them. "Keep your head down and stay there. You too," he told Jess firmly. Then he rolled back off her and Jess could only hear his muffled sounds.

"What are you doing?" she asked, her fear bringing her close to tears. "Ryan, what are you doing?!"

"Getting out of this thing. I have to get Jade out of there."

His shouted words were overly loud, for the battering outside had suddenly stopped. The wind only whistled now as it swirled back to a safer distance, ebbing with its fury a little further down the valley. Jess also shucked her bed roll and stood as Ryan's groping hands located the flashlight and clicked it on. The yellow beam revealed them standing looking at each other in horror. He swung the light to hover over the now non-reflective openings and then onto the closed bedroom door. He took fearful steps towards the side room, grief already showing on his face for the little boy had made no sound. Not a scream, not a murmur had come from the room, the loud shattering of exploding glass failing to raise even the slightest cry.

Edging the door slowly open, not wanting to see what he expected to find, Ryan stepped into that tiny room, Jess's footsteps dogging Ryan's in the limited light, both carefully avoiding the shards of purple glass littering the floor and glinting back in the torchlight. The golden beam illuminated the barrier of dressers.

Hesitantly, Ryan held the torch aloft to cast a brighter glow into the abyss within, his breath held with internal remorse. Jess heard his sigh before her eyes also found the babe sleeping within the glow of that yellow orb, not a sound except a contented purr coming from the makeshift crib.

"The cupboards must have protected him," Ryan whispered, directing the light beam upward over the walls. Light mirrored back from the window in the room, bringing a deeper frown to Ryan's face. The windows there had remained intact, untouched, yet the ones on the same wall in their room had been crystallised.

Backing out again, the movement edging Jess back into the other room, Ryan quietly eased the door shut again.

"I don't understand this," he hissed in the dim light, his head turning as the glow upstairs brightened. Gingerly treading a path back to his bed, he found his shoes and donned them. "This is really weird."

"What was it?" Leesa asked as her slim frame descended the ladder. "It sounded like all hell had broken loose out there."

"Just a bit of a wind gust." Jess tried to sound mild. "I've heard it tends to happen here a bit, something to do with the lay of the land creating pockets of air that get swept along the valley. It sometimes hits the ridge and bounces back against the hill. It's nothing to worry about."

"Can't happen too bloody often," Ryan challenged her local knowledge, "not if these windows have been in for that length of time."

She shrugged. "Maybe it's never hit the house before."

In the semi-darkness, they stood looking at each other huddled against the cold pouring in through the glass-jagged openings. With difficulty, Ryan relit the lamps, then went to work rebuilding the fire around which they sat shrouded in bedding until dawn's first light. As the sun tipped over the mountains in the eastern sky, Ryan took a slow walk around outside the cabin, assessing the extent of the damage the storm had created. He came back even more dumbfounded than before.

There had been no damage, no tin dislodged, no trees downed, not even the tools leaning up against the house knocked over. He felt baffled that a wind so fierce could blast the windows inward all along the house – bar one – yet leave less-resistant objects still standing. He shook his head and looked at Leesa and Jess with dark, brooding eyes, then, picking up the bucket, he headed for the creek alone.

Ryan stayed pretty close to the house after that, as if on guard. His gaze repeatedly scanned the length of the valley and then swept up around the girt of tall trees and saplings. By early afternoon, his nerves had settled somewhat, and he left Jess to strand the ever-vining roses up the wire trellis he had structured for that purpose and disappeared to other toil elsewhere. Yet Jess caught a glimpse of Leesa chasing up the hill after him and watched as they both disappeared into the timber there.

Looking at Jade, she smiled, felt the gentle rustle of leaves around them and started to hum, that old sea shanty coming pleasantly back to mind, that old song bringing back visions of a tall man with jet-black hair and piercing steel grey eyes, a strong square jawline and a harsh profile softened beautifully by the subtle cleft of his chin; she savoured the small dimple which would appear when his face lit up with humour. His breadth, too, was impressive, structured by toil, his skin darkened richly by the ocean-strengthened sun from which he came, the muscled contours of his massive chest visible through the open neckline of the fluttery white shirt he always wore. She sighed at his magnificence.

He, too, sighed deeply, for he was at last truly happy again. He smiled as Sarah hummed him another shanty as he played with Jarvis on the hill.

Ryan returned sometime later, appearing happier than he'd been before he'd left. Leesa looked worn out from the exercise and complained before disappearing back up the ladder to her nook that they could at least have inherited flat land.

"I can solve this strange wind phenomenon," Ryan announced proudly as he came up beside her, his presence stopping her song mid-chorus. "That full circle of trees creates the problem," he said. "It sends the wind swirling around close to the ground until it whips down the valley where it builds in strength. Then it comes rushing up the other side, hits the treetops there, which turns it into a vertical swirling current which then smashes back onto the hill. Now, if we cut a wide strip in the belt somewhere up there ..." He pointed to the slope. "... it will be an escape route for the breezes and would solve the whole problem."

"No!" Jess told him without looking up from the roses.

"What?"

From the corner of her eye, Jess caught a glimpse of his dark frown. "No!" she repeated. "I won't have the trees cut down!"

He laughed, a short, sharp sound. "Be reasonable, Jess. An opening on the hill would be an advantage, not only to this wind problem, but it could also double as a driveway in."

"No!" She felt her teeth gnash together determinedly, and straightened her back. "The trees must stay! They have been there since the very beginning, and I'll not allow anyone to touch them."

"Now you're just being petty. Hasn't anyone ever told you about sacrifice for progress? And we're going to need a driveway in for the truck to bring the sheep. And how else are you going to get a glazier to come and repair the windows if he can't get down here, huh?" His blue eyes had gone hard, and his jaw had set firmly. "Or do you expect him to walk down here pane by precious pane?"

Jess shrugged that she didn't care.

"Well, I'll tell you now, he won't do it, and neither would I!"

She shrugged to that as well. "The trees stay!" she impressed further and turned to walk away.

"Well, the windows stay broken then!"

"Fine." She started to walk away, but Ryan's hand gripped her arm and turned her back.

"Now you're just being stupid …"

The rising roar of wind rushing down the hill from Jarvis caused Ryan to look up in awe, his hand retracting instantly. They both watched as the breeze whistled away above their heads, its trail slightly ruffling their hair in its wake. Looking suddenly pale, Ryan's eyes followed its path down the valley; watched as it shook the trees with mirth as it went.

Jess's eyes smiled as she turned. "Strange phenomena," she said as she walked away, leaving Ryan standing, still watching the wafting breath of wind that bounced along the valley.

Ryan didn't speak much to her after that – didn't do anything around the place either. He just sat sulking on the hill beneath the sad oak tree, becoming further dejected that his own son found more pleasure in his toys than in his company. They left early that afternoon, much to his joy.

"Well at least we won't have to spend another weekend here," he sniped.

Jess frowned. "Why not?"

"No windows. And it's too bloody cold to be possible," he shot back at her as they climbed into the car.

"You are such a wimp. No windows won't stop me. I love it here. I can sacrifice the comforts of home for progress." She slammed the car door.

Ryan huffed and shook his head, his jaw tightening.

Jessie shrugged with indifference. She sensed the rift was growing and wondered whose side Leesa would take, for she'd been strangely quiet since their long walk together. Somehow, she didn't think she'd be surprised if she took Ryan's, for they were becoming closer as she drifted away from them both.

But she shrugged that thought away too. *Can't afford the time to let it bother me. I have the farm now.*

Indeed, she had finally succeeded in what her mother had tried so hard to avoid and felt extremely elated. For the first time in her life, she felt truly, ecstatically happy. She had found herself on *Whistling Gums*, and that was where she belonged. There she had a purpose.

Chapter Eight

Profound?

Life isn't what it always seems,
For we see only what's on the surface.
But delve into the heavens, finding history abound,
Then enjoy what you are, and who you be,
For you are your ancestors' product.
So now, look forward to the future as they intended.

Leesa Bradden (14)
18/12/76

16th November, 1991.
The drive back to Sydney was unbearable, the silence reigning making Leesa feel strangely alienated in the back seat. She dared not interfere in the problem; felt this was probably a good time just to keep her mouth shut and let them get on with their argument lest she be considered a meddler and lose the friendship of both. So she played with Jade, who was strapped into his car seat beside her, the darling baby she cherished so much clutching dearly to her hand in an effort to prise it open.

And he was a dear child, she noted, but he hadn't always been; he had been born an absolute terror, almost driving Jessie and Ryan crazy with sleepless nights, with refusing to suckle, then refusing to eat, with not being able to amuse himself for a second, with losing interest so quickly when they tried to occupy his time ... it had been just one trauma after another. Oh, it sounded like the usual parent frustrations, she supposed, but it hadn't been. It was far worse than that. So bad was it that Jesse and Ryan had to take turns in rocking the cradle, sometimes way into the early hours of the morning, only to find he would doze just long enough for them to both find comfort in the bed then he would wake again. They'd had him tested by all the specialists they could find, for every possible cause they could find, but nothing had eventuated. As far as the medical profession was concerned, young Jade Robinson was a perfectly healthy baby, barring his difficult behaviour.

She looked at him now, his happy smiling eyes glowing with life: the world his oyster, so to speak, and she was glad for she loved him dearly, probably almost as much as Jessica herself. A while back, she would have professed to have loved him more, for Jess had become rather callous towards him in his first year, maybe even been on the borderline of hating him. But Leesa could love him more, because she didn't have to live with him, spending most of her time at the university, either in Brisbane or Tasmania. She was assigned to Brisbane at present, but scowled that the fortnight's study leave was nearly at an end.

She shifted her attention to her two friends sitting rigidly in the front seat. They were beautiful people: Ryan was as handsome and perfectly structured as anyone could want to be; he was incredibly intriguing, and so mentally stimulating she felt comfortable in his company. And he was loving to boot. Jessica had caramel-honey blonde hair, many shades darker than Ryan's, and her olive complexion was a gentle contrast to Ryan's rugged depth of tan. Jess was a sweet, kind, and gentle soul, and they were made for each other. No one was happier than Leesa when they had finally married, their love exuding from the glossy wedding portraits. If she had really analysed her feelings back then, she realised she would have found a touch of jealousy seeping in, for deep down inside she had found Ryan to be as irresistible as Jessica had, only he hadn't the slightest notion of her thoughts. And she had never let on. She was simply Jessie's best friend. Right now, though, she felt truly sorry they were not on speaking terms – hence why she had kept quiet – she had an awful suspicion Jessie knew how she felt about Ryan, and didn't want to risk losing her friendship.

They went back a long way, she and Jess, way back into their youth, long before Ryan had come on the scene. Yet, in all her varied travels, she had never been so lucky as to find another man quite like Ryan, and so had never married. Oh, there was this rather-young-for-his-title Professor at the university she had found a little interesting; they dated a few times, but not enough to really get to know him. He'd asked often enough though, but he just seemed so sedate ... and she had this important thesis to prepare ... one that delved into the various methods of tracing heritage. It linked to rather controversial resources, resources of the sort that, when dead ends blocked all other means of progress, called for the use of a medium. The special insight they possessed made it possible to unlock a few hidden doors to the past, as had been proven in her recent research. She didn't relish going back to her superiors with her theories though, for not all on the panel could be deemed scientifically open-minded. Not all were in favour of the newly formed Department of PSI ... the Parapsychology Science Investigators – or Parapsychology Studies Incubus that operated in the deepest, darkest corridors of the university.

But that was her problem. It had nothing to do with the little tiff that had developed over the weekend, and she wondered if she could somehow help them patch it up before she headed back to Brisbane in a few days' time.

Slamming car doors signified the long drive home had done little to quell the animosity that had risen. Nor did the stomping footfalls up the stairs to the porch. She decided it was best to leave them to it, hoping a good night's sleep would see a better mood from both in the morning. Retiring early also gave her an excuse to sit quietly in her room and peruse the papers she had smuggled into her kit bag in the loft, papers which had stirred her interest the previous night and had seen her up into the lighter hours of the morning. At least here, the bed was softer, cushioning her butt comfortably as she sat cross-legged on it, pouring over the cluster of letters and forms she had pilfered.

Darkness soon fell on the house, and she too decided to call it a day, though she lay awake for long hours in the pretty pink room that had once been Jessie's, remembering how Mrs Kendall had once started to piece together the events that had led to her being. She'd come a fair way along with her research before suddenly shelving it for other things, and she'd promised Leesa she would get back to it at a later date, but never had.

Leesa's thoughts shifted back to a time when they'd sat together in mutual discussion, Mrs Kendall's interest seeming genuine in her new job – she'd been really pleased that someone really cared about what she was doing. Leesa's own mother had remarried when she was in high school, and had left to start a new life in Perth almost the day Leesa had left to study at the university. Leesa's father had never seemed to care about his kids. Never then. Never now. In fact, Leesa didn't even know where he was. In a way, she felt as alone as Jessica did, except that she had half brothers and sisters living somewhere on the West Coast. Maybe that was why Ryan and Jessica were so important to her, she mused. Maybe that was why Jessica's mother had seemed like *her* mother, maybe more like her mother for Mrs Kendall and Jess had never gotten along.

That small reminiscence brought forth other snippets of detail: things like how mean Mrs Kendall could be at times, such as giving John everything and Jessica nothing; how, at times, she seemed to go out of her way to create disappointments for Jess. And Leesa wondered too, as she had back then, if that was why Jessica could be so deep, if that was what had caused her to wonder about her existence even back in high school. A poem Jessie had written for a class competition came instantly back to her, the words committed indelibly to mind because they were so deep and thought-provoking compared to what everyone else had written.

> *What does life hold for Jessie Kendall?*
> *Born one day, yet has no belonging,*
> *Now to her teens she has come grown,*
> *Yet still without a soul she's sighing.*
>
> *Time will heal that dreadful longing*
> *Time will come to make a stand*
> *Never fear, soul's time is coming,*
> *And I hold Jessie's soul in my hand.*

Leesa had asked Jesse why she'd written that; what had possessed her to think so profoundly; what in her life had ever happened that she would consider herself without a soul. Jessica's reply had been simple – she didn't know where the words had come from; they'd just tumbled out of her head. Confused as much as Jessica had been, Leesa had dwelt long on those words, trying to determine their meaning. But she never had. Maybe that was why she had committed them to memory – it was one of those mysteries of life, and Leesa loved mysteries. Maybe that was why she loved her job so much, she mused deeply, digging up people's origins, finding the twisting turns of life and straightening them all out on paper to find their living history. She found it more challenging than being a private investigator or a detective as she'd once considered becoming, those cases being far too easily solved, too close to the surface while life's blood ran much deeper … much, much deeper.

Chapter Nine

The black moods hadn't changed overnight, Leesa noticed, the clipped words and terse replies drifting up the stairs causing her to stay longer in bed than she'd wanted. It was better that way, she thought: let Ryan get off to work, then she could talk to Jessie in the quiet and see what was bothering her so. It had to be more than cutting down a few measly trees. It had to be, for she had seen her suffer far worse suggestions rather than have a conflict with Ryan.

"How goes it?" she greeted Jess cheerily as she came down the stairs, Ryan's car having aggressively left the driveway some five minutes earlier.

"Abominably," Jessica snapped back, her blue eyes drifting upwards, their sharpness seeming to assess whether to turn her temper on Leesa or not. "The nerve of that man!" she hissed.

"I'm sure he means well, Jess." Leesa picked up Jade and gave him a little cuddle, tousled the velvety crown of baby hair that was starting to gain some length at last; she put him down again. "Don't let it bother you, Jess. Why not just let it drop?"

"Me? Let it drop! You heard him! He wants to cut down the trees!" Her expression bordered on hysteria, a look Leesa would have more expected had she seriously suggested murdering someone, and she knew the futility of continuing this line of discussion. She was, after all, on Ryan's side. What would be the harm in cutting down a few trees, *really*?

"I'm sure if nothing else is mentioned, he might change his mind." She tried to sound nonchalant: dealing with Jessie since her mother had died had become harder than usual, her friend apt to snap at the most harmless of comments.

"Well, he'd better," Jess huffed, "or he won't be welcome on the farm again!"

Leesa let it go, rather than keep Jessie's temper fuelled. And Jesse, she had come to realise of late, could raise a fine temper, the recent arguments with her mother proving that.

She hadn't always been like that though – she'd been more resigned to drifting from one day to the next, her outlook being she was going nowhere anyway – this was just a stepping stone along the road of life. And Jess had laughed at that.

'What a cop-out!' Leesa had chastised her when she'd first made that comment. 'What about fighting for what you want! Nothing comes to those who wait. Isn't life worth making something out of? Isn't making every day possible better and better?"

Jess had merely shrugged, which Leesa had taken as not caring. And she'd wondered what her mother had ever done to make Jess so despondent. And she'd questioned at the time why she had ever stuck around so long because she and Jess were just *so* totally different.

Yet, in the last few years, she had come to realise how callous the woman she had considered her replacement mother could be. When Mr Kendall had died some years ago, she had been totally devastated by his demise; she had become totally reclusive in the house that now was Jessie's. Jess had gone to visit her daily; she had taken care of all the household duties, saw to it her mother was washed and fed, that her gardens were tended with the same loving care her mother had bestowed on them. It must have slowly killed Jess, Leesa had finally realised, to go there day after day, tending the house and suffering the cruel criticisms her mother would deliver upon her with the utmost regularity. This until Jess had a special announcement to make, one she hoped would give her mother a new purpose in life. She was pregnant; she would make her mother a grandmother. And her mother was delighted – so delighted she called John back from Cairns on the very day Jessie went into labour and, taking him up to Amberlay, gave him the farm. She was not even in the hospital for the birth of her first grandchild.

Leesa had thought back then it was the most despicable thing that woman could ever do: to give away the family farm to a son who had not the slightest interest in it while Jessica had all her life been keen to go and live there. Jess had told her of the dreams she'd had of spending holidays there.

"It's sitting empty," Jess had fought, "just begging for someone to come and stay. No one would be put out by our visit," but her mother would never let her go.

"I don't want no city-girl of mine coming back farm-girl," Jess's mother had said. "I don't want you to have to put up with the discomforts country life can bring. I struggled hard to get off the damn land and make a decent life for myself, with all the home luxuries you now have, and I don't want any daughter of mine to have to go back there. The farm is a man's place!" And Ryan had backed her on that, saying, "It isn't much of a place for a man either."

Well, Mrs Martha Kendall had gained a grandson that day. She had gained a grandson and lost a son, the sudden storm that had lashed the mountains as they had driven to the farm produced lightning streaks that jolted earthward. One bolt hit the gate just as John climbed over, the violence of its spear killing him before he could take possession of his birthright. The heat of its strike had welded shut the hinges to *Whistling Gums* forever.

Had it not been such an unfair end for poor John, it would have been easy to say it was just desserts for the old lady. But Leesa couldn't be so mean as to say that to her face. Mrs Kendall was so distressed, and had been so kind to her over the years. But Leesa did feel sorry for Jessie. She had lost a brother, and gained a son who drove her almost to a mental breakdown with his unnatural behaviour. And she drifted further away from her mother – the woman barely able to sit with her in the same room without telling her it was all her fault. Incredibly, she blamed Jess for John's death.

Then Martha Kendall had turned inside herself and withered away, no one able to help her find her way back to reality. With her death, the farm became Jessie's, her mother's pleading voice giving it to her in one breath yet taking it away again in the next. "You must never go there," she had rasped with her last breath. Then she was gone.

That had been four months ago, and Leesa was not surprised when Jessie slumped into deep and suicidal melancholia. What an awful burden for one person to put on another; to be blamed for your brother's death, told you were ultimately responsible, and then to watch your last blood fade into non-existence, not wanting to be helped by anyone, especially by the one who cared for her the most.

Thinking back to just how things had been in the past, Leesa wondered if maybe she should warn Ryan to back off as far as the trees were concerned. The farm was Jessie's now and it was her right to do as she pleased with it: it seemed to be the one thing that kept Jessie wanting to go on. What did it really matter if it meant walking down the track pushing a wheelbarrow with their supplies?! Wasn't it better that they were all still together and keeping an eye on the situation?

Ryan didn't see it her way that night. He remained angry that the farm had taken precedence over his wishes, and still felt angry that Jessie had taken to making her own stand in life without giving him a thought. He vowed again that he would not go to the farm, not until Jessica agreed to open up a drivable track. It was a stalemate; one Leesa could not alter. So she left them to it: Jessie vowing to spend every weekend on the land whether Ryan went or not; Ryan vowing the next time he set foot on the place he would be carrying a mighty big chainsaw.

And Jade?

Well, Jade played on the floor quite merrily and oblivious to their quarrelling, his wonderful new outlook that life was too good to be ruined brightening Leesa's face in the gloomy atmosphere around her.

And so, on Friday, when Ryan took his rostered day off and headed for his family's farm in Penrose, Jessie loaded the car with her bedding and Jade and drove off to the farm in Amberley. Leesa was flying back to Brisbane late in the evening so stayed at the house to pack, gathering her items from around the various rooms as she cleaned up the mess their joint leaving had left.

The peace of the empty house was unbelievably blissful, and she wallowed in it. In that peaceful solitude, she wrote a note wishing them to make a pact—an old remedy from way back—and granted them her love.

She pencilled on the calendar the date she intended to return, noting at the same time Jessie's repetitive circling of a date in December. The thirteenth of December. She wondered what significance it held. Had she maybe forgotten something important? A birthday? Anniversary? ... Nothing came to mind. She made a mental note to prompt Jessica for the details on her next visit as she placed her bags in the hallway ready to load in the car later. It was still early in the day, and she wandered aimlessly about the house, gazing at the memory-provoking ornaments, reflecting back on how long ago this or that photo had been taken, on how young Jessica's father had looked in his time. Her fingers stroked one photo absently. Old photos always fascinated her for they always linked things. People to people. People to a time. Time to an origin. She thought now how wonderful it would be if she could just trace the Robinson/Kendall/Raybourne family back, secretly of course, so that later in life, when Jessica eventually found the need to know her beginnings, she could present her with the finished item. *It would be a marvellous gift for anyone.* That's what she told her paying clients, and she honestly believed it was true.

Feeling rather safe that neither Ryan nor Jess would be returning to the house for many hours and, burning with a guilt that what she was doing could maybe be construed as interfering in their personal belongings, she slowly entered Jessie's room – the room Mrs Kendall had occupied in her lifetime. In the tall, ceiling-high cupboard in the wall recess, Leesa knew she would find what she wanted: a very special book. Jessie would never miss it, which would allow her time to sift through the information at her leisure and return it to its rightful place on one of her next visits.

The book was old and edge-tattered, a scrapbook with pieces of paper sticking out at odd angles from its pages. Its present disarray indicated it had been packed away in a hurry and never reopened to tidy away the files. This was the book Mrs Kendall had pencilled her research in and contained data that would save Leesa much time pouring over State Records at the Historical Library. Eagerly, her hands itched to open the pages just to see how far Jessie's mum had delved. But she didn't. There were more important things to do.

Returning everything to exactly how it had been, barring the presence of one family journal, she left the room, a slight tremor running down her back at the thought of how improper she was being while further thoughts begged her to renege on her original plans and return to Jessie what was rightfully hers. But she didn't do that either. Instead, she stashed the journal in her bag, then ducked outside to fetch the small step ladder-cum-stool. This she placed under the overhead man-hole to the ceiling.

'She kept what she didn't have a use for in the ceiling,' Jessie had told her.

What treasures are bestowed to that high place, Leesa wondered obsessively as she stretched tippy-toe on the stool to increase her reach into the roof cavity. Groping into the darkness, her hand touched a handle – a small leather handle – which was attached to a small leather suitcase of ancient origins. It moved easily her way until it teetered on the edge of the opening. From there, Leesa needed two hands to extract it. Gently lowering it to the stool, she climbed down, flicked open the latches and examined the contents. It was indeed what she was looking for; age-yellowed parchments, Bibles, photographs and etchings, the full family treasure.

As pleased as any archaeologist with a major find, she again covered any evidence of her doings and added the suitcase to her baggage. Her adrenalin was now really flowing, an excitement building so intensely within her that she felt tempted to open the box and turn those pages right then. But she didn't dare do that, not while in this house, not when one of them could change their mind and come back unexpectedly in the hope of making peace with the other. She could be caught red-handed, forever held with suspicion for taking liberties far beyond the realm of their friendship. She shook the thought away as often as she did the growing temptation to get started. She would be back in Brisbane soon enough where she would be able to work in complete security.

By late afternoon, and giving herself plenty of leeway to make the airport with time for the 'pre-flight nerves' coffee, she prepared to pack the car. Hoisting the black overnight bag and newly added brown suitcase, she headed for the door.

A shadowy figure hovering on the other side of the ripple-glassed panel froze her mid-step.

Ryan! Ryan's come back early! She chilled instantly. *Now what the hell am I to do!*

The flywire outer screen door creaked open.

Instinctively, Leesa dropped the baggage back onto its pile, kicked the unfamiliar case under the bigger, more saggy night bag, and sighed that it was completely concealed.

The blurred figure reached for the latch and she backed away, reluctant to show her nearness. Then came the knock, a very light rap on the wooden door frame. She knew then it wasn't Ryan. And it wasn't Jessie, for both had keys. After a short pause, the knock came again, followed by a voice.

"Hello. Is anybody there? Martha?" It was an elderly voice; one Leesa didn't know.

Frowning with suspicion, she went forward and gingerly opened the door a crack. A well-aged woman, finely dressed in a blue summer suit topped with white gloves and a petite crown hat, stood on the porch, looking just as startled at her presence as Leesa must have been at hers. The lady was tall, her flesh withered by time and laying in tiny folds over the diminished skeleton of her slender frame. Apart from the decay of years on her skin, she looked remarkably healthy, her bright eyes shining from the gauntness of her features, the hue of those smoky-grey orbs matching the silver-streaked short, tight curls on her head. The woman looked a little taken back as Leesa stood there staring at her then she turned and glanced back down the path as if to assess her surroundings.

The grey orbs cast back her way again. "Oh dear ... I was looking for Martha Kendall's," she said hesitantly, her words sounding as if she was starting to feel foolish. "It's been so long. Don't tell me I've come to the wrong house."

Opening the door wider, Leesa smiled, feeling a sudden warmth generating from her dilemma. "No," she said, cringing inwardly that she was now faced with the awful task of relaying bad news. "This is the right house."

"I'm Mrs Castle," the lady introduced herself tautly, her pride in who she was and her ramrod straightness showing her confident nature. She reminded Leesa of a primary school teacher she'd once had, the old school ma'am type. Very prim and very, very proper.

"Martha and I go back many, many years," she said, starting to look uncomfortable at being left standing on the porch. "... though we haven't seen each other in a long, long time. Is Martha home?"

"Umm ..." Leesa faltered. "Umm, no ... but please, do come in."

The best place to break the bad news to her was inside, and Leesa dreaded she would take it badly.

The lady wandered with interest, casting keen scrutiny over the passage and lounge, noting, Leesa presumed, the new decor Jessie and Ryan had applied over the past few months. They stopped in the lounge room, the woman ready for her as Leesa turned.

"You're not Jessica, are you?" she said, straightening as if certain of her observations, her faculties obviously in full order.

"No. I'm Leesa Bradden, a friend of Jessie's."

"I didn't think you were Jessica." Her gaze drifted further around the room. "That young girl had the loveliest dark-blonde hair. She would never have gone as dark as you are."

Leesa nodded her an acknowledgment. "She still has the blonde hair," she told her.

The lady looked around again and adjusted her handbag on her arm, and Leesa sensed her nervousness.

"May I make you a cup of tea, Mrs Castle?"

The lady nodded slowly, apparently prepared to stay for a reasonable visit. A few minutes later, they were sitting in the dining room, steaming cups before them. The lady had gone quiet as if waiting for Leesa's words.

"I'm sorry to have to tell you this, but Mrs Kendall died about four months ago." It was the best way Leesa could think of to broach the subject – straight to the point and take it from there. "Jessica and Ryan live here now."

"Jessica is married then?" It appeared she hadn't heard her first words.

Leesa nodded. "About three years now, to a wonderful man who thinks the world of her." Leesa hoped if they ever bumped into Mrs Castle they would behave a little better than they were behaving right now. "And they have a young son who turns one in a few weeks. It's a shame Mrs Kendall isn't around to enjoy him," Leesa impressed a little louder.

The woman lowered the cup back to its saucer. "Is Jessica happy now?" she asked, her eyes calculating the truthfulness of Leesa's next answer.

"She wasn't for a long time, but she is now." Leesa wondered if the woman had deliberately ignored the more important words.

"She was never a happy child. Tell me, how did she take it when John inherited the farm? That would have been so hard for her to accept."

Putting her cup down on the saucer, Leesa swallowed slowly. "Hadn't you heard? John died a year ago … he died before Mrs Kendall did."

That seemed to create an effect on the old woman. Clasping her hands tightly, she lay them on the table as if in prayer, then shook her head ruefully. The grey eyes went cold and stern more than sad.

"Who has the farm now then? Who did Martha leave it to?" It was a definite demand to know.

"To Jessie," Leesa answered meekly, somewhat aghast at the woman's sudden tone. "There was no one else, you see. She had to leave it to someone. And Jessie did love it so."

"Jessica must never go there. Never! No good can ever come of it!"

"But I don't understand …"

The woman started delving into her handbag. Fossicking hurriedly, she withdrew a pen and tore a page from a small notepad she'd also extracted. In rapid scrawl, she wrote a number across the page.

"Please, tell Jessica to ring me. There is much we need to talk about."

With that, she rose, curtly thanked Leesa for the cup of tea and closed her handbag. She was leaving, somewhat abruptly. At the door, however, she turned back.

"If you are Jessica's friend … truly Jessica's friend … then you must stand by her. You must do what must be done to save her soul."

"Pardon??"

"You will know the steps you have to take," she said stiffly. "I can feel it. I feel everything. I only hope we are not too late."

"Too late for what?"

The lady had already started descending the stairs, and did not turn back at her question, though Leesa heard her muttering to herself as she walked short, purposeful steps away. "I should never have left." She shook her head in private conversation. "… should never have left."

Leesa left the note and the message for Jessie on the dining room table, then loaded the car and left, those words of self-chastisement filling her thoughts for much of the journey. Why should she never have gone? And where had she gone? There was so much left unanswered.

Chapter Ten

The silence surrounding Brisbane University was expected in the late-night hour. The pile of messages shoved under the door of her campus unit was not. It looked like Saturday was going to be occupied with catching up with the letter-writers rather than taking it easy and starting on her new project as she'd hoped. The baggage safely transferred from the taxi to her room – her car checked for scratches that may have happened in her absence, its precarious parking spot by the stairway saving it from theft but not from inconsiderate passers-by – Leesa settled down to a steaming cup of cocoa and perused the notes more closely.

One was from Marion Wakely, a student who had recently joined the Parapsychology unit. She was interested in helping with her thesis, stating she wished to fully test her abilities and, therefore, would make herself available whenever Leesa needed her. She couldn't do much to help her, seeing her thesis was already completed and just needed a little more organising on the delivery presentation.

Another note was from Dorothy Maitland. Dot was eager to show her the results of further experiments undertaken at PSI in her absence. CONCLUSIVE EVIDENCE, she had double underlined.

Ah, and one from Professor Dean Morrison asking why the hell she didn't answer her damn phone!! *Oops! I forgot to tell him of my trip to Sydney. My bad.*

Several more were junk mail, a couple more letters from people wanting to start delving into their families' past, or wanting to know where to start so they could do it themselves. Leesa put those aside for early personal attention. Maybe she would run a short Genealogy course over the summer break. But for now … a quick phone call to Dot to set a time for the morning.

The lady sounded more happy than usual to hear from her. *Something must have really blossomed in my absence,* she realised, but Dot Maitland wouldn't say what, making Leesa look keenly forward to morning.

The polished hallways leading down to her office echoed in their loneliness, Saturday finding few students willing to partake of extra curriculum. The jarrah staircase was just as easily descended without the usual crush of bodies thumping up and down, and Leesa soon reached the doorway to her rooms. If there were few enthusiastic scholars on the upper level, there were even fewer on this one. The newly resurrected basement was home-base for the little and lesser-known departments – the Department of PSI, being one – the bowels of a building most suited to such an incubus subject as the Abstract Sciences – and while Genealogy studies didn't exactly fit into this field, it was better than having no Department at all or, shudder the thought, being attached to the Histories wing where all the students and professors were prematurely fossilised. Leesa excluded Dean Morrison in that regard, though his outlook on life could be pretty narrow at times.

The quietness of the basement level had actually motivated the choice for her rooms, a decision that had brought her into acquaintance with the ladies of Parapsychological Studies. Knowing little except that the Department existed, she'd expected to find an assortment of weirdos patrolling the halls chanting mantras and holding hedonistic rituals, but that hadn't been the case at all. In fact, it would have been difficult to determine the perceptive souls behind the doors opposite hers from some of the students' own mothers – from her own mother for that matter.

Opening the door and flat-tossing her file onto the dark wood work desk, she crossed the passage to the door with the light glowing outward through the small glass panel. Knocking once, she entered.

Dorothy Maitland sat at her desk in the far corner of the expansive white room. Other tables sat diagonally across the adjacent corners, but these were empty and bare, the files cleared for the days of rest and stored away for security. Dorothy was a good twenty years Leesa's senior and was neither young for her fifty years, nor old, yet something about her told of a wealth of knowledge. Maybe it was the heavy grey-framed glasses she wore for reading. Maybe it was those depthless blue-grey eyes that saw far beyond what anyone would ever expect to see, with or without the glasses. Leesa didn't know why, but Dot's eyes had always fascinated her.

She'd heard some of the students once call her 'the Guide Dog', not derogatorily, of course, for everyone seemed to find Dot Maitland easy to work with. The title was more complimentary, for the woman could lead the seeing where they could not see.

She smiled now as Leesa entered, and looked up, her pen ceasing to scribe as Leesa approached the desk. Pulling the chair in front of her out and sitting, Leesa tried to decide yet again if Dot's hair was red or blonde; both shades seemed to dominate yet without definite result.

Dot slid her glasses down on the table, smoothed the page-boy style haircut back from her heavily powdered face and became more perceptive. "I sense the trip didn't completely assail your worries, Leesa. Did something go wrong?"

"No, not really." But Leesa sighed deeply. "My girlfriend seemed to be coming good for a while but I'm not so sure now. Maybe one obsession has just been replaced by another."

Dot shook her head consolingly. "Never mind, dear, your new project will take your mind off it for a while."

Ordinarily, that would have surprised Leesa, but nothing Dot said phased her any more. She did indeed know all; see all. She, therefore, simply nodded.

"Well, I know you are keen to hear about our find," the lady said, opening a drawer to her right. She extracted a cream manilla file. Flipping it open, she spread a stack of photos across the desk, the images depicting an assortment of people and places of various eras. Catching her confused frown, Dot selected one of a time long past: two moustachioed men in gentry clothing posing for what would have been an equally ancient camera.

Taking it, Leesa studied the snapshot, looking for what she wasn't quite sure.

"The two men are father and son," Dot informed her. "The photo was taken in 1870."

The period looked about right yet Leesa couldn't see the significance of the point.

"The point is," Dot gave her a keen look of interest, "the father had died ten years earlier … before the photo was taken."

Her words took a while to sink in, Leesa's dark scowl an indication that she needed no further explanation.

"It could be a hoax," Leesa warned her, looking up again. "The photo could be a fabrication."

The wry grin creeping slowly over Dorothy's face told Leesa she had further evidence up her sleeve. "We've done all the testing possible, including using our newest protege. All tests are conclusive. That is an apparition standing there. And that fact is further backed up by the death certificates provided by the family."

Leesa's rising eyebrow told Dot Leesa was quickly putting two and two together. She fished for another age-yellowed print.

"This one … see the face in the painting on the wall? It's the great-great-grandfather of the boy on the chair. He died a decade and a half before, yet returned to be seen in that most recent family portrait. This one …" Dot fossicked through the stack and flicked out another one. "The lady on the left of the garden was the other woman's best friend. She was killed in a horse-riding accident two years earlier. And this …"

"Whoa! Whoa! I get your point," Leesa gushed, taking a moment to examine the images more closely. "Does this now mean that I was right in saying Joseph Morrison died before his own father?"

"It does. The figure beside James Morrison was his son in the spirit, not in the flesh. I feel you can safely say the documentation you unearthed was correct and that he did indeed die some five months before his father." Dot looked pleased.

And Leesa's pleasure sparkled in her eyes. *Professor Morrison will have to eat his words as far as this startling little piece of evidence is concerned,* though it wouldn't surprised her if he wouldn't listen to that either. He wasn't one for believing in supernatural occurrences. And she probably didn't really blame him. She had felt much the same in the beginning; she had been very sceptical until the students had challenged her to sit in on one of their demonstrations. Awed, Leesa had watched objects move from place to place without being touched. Her fortune had been told – the information scoffed at until the very predictions fell into place like clockwork. The final touch was when a young girl had held her hand and told her the exact location of a wristwatch she had lost months earlier. That wristwatch was now back in its rightful place on her wrist. She glanced down at it. *Mid-morning.*

Dot restacked the pile of photographs, stowed them back in

the file and returned it to the drawer. "Do keep this under your hat for the time being," she said. "We haven't told anyone else about it yet."

Leesa nodded her assurance.

"If you wish to put it in your thesis though, we would be agreeable to have our submission prepared and delivered at the same time as yours."

A sure way to go. One branch of the Abstracts helping concrete the other's findings. Rising, Leesa smiled, for it would be one incredible release when the time came. She heard Dot's stifled mirth, the lady's eyes bright with similar thoughts. This would undoubtedly push their work even closer together.

Filled with thoughts of past lives and returning spirits, Leesa headed back to her office, anxious now to get started on Jessie's papers before she needed to put her efforts to more academic purposes. She found herself ringing Dean's number, wanting to gloat. He was out, probably taking the opportunity of the fine day to take his plane up, so she left a message on his machine telling him she was back. Then she rang Ryan.

He sounded lonely. Jessie had not come home from the farm as he had hoped. But no, he wouldn't change his mind and go after her. He said he missed her, and Leesa had mixed feelings about that, wondering if he really missed her or just missed someone to talk to, or did he just need company of any kind. She told him she hoped everything would work out and reminded him to tell Jessie to ring Mrs Castle, then hung up. Hopefully they would have it all sorted out when she returned in a few weeks. She would use the interim time to finalise her report, the success of which would hopefully facilitate another grant.

Absently pulling some blank charts from the wall niches, her thoughts still on Ryan, she flipped open the tattered journal she had misappropriated and started sifting. Mrs Kendall had indeed made her task very easy, having done most of the footwork of hunting down certificates that registered births and marriages, deaths and burial places of past relatives. Separate was a list of Charter, names of those who had come from other countries, some of whom had left again. It was all there – well, it was for Martha's side of the family – and Leesa was surprised at just how far she had come with her work, the depth of her delving making her wonder why Mrs Kendall had stopped so suddenly.

Scrutinising another scrap, Leesa noted Mrs Castle's name written – scrawled actually – not in Mrs Castle's hand from memory – that lady had had such a precise flair even in her fluster – but probably in Mrs Kendall's, yet shakily so. Mrs Castle's name was the last item pencilled in the journal, and Leesa wondered if there was a connection.

Returning to the journal's first page, she started transferring the data across to the forms she was more familiar working with. The entries started with the present family and worked back into the past, so, for ease, she followed suit in her transcript.

Extending the data to include Jade, she wrote his full name: Jade Damon Robinson. Born 20th December, 1990. Mother: Jessica Linda Robinson, nee Kendall. Born 11th July, 1963. Father: Ryan Philip Robinson. Born 4th October, 1959. And that was as far as Ryan's tree extended; the rest of his details were blank, as were the spaces extending from Jessica's father. It was obvious Mrs Kendall was only interested in her heritage, but that was how the woman was, and had been for as long as Leesa had known her.

Leesa transferred the data from the rest of the pages quickly, asterisks showing the lineage in the unions she was most interested in. The years rolled back to the founding of the country; Martha Rose Kendall, nee Raybourne occupying dates from 1926 to 1991; her mother Elizabeth Rose Wentworth-Moore from the turn of the century to 1963. At that point, the line turned to Wentworth with Philip Kenton Wentworth living in both centuries ... 1876 to 1927, his father John William Wentworth from 1836 to 1886. There, the entries were nearly at an end. John Wentworth's son, Ken, married Jane Sanderson (the asterisk was on Sanderson), and I remembered Jessie having said something about the Sanderson line. Jane was born in 1803, died in 1836 at the age of 33. Her father was the last starred entry. William Kenton Fintish Sanderson.

The name took up nearly a whole line and Leesa stared at it, bewildered. *How the hell did anyone come up with a name like that!!* She shook her head in wonder, thoughts stirring about the past generations, and what would the man have been like to issue a moniker like that to his offspring. Thankfully, someone had the foresight to endow his wife with a better name: Rebecca Morton.

From there, the list ended, Mrs Castle's name the last scrawled message. It didn't seem to fit that it should be on a page of family members, and Leesa wondered if maybe the old lady was related, but to whom and along which line would probably never be known unless she wanted to go much further than Mrs Kendall had.

For now, though, Leesa chose not to. Mrs Kendall had provided enough history to keep her occupied for several days without flitting off on tangents. Other pages she turned at random, just sifting through information in an effort to decide how to structure her other charts, wanting an easy display of facts so Jessie could follow them without a great deal of effort.

What did appear from that brief browse was the Sanderson clan's origins: the Americas – or at least that they had travelled somewhat before arriving back on our shores. There was little information on Rebecca Morton, just a set of numbers she would need to follow up on in the Historical records, and she hoped the contents of the boxes and suitcase would fill in the gaps. Apart from that, the Charter list showed they were a fairly settled family; that, once William Kenton Fintish Sanderson had stepped off the decks of the *Bellona* back in 1793, they stayed fairly close to Sydney. One or two in later years were listed as passengers to the west coast, but they, too, had returned within a year or two of leaving.

There was not much else, except the burial records, and those she pencilled in alongside the deceased's name. Glancing across at the now documented chart-forms, it became suddenly obvious that she'd spent much time in her doings. The clock above the computer verified her thoughts. She had whiled away a good seven hours, and it was now late afternoon. *Time to think about closing the file for a while, maybe even phoning Dean to see if he is back yet.* With an exuberant yawn, she did, closing the file and the journal and stacking them ready to take back to her unit. Tidying the remnants of her day's work, she thought again of Ryan and the words he'd said. His loneliness increased hers, and she felt the need to secure some company of her own for the night.

Dean's answering machine activated, so she just said "Me again," and hung up. Maybe she too would sit alone all evening.

I could phone Ryan again, the thought embedded warmly, … *just to see if he has heard from Jessie* … But she knew she wouldn't. As much as she liked the sound of his voice on the phone, Ryan and Jessie would have to sort out their own problems.

She dimmed the office lights and listened to her solitary footsteps squeaking down the corridor, the rooms of the Parapsychology wing already in darkness. *Some people apparently have other things to do with their weekends.* And she wondered again where Dean had gone.

The campus looked deserted as she crossed the green expanse of freshly mown lawn to the block of units at the southernmost perimeter. Way across the gardens, beneath the spreading reach of Jacaranda trees, the space where Dean always parked his car sat empty so she knew it would be pointless phoning again when she got in.

Although cosy, her small flat on such a grim Saturday night seemed uninviting; she made a coffee and sat on the lounge floor in front of the small TV to drink it, idly pushing around the scatter of books and news clippings in the small, open, brown suitcase on the armchair.

The items were very dated, portraits of men in very distinguished dress, straight-backed in their prestigious gentry stances; ladies in stiff frills and laces, hair in tight buns further accentuating their stern, angular faces; some held small babies garbed in long flowing garments, the obvious pride of their household. The contents of the case showed the family growing, and spreading, and her doldrums soon deteriorated into rising interest. This was Jessie's family, and Leesa felt so close to her it was like watching *her* family, and she wanted to know more.

The books enticed her hands to touch, to open, but she knew she had to be careful for they were old, the pages flimsy and easily damaged. The biggest book was bound in smooth blue leather, and proved to be a Log, the entries hand-written in a flourishing style, yet more in a man's hand than the gentler hand of a woman. Her theory was correct for, on opening at the book's centre and turning several pages midway through it, a signature ended the entry. It read ... William Sanderson.

Her jaw dropped open. *This is the beginning! This is where Australia's family branch started,* and her heart soared at the luck she'd been granted. This volume of memories was the written history of the Sandersons ... seven generations past!

Chilled with anticipation, Leesa turned back to the very first entry, a water-stained page with blurred inkwork. Holding it to better light, the words *I go to find a new start in a new world* became readable. The entry was dated in a similarly smudged style ... *May 15th, 1789.* How gently her hands touched the paper for fear of destroying the fragile parchment. The next page refused to turn easily; it had stuck firmly to the next and then to the next. There appeared to be a thick band of written work bound together, perhaps the result of whatever had stained the first entry. Her fingers shaking, she gingerly tried to prise the edges apart, her eagerness to read on almost overcoming her patience to go gently. At least ten pages refused to succumb to her teasing nails, nor did they surrender to the extreme point of a sharp knife.

With a brittle crackle of parting substances, a sheet finally yielded and eased stiffly over. She leant over to read the faded print, wondering at the same time just how to coax the resisting leaves open. There had to be a way to expose the wealth of words fate had sealed from her eyes and she frowned deeply as possibilities raised themselves. *But not tonight.* Tonight, she would pour over what was willing; glean as much as she could from this gentleman of the past.

The word *Bellona* caught her attention immediately, and so did the loud rap on her front door. Warily, she closed the ancient diary and rose to answer it, her heart skipping that Dean Morrison stood there in the rather dishevelled casual wear he was renowned for. His hair was boyishly tousled as usual, and his gold fine-rimmed glasses gave him that windswept John-Denver-look she was accustomed to. With a minimal smile, his deep green eyes glinted behind the clear lenses, revealing he had something on his mind.

"Me again," he said, amused. His smirk spread. Obviously, he held no malice for her sudden departure to Sydney. "Can I interest you in a meal at the Golden Arches, or by chance have you already eaten?"

"No … no, I haven't," Leesa floundered, half torn between the gnawing reminder in her stomach that she hadn't eaten since yesterday and her overwhelming desire to continue with the writings of one Will Sanderson.

She didn't get a choice as Dean's hand took hers and hauled her out into the corridor. He never was one to dally over matters, and Leesa was thankful McDonald's dress code was pretty flexible. At least she now had someone to share her excitement with.

As usual, Dean listened to her constant prattling about her work though she sensed he was still very sceptical since the flaw she'd revealed in his own family records. She wanted to tell him about the amazing discovery Dot had made, about the single photo that would convince him of the records' accuracy, but she held back. For one, Dot had asked her to keep the information a secret, and secondly, Dean was too academic to believe in psychics, mediums or the paranormal in general. So she let it drop. Instead, she listened to how his day had gone and somehow, by the end of the night, she found herself coerced into joining him for a day's flying on the morrow.

Consequently, she didn't get back to Jessica's papers until Monday morning, when she was able to double-purpose a visit to the State Registry Building. There, she delved a little further into the Sanderson's Death Records, as well as acquiring a copy of the death certificates for James and Joseph Morrison: Dean was going to have to eat his words before she was finished!

The rest of the day rolled on, fairly uneventful. The ladies in Parapsychology had left that morning on a field trip, so the lower bowels of the Sciences Wing held an eerie, eerie silence. Dean was heavily committed to classes so therefore, once Leesa returned to her office, her time promised to be totally uninterrupted. Reluctantly, she put Jessie's project aside and put some time into the all-important Thesis which was soon due for delivery. But she needed some ideas on how to broach the inclusion of Dorothy's discovery without sounding like a perfect nutcase.

By the end of the afternoon, she was no closer to a solution and hoped Dot herself would have some suggestions. Closing her books, she returned to her unit, hurrying the last few steps to reach her door and open it before the phone stopped ringing.

It was Ryan, the worry in his voice evident over the distance.

"I hate to impose on you like this, Leesa, but can you come back down again? Jessie's got me really worried."

"Why? What's happened?" she asked, not yet even registering the expense and time involved with trying to get away.

"She won't even speak to me now. She came back from the farm late last night, gave me the cold shoulder right from the get-go and went straight to bed. She wouldn't even get out of bed this morning to see me off. I don't know what to do. I thought maybe you could talk to her."

"Has she rung Mrs Castle yet?" Leesa didn't know why, but that point seemed very important right then, more-so than whatever else was happening in the house.

"No. She's not going to."

"Why not?!"

"I don't know. She just said something about her being an interfering old biddy and that she could just butt out. You see what I mean, Leesa? It's just not like Jess. She's changing … she's becoming so distant."

He sighed with deep frustration. "I don't know what else to do. If anyone can help her, you can."

His anxiety made the decision for her. She promised to be there on the coming weekend.

The rest of the week was taken up with preparing to get away again, squeezing in extra time on her schedule so she would be well ahead of her duties by Friday. Thankfully, she was. Leaving a note for Dot, and one for Dean, she hopped a plane for Sydney, the stewardesses now starting to know her on sight from the frequency of her visits.

It was a late flight and Ryan looked extremely tired when he collected her at the airport. He was alone, Jessie and Jade having gone up to the farm earlier that afternoon. He expressed his concern that she seemed to spend her whole week preparing for her escape at the weekend. The lines of strain on his face told the rest of the story.

They decided Leesa would take his car the next morning and go up to the farm alone and talk to her. For one, Jess might just confide in her if Ryan wasn't there, and secondly, she would still not allow him to set foot on the place.

The drive up through Oberon was pleasant enough, even more picturesque through the sleepy siding of Amberlay, and the solitude allowed Leesa's thoughts to flow on just how she could broach the subject of Jesse's conflict with Ryan. Jess had been so adamant not to give an inch last time.

Soon enough, the rusted gate blocked further progress.

The mid-morning sun felt pleasantly warm as she climbed from the car, straddled the gate and started the long walk down to the valley, her gaze watching for signs of Jessie below. Leesa didn't see anything. The parked Ford was the only indication Jessie was there at all.

The cottage also looked lifeless when she arrived yet, on pushing open the door, she found the previously dusty living room very homily decorated. The glassless windows now had plastic taped over the vacant spaces, and curtains of red gingham draped attractively across each, somewhat concealing the substituted glass. The cane wicker chairs dotted around the fireplace now had cushions that matched the curtains and a large oblique grey carpet spread across the floor to warm the feet. The fire itself still emitted smoke from the soft glow of embers visible in the grate. Obviously, Jess had made herself very comfortable indeed.

Turning, Leesa wondered where Jess was, where the hell she could go, and, as an afterthought, why she would want to go anywhere.

"Leesa?"

The voice outside the door made her turn further.

"Jess?"

"What are you doing down here?" her friend questioned, her eyes narrowing with suspicion. Entering, she placed Jade down on the circular mat.

Leesa knew she would have to be careful if she was to keep her friend on her side. "I had to come down on business," she lied. "Ryan said you were up here so I bummed his car for the day to come and see you."

"That's nice," Jesse said drily. "What business?"

"Oh, just a very financial client with an interest in holding a seminar in Genealogy for the Interested Amateur." The lie thickened. *Well, it really isn't a lie;* Leesa excused herself – it was something coming up that would require yet another trip at a later date.

Jess didn't answer straight away, instead filled the kettle. She had obviously come in for a break.

"The cottage looks lovely," Leesa said. "Really homely."

Jessie cast a more friendly look her way, her eyes glinting with the compliment. "You really like it?" she tested.

"Love it! The curtains are divine … just the right choice for in here."

Jess's smile looked warm and genuine. "Would you like a cuppa?"

Leesa nodded.

They pulled the chairs up at the table – made from an old door and two petrol drums – and set cups down on it as comfortably as if we were at home. Leesa noted Jess certainly appeared to be; noted too she was becoming more relaxed the more they chatted. For that reason, she hedged on discussing Ryan, and of mentioning Mrs Castle.

"So, what have you been up to while I've been gone?" she probed gently.

"Lots." Jess smiled. "As you can see, the house has taken a lot of my time." She waved her hand around to encompass the room. "… and the outside is certainly shaping up nicely. We even cleared a patch for the vegetable garden last weekend."

"We? Who's we?"

Leesa caught the sudden apprehension strike her face, and then a blank look of terror momentarily flitted before a smile slowly touched Jess's lips again.

"Me and Ryan's ghosts," she grinned pertly.

"Really." Leesa raised an eyebrow at her joke "Anyone I might be interested in?"

Jess laughed lightly and shook her head.

"And how is Ryan?" *Opportunity knocks*, and Leesa grasped the moment to ask, seeing Jess had brought him up.

"You saw him!" Her voice became brittle. "He hasn't changed a bit. And he doesn't understand. I really think he doesn't want to."

"Oh, I'm sure he does …"

"He does not!"

Taking the hint, Leesa regressed and pushed back to a happier conversation. "Whatever," she shrugged, avoiding having to take sides. "So, tell me about your ghosts."

The look Jess flashed her was surprising to say the least. It was a mixture of total shock at her asking, and wariness, as if she had touched on a secret Jess wasn't sure she wanted to share. "I didn't think you believed in ghosts," she challenged.

"People are entitled to change their minds." Leesa shrugged again, remembering the photos Dot had shown her. "Sometimes things happen to change one's mind."

"Oh. And what happened to change yours?" she tested.

Unable to divulge that information, Leesa said, "Just something."

"So you believe in ghosts now?!" Her eyebrows rose mockingly, the look on her face brightening as she rose to reheat the kettle on the gas stove.

"Don't you?" Leesa teased.

"Hell no!" came the sharp retort. Then she turned back to her friend, the twinkle in her eye glinting with humour. "You want to be careful. You hang out with Ryan so much you're beginning to sound like him!"

Leesa cringed at the subtle accusation and decided to tread warily for a while. "Why? Does Ryan believe in ghosts?" She forced a smile back at her.

"I didn't think so, but lately he appears to." Jess straightened and looked her straight in the eye, a blatant perusal of her next thoughts. "Do you know, he actually accused me of coming up here because I was having an affair! When I asked who with, he laughed and said he didn't know. All he knew was that I was more interested in someone other than him."

Jessie's eyes narrowed slightly at Leesa's expression. *She's picked up on my thoughts. Shit. Be careful.* "And?" She forced a cheeky grin.

"Well of course I said I wasn't. But he didn't believe me." She also half laughed, falsely. "He said I go home from here starry-eyed as if I'd had a romantic interlude. Can you believe that?!"

Shrugging again was Leesa's only answer for she knew not what else to say. This side of the argument she'd definitely not heard before.

"I told him he was being ridiculous, that no other man comes on the place but him, but he wouldn't hear of it. He said if that was the case, then I must be having it off with a ghost.

Personally, I think Ryan is the one with the mental problem." She shoved the freshly filled cup of tea down in front of her friend, and Leesa noticed the assessing glance she flicked her way.

"Ryan's just worried, Jess. He really is worried sick about you."

"Well, he has a funny way of showing it! Sometimes I feel it would be better if I moved up here permanently." She slid down onto the crate opposite Leesa again, and looked thoughtfully out the window behind her. "Are you staying long in Sydney?" she finally asked.

Leesa shook her head. "I have to be back by Monday."

"Are you staying over here tonight?" Jess's eyes glanced up to the loft.

Again, Leesa shook her head. "Ryan will need his car and I must get back to business."

Jess seemed to accept it well enough though Leesa wondered if she would put any connotations to her spending a night alone in the house with Ryan. They talked for a long while before lengthening shadows warned Leesa it was time to make a move to leave, and then, for a moment she looked sad.

"Is there anything I can do for you back in town?" she asked, hoping she would send a message or acknowledgment to Ryan.

Nodding, Jessie rose and picked up the notepad hanging by the back door; she started writing. "You can drop this list off at the Amberlay store on your way past if you will. Just some items I need for tomorrow. Tell Mr Bateman I'll be down in the morning to collect them."

Tearing off the top sheet, Jess handed her the list; and Leesa absently flicked a quick glance down at the page. Then frowned.

"Sarah?!" she queried.

Jessie turned, looking equally confused. "What?"

"You signed it ... Sarah."

Peering over her shoulder in verification, Jess looked just as puzzled. "Did I? Now why did I do that?!"

"Don't ask me. And who is Sarah anyway?"

Jessie looked taken back, and her blue eyes widened. "Don't ask me!"

Shrugging with her own lack of answers, Leesa headed for the door, Jessie following her out to the verandah, apologising for not walking her to the car. "Jade's getting heavier and heavier these days," she excused, to which Leesa nodded that she understood and started walking up the slope.

She hadn't gone far, though, when she heard Jessie call. "Leesa?"

Turning, she waited for her to continue.

"What made you change your mind about ghosts?"

The question was posed in a way that deserved an answer, and she obliged as briefly as she could. "I saw some ... in a way."

Jess nodded wordlessly, her eyes slowly panning the sky as if deliberating the possibilities. Again, Leesa started walking, though, after a short distance, her annoyance grew that she had not thought to give her a message for Ryan. She turned back again. Jess still stood on the rickety verandah, though her attention had gone to the hills on the far side of the creek, to the breeze gently wafting through the treetops.

"Jessie," Leesa called to her.

There was no response, so she shouted louder. "Jessica!"

Still Jessie stared upward to the trees.

"JESSIE!!"

Not the slightest motion came to indicate Jess had heard, yet Leesa was well within hearing range. Annoyed, she called again, but this time, for reasons she was unsure of, she called, "Sarah!"

Jess turned promptly, smiled and waved her goodbye.

Bewildered, Leesa stood staring down at her, all thoughts of Ryan gone. *What the hell is going on?! What the hell has happened to my friend?!* Frightened, she turned and hurried away, leaving Jessie standing there happily waving. She wondered if Jessie had really answered to the name she had called her, or had she just finally heard her voice? In light of the scrawled note, she shuddered to think of the answer.

Her duty done, albeit fruitlessly, Leesa returned to Brisbane on the first available flight north, after telling Ryan he was right. Jessie needed help – professional help. Between them, they had done all they could to help her. Her problem was far beyond their capabilities. She felt traitorous leaving, but there were things she had to tend to, things she wished to have fully completed before being needed again in the South. And needed she would be; she knew that. Things had certainly taken a turn for the worst. And she sensed they weren't going to get any better.

Chapter Eleven

By Monday Leesa was back in her subterranean office, idly poking about amongst Jessica's papers, trying to force her concentration to stay on the thesis that was running to its deadline. Neither project held her attention for long though; thoughts of Jessie kept drifting in, thoughts that dwelt on her reaction when Ryan insisted she get psychiatric help.

Rubbing the tiredness from her face, Leesa pondered guiltily that maybe she had said the wrong thing. Was she really helping Jess? Or was she just creating further stress? For a moment, she had a strong need to cry, to let out her anxieties, for the only family she had ever really known was falling apart around her, and maybe she was partly to blame.

A tear threatened to fall, the gentle rapping on the glass panel of her door the only thing stopping it. She didn't have time to answer before the door partially opened. Dot Maitland peered in through the gap.

"Do you want to talk a bit?" the woman asked in a motherly whisper. Leesa guessed she'd sensed her misery, and while she knew she could talk to Dot openly, this time she shook her head.

"My, you do look down. Are you sure there is nothing I can do to help?"

"I'm sure," Leesa assured her. Dot was very sweet, and she didn't want to burden her with any more of her problems.

"Don't worry, love. This will soon be over, and you will be strong enough to handle the problem when it arises."

"What problem?" Leesa asked, one eyebrow rising as she looked up. *Lord, the problem I'm having now is great enough without Dot intimating there's another.*

"You will know when it comes," she said.

Blinking heavily, Leesa reluctantly accepted that was her answer, for Dot could be stalwart in her decisions when she wanted, and only ever said what she wanted someone to know.

"Seeing you wish not to talk about your dilemma, could you spare a moment for mine?" the woman asked coyly.

Leesa nodded, smiling, and beckoned her to enter. She did so, opening the door just wide enough to allow access to herself and one other woman, who looked to be in her early forties.

"Leesa, this is Marion Wakely. Marion … Leesa Bradden."

Leesa remembered the name instantly and her guilt pushed a little higher that she'd not responded to the woman's earlier message. Saying hello, she quickly noted the woman was slightly smaller than Dot in height and shape, her hair a deep shade of brown, its length pulled back into a clip at the back of her neck. Her eyes, though, took Leesa's mind from the rest of her. They were more gold than brown – eyes that commanded attention – eyes that instantly sent thoughts flowing on what was going on behind them. They were unusual, to say the least, if not alarming, but they suited this woman perfectly.

Marion smiled warmly, and Leesa knew she didn't hold it against her for not contacting her. And felt easier.

"Marion has been keen to meet you," Dot said. "She's only just joined our team and we feel she'll be invaluable to all of us. Unfortunately, we've run out of things for her to do just now so we thought we'd drop in and let you know she's available for anything that poses a problem in your research."

Marion stood, giving Leesa's office a casual once-over, the eagle-like eyes gliding across the walls and benches with minor interest. Still smiling, she leaned back against the bench where

Leesa had been working earlier, her attention now back to where Leesa sat.

"Well, unfortunately," Leesa started, "I've got nothing on the go at the moment. My presentation is nearly ready and I haven't taken on any new clients because of the coming holidays."

She noted Marion's attention drifted again, this time to the desk she leant against. Glancing back, the woman drew a deep breath and Leesa noticed her eyes narrow slightly. Then she half-turned and placed her hand flat on a file that lay closed on the table. The gold eyes narrowed further, her expression sobering with deep concentration. Then she turned fully; let her other hand lay beside the first.

"Oh, these poor people," she said breathily, her words not quite a whisper but soft enough they could have been meant only for herself.

Dot and Leesa glanced at each other, their expressions simultaneously questioning.

"What do you mean … poor people?" Leesa asked.

For a long while, Marion Wakely just stared at the cream folder that enclosed the many papers of the Kendall family's past.

"They're lost," she said with sadness. "They're caught up on the plane, unable to move on." Her eyes looked heavy as if she was receiving heartfelt news, then she shook her head in slow deliberation. "The poor, poor souls," she repeated, in barely a whisper.

"What is it? What do you see?" – Dot's question.

Marion's long fingers spread out across the folder. "This is a very sad family," she said, looking up at the wall as if movie images played there. "They are torn and tortured by their past."

"Her insight is incredible," Dot whispered sideways, resting her ample butt against the back of the chair next to Leesa. "She has an amazing gift."

Leesa's brow creased deeply. "But what does she mean?" she murmured back. "And what is she doing?"

The woman, by this time, had both hands on the file's cover, the fingers of each hand spread fully. Her eyes lay lightly closed.

"She's reading the past," Dot said, hinging forward as if waiting for the climax of a suspense-filled thriller. With a sideways glance, she queried quietly, warily, "Whose family is it?"

Chilling before the answer was even spoken, Leesa looked darkly back at her. "Jessie's."

"Oh, dear," the lady drawled deeply. Her hand closed over Leesa's consolingly.

That response worried Leesa more than she cared for, but she said nothing; just watched the dark-haired woman as she let her fingers glide over the blank binder. Then, as if whatever had occupied her mind was gone, she looked up, inhaled deeply, and let it out again. She turned and took Leesa and Dot into her vision. The gold eyes blinked quickly once or twice then her fingers went up to rub firmly at her temples.

"Are you alright, dear?" Dot prompted carefully.

The other woman didn't speak for a long moment, just stood, seeming to catch her breath. Then she nodded slowly and sighed tiredly.

"What was it? What did you see?" Dot prodded again.

Another sigh preceded the answer. "I could see very little actually," came the dull reply, "for there was little to go on, but I could feel the pain reigning over those people. Much pain. Much sorrow."

She turned and picked up the folder then looked straight at Leesa. "What is in this?" she asked, holding it out to her.

"Papers mainly," Leesa told her. "Certificates of Births, Deaths and Marriages ... some charts I have formatted to record them ..."

"Maybe that is the barrier," she said, her words still subtle, her eyes still on the file. "Too many other hands involved. Yet even so," – she looked up to take in both women – "I feel there is need for concern. I feel a tension, as if something is going to happen."

Leesa's face paled and the chill on her skin increased threefold.

"Leesa, have you got any other material? Anything belonging to members of the family?" Dot's words were pressing, her expression worrisome.

Leesa nodded. "Lots of things. But they're all back at my flat. Look ... what is this all about?"

Dot gave a look that bordered on impatience. "Marion is psychic," she impressed slowly, "but she also has the power of communication."

"And what does that mean?"

This was all still fairly new to Leesa. She knew a clairvoyant – like Dot – had the ability of second sight and the power to pick up others' thoughts, and she knew a psychic was different from that. But a psychic with communication skills? Her lips twisted.

"To put it simply," Marion cured her confusion, "I can see or sense happenings of another time or place. I can also reach those of the past world and be reached by them. You may have heard the term ... medium?"

Leesa nodded once.

"Then I am what you call a medium ... and a psychic."

Leesa's tilting head warned Marion she had just confused her further.

"I can sometimes see the future and the past," she clarified.

Now Leesa understood perfectly, but her quick acceptance of the medium's revelation surprised the woman. Glancing at Dorothy, she received a slight smile that confirmed Leesa was indeed a believer, albeit one who was still learning.

"Are you interested enough to take this further?" Dot queried softly.

Leesa nodded decisively.

"Good! Now, when do we get to see that other stuff?"

"Now?" Leesa offered keenly.

Exchanging glances of approval, they rose and headed to the door.

Following the curving pavements past the Sciences Wing, the three fit comfortably side by side on the near-empty path, which was clear due to the popular lecture hour. All the while, Leesa's thoughts dwelt heavily on what the woman had said in her office.

"You said Jessie's family was tortured," she reflected verbally, looking across to the medium/psychic. "Exactly what did you mean by that?"

Leesa noted Dot dropped back a little so Marion could walk beside her, the psychic drawing a deep breath and exhaling as if preparing herself for some major physical effort. The golden eyes took her in for long seconds. "They are in conflict with each other," she said. "Much hatred passes between them. And there is fear … much fear." Her voice reflected a sensitivity as if she were closely involved; her words brought them to silent thought.

Passing beneath the wide spreading branches of flowering Jacarandas that bordered the final path to the almost suburban sprawl of Staff/Student living quarters, Marion finally spoke again. "You do realise we must help these people," she said bluntly. "We must try to help them find their next path."

Leesa looked wary. "But how can we do that?"

"There are ways, but you must keep an open mind." It was Dot this time. "What you have seen of our work so far, Leesa, is only a scratch on the surface. There is so much more to it, it would be hard for you to imagine."

They had reached the stairs to her unit and started to climb,

Marion directly behind Leesa.

"I can't promise I'll be able to see everything," she said, "nor that I'll be able to piece it all together. But we must try ... Lord knows, we must try. The vibrations are coming so strong ... it's as if someone is reaching out in desperation. That much I do feel!"

They arrived at Leesa's door, the three women of mixed ages planning to take up the salvation of lost souls. At that realisation, Leesa almost laughed. It was like something out of a poor B-grade movie with a totally unbelievable plot. *Three average-looking women taking on the spirit world. Title: 'Three gals and a Spook'.* Then she bit her lip, the seriousness of the other two holding back her mirth. Shuddering, she turned the key and opened the door. And she had a right to shudder for she'd already had a taste of what one of these ladies was capable of. The second was yet to prove herself.

As if instinctively drawn there, Marion crossed the room and went straight to the papers spread across the circular dining table. Her hands wandered slowly over the case and closed journals while Leesa and Dot stood back in silent scrutiny. They glanced at each other as Marion's hands lifted again. For a long moment, the woman stood, her hands softly clenched as if holding onto whatever vision she'd extracted. Then she exhaled fully, her tension exuding with the breath. Blinking with empathy, she turned and looked straight at them.

"A meeting is necessary," she said, directing her words to Dot. "It should be as soon as possible."

Dot nodded acquiescently. "How many?"

"Six will suffice. It will take too long to organise more."

Again, Dot nodded.

"Six what?" Leesa asked, noting the student seemed more like the tutor right then. "And what sort of meeting?"

Her eyes returned to the disarray of papers and books on the table, then back to the two parapsychologists. Somewhere, they had left her far behind.

"A seance," Dot said drily, her tone signifying the apparent normality of the event. "We're going to contact Jessica's family."

Leesa's jaw dropped open, but the others planned on regardless. "You and I and Leesa, that's three," Dot counted.

"We can bring in Karen and Roger."

Leesa knew the two mentioned were involved in the parapsychology field.

"And we should have an independent party," Marion filled what appeared to be a criterion.

Seeing Leesa had been unceremoniously included, she thought, *Why not!* And, grinning, offered, "How about Dean Morrison?"

"Professor Morrison ...?" Marion deliberated carefully, her eyes narrowing with assessment. A smile slowly spread and she nodded. "I gather he would be rather sceptical about all this?"

"He would indeed," Dot chuckled.

"Then if you can get him, get him."

Leesa promised to do just that and, upon those arrangements, both women left to organise the other participants of what was to be her very first seance. It would be held late at night, the venue to be decided when they all assembled in the courtyard outside the Administration building.

Dean Morrison was receptive to spending the evening out, a quick message left on his answering machine responded to immediately after his last class. They would dine at The Arches, her shout she'd promised, after which he could escort her to a function still to be arranged. Dress was informal.

His eager agreeance stirred her wry smile.

Dinner was a pleasant affair, as it usually was, and Leesa noted she was finding the professor's casual manner rather relaxing of late. He was an easily liked companion, and she felt good that their friendship was building. Only once during the course of the evening did his words cause a shiver, and that was when he asked what was on the agenda for their late entertainment.

Swallowing apprehensively, Leesa responded indifferently – lied – that it would depend on what the rest of the party decided when they gathered, and hid her sigh of relief when he cordially accepted her answer.

Deliberately, they were the last to arrive in the campus courtyard, her arm linked through Dean's, looking rather old-fashioned, yet a planned precaution against him escaping. Either the vibes going out from the rest of the gathering forewarned him, or the mere presence of half the university's PSI Department, he soon caught on that something was about to happen, something he wasn't exactly going to be too keen on. Leesa's arm increasing its grip around his bicep further set his mind.

"We're going to a seance," she explained with forced brightness, her smile intended to win him over. "I've never been to one before."

"A seance!! You've got to be joking! ..." Her theatrical, pleading puppy dog eyes caused him to grin. "You don't really believe in that crap, do you?!"

"He's definitely an independent party," Marion said, smiling her approval.

"Oh, come on, Professor. Don't tell me, you of all people are narrow-minded to the ways of the world!"

Leesa wondered how Marion felt coercing a full-fledged professor a good ten years her junior.

"I believe in the facts," he grinned widely. "The facts. The whole facts. And nothing but the facts."

"Then let us show you the facts."

His scoffing chuckle hinted she had twigged his curiosity or his conscience, and he glanced at Leesa, a little sternly if she really wanted to assess it. Then he smiled, a slow indication of his agreeance, the glint in his eye implying Leesa would later suffer for her subterfuge.

"Okay," he finally said. 'But I have my conditions. Seeing I've been coerced into sitting through a night of hocus-pocus, the seance should be held in my rooms where there is no possibility of human falsification. This thing will be real, or will die a dismal death, a just end for such a meaningless shenanigan.'

Glancing at each other, Dot and Marion smiled. It had fallen together perfectly.

Dean's place was a short walk through the university grounds in the opposite direction to Leesa's, and she was surprised to find it so tidy and well-kept, seeing his personal appearance always looked as if he had thrown himself together in a windstorm. The main room of the three-roomed flat was decked out with capacious brown armchairs and low tables. It looked able to cater for casual chats with a number of students who might be finding difficulty with the work. (She'd heard Dean was well-liked on campus for the genuine concern he showed his students and could see him seated amid his worried disciples, guiding them wisely towards a solution. The room purported solution.) It was a place where one could feel relaxed, and Marion nodded that it suited her needs perfectly.

Without much ado, the large chairs were drawn closer together so each could sit in comfort and still hold hands. Leesa had no idea what hand-holding had to do with spiritual contact, but the others seemed to be accustomed to this rule, so they obliged. Dot had closed the heavy curtains and dimmed the lights, leaving only one light burning: a small night lamp over the

TV. It bathed the room in a subdued deep gold glow.

"Bright light hinders communication," she offered in undertones. The others were obviously aware of that.

Marion settled down into a high-backed chair directly in front of the light, her features darkened by the room's umber shadows. Her eyes closed as she prepared herself for total repose, her arms outstretched so Dot and Karen could link their hands in hers. Several long moments passed in the eerie stillness, nobody daring to break it lest they break her concentration. Leesa's eyes glanced from one to the other ascertaining their responses – their eyes were also closed. Dean's hand squeezed hers, a substitute for laughter, she imagined, catching sight of his expression.

"I leave this night open for whoever wishes to speak," Marion said boldly, her voice somewhat deeper than usual. "I feel your trouble. Please come forward."

Quiet filled the room. No one moved or made a sound, except Dean who moved in his seat, his foot starting to swing small circles at the end of his crossed-over leg.

"Your presence tonight is for your benefit," the medium implored again. "Please, come forward. We wish to help you."

Again, nothing.

Dean smirked and Leesa squeezed his hand harder, really hard, thankful Dot and the others were so preoccupied with Marion they seemed not to notice. Marion's head had tipped well back against the chair as she spoke. Then suddenly, it fell forward to her chest. Unsure of what was happening, Leesa's attention turned her way, a frown forming. Then Marion's chin lifted again, and though her eyes were still closed, her lips began to form words.

"You cannot help us. We are beyond your reach. But save the others from him."

Her eyes widened, and Leesa gasped and looked at Dot. "It's Martha Kendall's voice," she whispered.

Dot nodded back, then turned back to Marion.

"Save who?" she prompted, her voice barely a breath in the night.

"Save them. He must not take them ... must not ..."

"Who is 'Them'? And who is 'He'?" Dot questioned more pointedly.

"He took her mother and father ... took her son." The voice wailed then started to cry. "He took them from me."

"Who is *he?*" Dot's voice pressed through the darkness. "Who is *he?*"

Leesa's hand gripped Dean's tightly, the cold air suddenly filling the room chilling her more than the dead woman's voice. The hairs on the back of her neck prickled eerily then stood high on their roots, chilling her even further. She felt Roger's hand close more firmly over hers on her other side. His gaze had gone to scan the room.

"He ..." Marion began cautiously.

Then over the top of her words, came a deep and resonant order, a male dominance issuing harshly from above them. "Silence, Martha! *SILENCE!*"

The medium stopped immediately and sat rigidly in her seat. Then, her breath heaved in and out in childlike defiance. "You took them all," she accused in Martha's voice, her chin dimpling as if she was about to cry.

"I needed them ... needed them both," the second voice came again, the tone a little softer. It seemed to project from a point somewhere ahead of and high to the ceiling above Marion. "You could have helped, but you didn't."

The tone became angrier, and Leesa felt Dean's hand go clammy. Or maybe it was hers.

"You ruined it!! I will not go without them!"

"You killed them all. You killed her father," Marion sobbed, yet Leesa knew it was not Marion at all.

"He was going to harm her trees ... Nobody touches her trees ... *NOBODY* ..." The voice trailed off to nothing, a remorseful fading moan. Marion slumped forward, her chin sagging wearily onto her chest, and Martha was gone too.

For a long while, they just sat staring at Marion, the woman's head drooping as if in a deep sleep, nobody game to make a sound or motion. Looking around the group after several long minutes, Dot broke the link of hands and, reaching over, placed hers on Marion's arm. The medium stirred slowly; her gold eyes hazed with confusion. She looked exhausted and inhaled deeply.

"*He* is the Control," she said dully, stifling a long yawn. "We can do no more tonight." She wiped her tired eyes.

The circle of arms broke immediately, Dot rising to turn the lights back on. Her attention turned from the stunned look on Dean's face back to Marion. The medium hadn't moved; she seemed to be fighting the weariness that had swept over her. Reluctantly Leesa waited, filled in the time by assisting Dot make coffees for all. Marion was most appreciative, for it seemed to restore her energies. They then sat in a close arc, Dot on her one side, Leesa on the other, both keen to quiz her on the experience. Dean, on the other hand, had risen and was giving close scrutiny to the ceiling from where the voice had emitted.

There was nothing there. Not a hole. Not a scratch, nor a mark. Nothing. He returned to the ring of chairs.

"What did you mean by ... the Control?" Leesa asked, hoping Marion was ready to talk. She had waited as long as she could.

Looking pensive, Marion heaved a deep breath and let her gaze drift from her to Dean and back again. Her jaw flexed as she answered her question with another. "Do you believe in metempsychosis?"

Leesa's perplexed frown showed her ignorance and she added bluntly, "... Reincarnation? Life after death? The immortal soul? ... That sort of thing!" Her voice sounded dry, too tired to be drawn into an argument over philosophies.

"I don't know really," Leesa answered honestly. "I've never really thought much about it. Life is life and death is death to me."

"But you believe in ghosts!"

"Sure, doesn't everyone?" Marion's gaze drifted to Dean, the academic professor who believed in the facts, the whole facts and nothing but the facts. He was stifling his amusement.

Marion ignored him. "Well, what do you think dead people are?" she asked, lifting her cup hesitantly to her lips.

At that, Dean laughed openly. "Dead people," he chipped in cynically.

"But we bury dead people," Dot interjected as she lowered her coffee to one of the low tables. "We stick their bodies in long shiny boxes and bury them deep in the ground."

"Yes," Leesa agreed astutely. "But the soul leaves the body at death."

Marion's eyes twinkled. "And then where does it go?" Her eyebrows rose, anticipating the answer.

"To Heaven, I guess. I mean, where else would it go?"

"Or to Hell," the pert professor added, "if any of you went to see *Ghost*."

They all smiled, for they'd all seen the movie several times. Marion's smile was the first to diminish; she had a point to make.

"Well, not exactly," she countered. "Look, seeing we're talking about movies here, I guess we've all seen various ones about dying and the person arriving at the Pearly gates …"

They all nodded.

"Well, according to the movies, that is where the decision is made as to whether you have reached your ultimate goal and can go forward into Heaven, or whether there have been things left undone and you must return to earth to rectify them. Right?"

All but Dean nodded.

"Are you still with me, Professor Morrison?" she solicited firmly.

His expression now serious with the sparking of his interest, Dean slowly nodded.

Huffing another breath of fatigue, Marion continued, her words stirring the mind with possibilities. "Well, I guess that's not far from the truth, but the movies do leave a bit of the journey out. You see, there are several planes one must achieve to even reach as far as Heaven's gate, if you'll excuse my simplicity. You have to realise that before you start the climb, your soul first enters the Plane for selection."

Dean's eyebrows dipped and his brow creased. "Run that past me again."

"Your soul first enters the Plane," she repeated. "The Plane of Souls. It's like an atmospheric pool of disembodied people; the place where your ghosts reside. It is here the soul is selected, either for a higher plane towards the ultimate goal, or is returned to earth to redo a part of their life, to correct any errors they may have made. In short, it's the first step to being reincarnated."

"And where did you read about all this?" Dean said, rudely sceptical.

"Marion didn't read about it," Dot shot him down. "She experienced it."

Blinking heavily, the medium swallowed thickly and drew another breath. "I had one of those near-death encounters," she explained softly, putting down her cup and leaning forward, her hands clasping tightly together. "About two years ago, I had a car accident. A bad car accident. On the way to the hospital, I died ... twice, and twice they brought me back. In that period of death, I saw the light; I saw my soul leave my body and float onto the Plane." She sighed again, jadedly.

"I didn't always have this specialty, you know. Not like some people who are born with it. Mine was acquired; I think I brought it back from that place."

"Now she can contact them whenever she wishes. And they contact her," Dot interrupted.

Marion stifled a yawn, then rubbed a kink from the back of her neck. Her sudden silence caused Dean to lean forward on his chair, his expression keen.

"And what did you mean by ... the Control?" he repeated Leesa's original question.

Nodding her acknowledgment, Marion blinked quickly to clear her thoughts. "The Plane is a vast place with many in residence – a world of its own," she explained somberly. "With so many voices wanting to reach out and be heard, it somehow developed that one would be designated the Controller, the soul that would lead the rest, a soul that would be most suitable to convey their messages to our time. The Control is the go-between between us and them, and He has much power."

"But your voice was Jessie's mother's voice," Leesa said with confusion. "Is she the Control?"

Marion shook her head firmly. "No, I don't think so. She submitted to the other voice, so I'd say *He* is. Sometimes others have a message so strong, they can override the Control, but only temporarily. He will always dominate in the end."

"She sounded so scared, so anguished," Leesa reflected, a hollow spot touching her heart at the thought of Martha's words. "And what did she mean by ... *He* had taken them? And who the hell is 'He', anyway?"

Marion shook her head slowly. "That is not my field. All I can tell you is that ... Jessie's mother? ..." Leesa nodded in confirmation. "... and He are related. But finding who and how is a totally different area altogether."

Another worry pricked insistently. "She said we have to save the others." Leesa looked about to see if recollection touched other faces. "What others? And from what?"

Marion stared blankly into thin air; shrugged. "I don't know," she whispered glumly. "I still don't know."

Silence fell on the room as they sat, Leesa's heart thudding as she thought of Jessie and the bitter conflicts that had plagued her family all those years. They had gone on during life and after death. They were still going on. *And now* ... she pondered, *when will it stop? Will Him taking the others stop it? or will us saving them stop it? And who the hell are THEY?*

Somehow, she had to find out. Somehow, she ... they ... had to save 'the others'.

"Where do we go from here?" she asked, not much caring which of the parapsychologists answered. *Surely one of them has a plan of action. Dot said what I have seen is only a scratch on the surface.*

"Are you really sure you want to take this further?" Marion asked seriously. Deadly serious. The golden eyes were hard and arresting, her question cold.

"What else can we do?" a voice cut in before Leesa's. It was Dean, and her mouth fell agape. He looked levelly at her, concern showing at her bewilderment. "What else can we do?" he shrugged.

Long moments passed as Marion sat silently assessing them, her obvious scrutiny deciding whether they were suitably ready for whatever lay ahead. Her long deliberation indicated her doubt. Her answer when it came was blunt.

"We call in a regressionist!"

"And what's that?" Dean beat her to it.

"Let's just say it's a tracer of lives," Dot told him.

"That's what Leesa does. Won't she do?"

"Well, no." The accompanying smile was warm. "It's a little different to genealogy."

About there the night's excitement ended, each agreeing to avail themselves the approaching Wednesday for an afternoon flight to Sydney, except for Karen and Roger, who would manage the PSI Department until Dot's return. Dean graciously offered to charter a four-seater plane and fly them all down, his sudden interest in the occult surprising everyone no-end.

Chapter Twelve

Landing in Sydney late Wednesday evening, they hired a car and Dean drove them into the city. At a cosy-looking motel, they booked three rooms – the shared room for Dot and Marion – and took a well-earned rest. Dot contacted the regressionist they'd come to see and arranged a meeting for the following morning. Leesa, on the other hand, absconded with the car and visited Jessie in Mosman.

"What are you doing down here again?" Jessie quizzed sharply on opening the front door, her hands continually wiping dry on a tea towel. As an afterthought, she laughed lightly, then added as she pushed open the flywire door, "Why didn't you ring to say you were coming?"

Shrugging nonchalantly, yet slightly disturbed at the seeming resentment of her visit, Leesa replied, "It was a spur-of-the-moment thing. Why? Have I caught you up to no good?!"

Jessica's eyes hardened like flint, just for a second, but Leesa picked it up before Jess covered it with a smile before her arms encircled her in the customary hug. But the usual warmth that went with it wasn't there. Her friend had changed, just as Ryan had said. Either that or her guard was well up, for what reason Leesa didn't know. She just knew she'd have to be careful to keep Jess passive. *I have to keep her on side.* But Leesa already knew how to do that.

"How's the farm?" she asked, following her down the passage

to the kitchen, their mutually favourite room. "Done any more to it since last time?"

Jessica shook her head, a wave of tresses flicking back over her shoulder as she did so. "I've done enough. We're happy with it just as it is. Now I can just enjoy being there."

She raised the coffee pot, silently asking, to which Leesa nodded eagerly. She noted the word 'we'. Had Ryan been accepted back on the place? Or was she still referring to her and Ryan's inference to ghosts, and the rift with him was still rife?

"How's Ryan?" she asked, glancing around the room for evidence of his occupancy.

"The same."

Jess switched off the kettle, her answer given without even glancing her way. Her bluntness made Leesa change tack.

"Where's Jade?"

"Sleeping. He's finally decided to start walking and he gets so tired. Are you staying for dinner?"

It wasn't an invitation, her dryness possibly designed to ensure she didn't.

"No. I'm actually down with Dean and a few other associates so I'll be dining with them."

That caused Jess to glance sideways, one eyebrow lifting. "Dean Morrison?"

Leesa nodded.

"So, it's progressing?"

"What do you mean by that?" Leesa smiled somewhat; her guard, however, rose about ten feet. "We see each other a bit."

"That's nice. I thought you only had eyes for Ryan."

"Jessie!" Leesa's jaw set in anger. Her fists clenched likewise. The Jessie she knew would never have said such a thing!

Her friend then smiled, a tight, teasing grin as if she knew she had hit a sore point. "Just kidding," Jess gibed.

"It was very funny. You know no one wants you and Ryan to

solve your differences more than I do."

Jessie shrugged indifferently. "I know. But it makes little difference now. It's gone too far."

"What do you mean? Gone too far."

Jess turned and leant back against the sink. "He's still pushing this thing about me having an affair," she said feistily, her jaw tightening. "Just because I like to spend my weekends at the farm ... just because I like to get back to nature, he has to go and ruin it by accusing me of that!!" Her chin dimpled as moisture touched her eyes. "I've had him, Leesa! He's finished it!"

"Oh no, Jess. No ... Ryan's just very concerned ... and he's hurt that you don't want him to help you."

"That's not it at all! He doesn't trust me, and I don't know now if I trust him. Maybe you two should have been the ones to get married. You understand each other so much better than we ever did."

"Jessie, don't. You just need to sit down and talk to him. You two belong together."

Jess shook her head adamantly. "I belong at *Whistling Gums*. That's the only place I could ever be happy now ..."

Leesa's heart thudded with horror. "But what about Ryan ... and Jade?"

Looking slightly horrified, Jess glared back at her. "Jade will come with me, of course! And Ryan ...? Well, he can just go to Hell!"

Leesa's astonished look made Jess turn back to the sink. She poured the coffee, leaving Leesa to cast an embarrassed eye around the room. It fell on the calendar on the wall, and again she briefly noted the large red circle around the 13th of December. It looked significant, more circles appearing to have been added since Lessa was there last, yet it still didn't jog any noteworthy memories.

"You intend to go, don't you?! You've made up your mind to

move up there."

Jess's silence confirmed her assessment. She didn't ask her when. Maybe that was the big indication written on the wall, circle after circle of deliberation.

"Hell!" was all Leesa could think to say, as *Damn! Poor Ryan will soon be all alone* ran through her mind.

Jess shot Leesa a harsh look as if she was taking sides, but Leesa ignored it and drank her coffee in silence. If she said anything, it would probably be something along the lines that she thought Jess was going crazy, and that maybe she did need a psychiatrist. They both fell silent.

Leesa left soon after, without seeing Ryan or Jade and feeling very much unfriendly towards the person who had been her best friend forever. Her tears streamed as she drove away, the rift developing between them hurting terribly because she had done nothing to cause it. Jessie was changing dramatically, and she could do nothing to stop it.

For her peace of mind, she rang Ryan that night, just to hear his voice and be available if he needed to talk. He didn't. Surprisingly, he didn't sound too distressed at all, and she wondered if he even knew what Jessie was planning, or that she had even set the date it would happen. Talk of Jessie brought only short answers, so she gathered they were still openly hostile towards each other and let the matter drop. He was surprised she was in Sydney and was sorry to have missed her visit; he laughed ... rather loudly when she told him she was in Sydney with parapsychologists. It was the first time she had heard him laugh in such a long time and it was a nice sound, even if she would have to suffer the chiding in the long run.

Her smile lingered when he rang off – he'd called her 'Ghost-hunter', and she shuddered that he didn't know just how close to home her hunt was heading.

A long night of tossing and turning found morning dancing at her window sooner than she wanted. Her eyes were sore and dry from lack of sleep. She turned over and tried to let the tiredness claim her again; tried to let the pillow push the day away, but her conscience nagged against those wishes. She had a meeting to attend at ten and needed to shower, dearly hoping she could wash away the 'friendship blues'.

It didn't, but Dean's cheeky face at her door soon after managed to reduce those thoughts to a lesser degree. He seemed extremely keen to get started, and that astounded her – this man of the academics, this pedantic educator of the facts, (the whole facts and nothing but the facts) was out on a ghost hunt too. It gave her an outlet to reclaim some of the chiding she would undoubtedly receive later. Like two school kids out looking for adventure, they were, at this point, finding it fun, even more so in light of their inadvertent 'escape from school'.

Only Dot's and Marion's presence returned seriousness to the event. They arrived punctually, ready to work. On checking that Leesa had the material the regressionist had requested, they headed south to Randwick.

The narrow street Dot directed them down was lined with old – no, more than old – absolutely ancient weatherboard houses, each adorned with ornate lattice work and wide, cool verandahs. The one they parked outside looked neat and white and was surrounded by a picture-perfect, white, chest-high picket fence. Inside this nestled an elaborate tropical garden of ferns, palms, and variegated ivies.

A minor squeak from the garden gate warned those inside of their arrival. The front door opened as they reached the verandah steps. Just inside the door stood an elderly lady, who pushed open the fly-wire barrier and stepped out to meet them. She greeted Dot and Marion with as warm a smile as her old thin lips could achieve. A dubious glance and a raised eyebrow greeted Dean before her grey eyes found Leesa. Wordlessly, she nodded her approval, her gaze dropping to the case in Leesa's hand for a brief instant.

"Let's go inside," she said softly. "We have much to do."

Following her into a dimly lit but elegantly arranged lounge room – undoubtedly what she would call 'the parlour' – Leesa's gaze swept the room before returning to the lady in the soft blue dress. Then her interest drew to the subtly embossed gold and cream wallpaper that lined the room, upon which hung delicately bordered frames containing etchings of the star signs. They were all there: Taurus, the Bull; Cancer, the Crab; Capricorn, the goat; the Twins of Gemini; Scorpio with its sting; Sagittarius; Virgo; Pisces; the Ram and the Lion; Aquarius and the Scales. Yes. So assessed, her focus went back to the old woman.

She had stopped beside a large, oval, oak table and there she turned back to Leesa.

"Jessica never rang me, you know," she said, openly concerned, her tightening lips showing her annoyance.

"I left her your message, but I doubt Jessie will do anything anyone asks any more."

"Well, I'm glad at least you came," Mrs Castle confessed. "I knew when I saw you last that you would be involved when the time came."

"When the time came for what?"

Leesa glanced at Dean. He looked as puzzled as she was. Avoiding answering seemed to be a knack to this woman, for she just let that question go by her.

"Please, Leesa, sit down." She motioned to a chair. "Did you bring the papers with you?"

"All the ones you asked for."

Setting the cases on the table, Leesa clicked open the latches then sat at the end of the table where the lady indicated. Mrs

Castle gestured with a sweep of her hand to the others to also be seated, Dot's surprised look remaining as she did so.

"I didn't know you two had met," she half-posed the question.

"Just briefly," the old woman informed her tautly. Remaining standing, she lifted the lid of the brown case and gazed down at its contents. "... but I knew then we would be meeting again on a mutual cause."

"Did you know that when I rang you the other day?" Dot again.

The woman laughed, a tittering sound that brought comparisons to the very young, and Leesa mused that age probably did run in such a cycle. Like being born small, growing with age until old age shrunk the body back small again. Like being helpless at birth and mastering skills only to be left helpless again in aged frailty. For her vast years, Mrs Castle looked nowhere near frail.

"Most certainly not!" she chuckled, her eyes lighting up and making her look even younger. "My powers are not as strong as yours, Dorothy. And thank goodness. I have enough trouble coping with what sight I do have."

Dean lowered himself to a seat next to Leesa. "We were told you are a regressionist. What is that exactly?" he asked, his eyes momentarily scanning the celestial outlines on the wall again.

Mrs Castle's hands rested in the case. Pausing to structure her explanation, she started slowly. "Yes, I'm a regressionist ... and a psychic ... and an astrologer. They all go hand in hand, you know. You look puzzled, Mr Morrison. I guess this tenet is not commonplace in your field." She smiled as if making a subtle joke.

"No, it's not," he agreed amiably. "Someone also said you trace lives."

"That is correct. If you study the word regress, Mr Morrison, it means to go back. And I do go back ... tracing back people's lives." She saw comprehension in his eyes, and quelled it in an instant. "I trace lives back to the very, very beginning."

"Leesa does the same."

"Leesa does it differently," she corrected him, her hands now delving idly into the layers of paperwork. "And my," – she looked down, frowning – "this family is so entwined." She scanned the gathering at the table with concern.

"What do you mean ... entwined?" Leesa queried. *How can a family be entwined? They can be close, maybe. But entwined?!*

The grey eyes lifted and blinked slowly, clearing the way for whatever she had to say. Her long pause heightened everyone's curiosity. Closing the lid of the case, the old lady's face straightened, became almost rigid if one could describe a face as being so. Hers definitely was, the eyes gone cold and penetrating.

"You've been told about reincarnation?!" She quickly summed up their knowledge. "You understand that the souls return?"

Firm nods confirmed her supposition.

"And you know they usually return to family groups!" At that point, Leesa's and Dean's frowns showed the limit of their knowledge.

"We all return, you know. We all come back, time and time again until we learn the lessons and get them right. Then we can pass over."

Their continued silence allowed her to tell it all.

"Some of us have been back forty ... fifty times. Some go back thousands of years, but regardless of when we began and when we end, we will always suffer for the mistakes of our past."

"You said we usually return to our family group ..." Dean reiterated.

"Usually, but not always. It's quite possible, you know, to come back as a brother of your returned father or a father of your grandfather, depending, of course, on when their souls returned and what lessons have to be redone. Why ... you could even find yourself in generations hence remarried to the returned soul of your past wife. Imagine it, paying for indiscretions committed against her. Uncanny, isn't it!"

She smiled at the concern on Dean's face.

"When do we stop coming back?" Leesa broke in softly.

"When all the lessons are learnt. When you have truly found yourself and life acceptance, when you have lived purely and without error ..." She blinked softly, almost angelically, as if her words were purity itself. Leesa thought she understood what she was feeling.

Looking fleetingly around the walls, Dean grinned that impish smirk Leesa was used to and she dreaded what was coming next. "I want to come back next time as a Pisces. Cancerian men have the worst reputations."

The smile cast back from the old woman was tinged with similar devilment. "Oh no, Mr Morrison. A soul has its own personality, and that it will always keep. You will always come back as the same astrological sign. So therefore, it is up to you to change the reputation by careful living in this life."

Grinning, he shrugged as Mrs Castle lifted the case's brown lid again, her attention returning to its internal contents.

Until now, the other two women had sat quietly, as if very much accustomed to this explanatory banter. Then Marion spoke, obviously wanting to get down to business.

"Joy, the woman's voice said we had to save them. She said he had taken her father, mother and son, but we still had to save 'them'." She looked straight at the old lady and added candidly, "We need to know who 'they' are and how we can save them."

Mrs Castle nodded that she'd heard, then looked at Leesa. "There are photos of the family in here?"

Leesa nodded yes. "There are many, dating way back to the

early days, plus some more recent ones I put in of Jessie and her immediate family."

Flipping open the files, Mrs Castle quickly located the one containing the visual history. She briefly glanced over several of the prints then proceeded to lay them out in rows, organising them, seemingly, in ages. The past at the top – the beginning. The present at the bottom. The table near where she stood was soon covered. Only then did she sit down, taking the chair on Leesa's right.

As she sat beside her, Leesa's gaze drifting from age-yellowed images to clear, vivid snapshots, her thoughts drifted to the events of the past. Mrs Castle had been the first to make an attempt to contact Jessie; she had made the need for Jessie to contact her sound imperative. Had whatever they were here for been known in advance? Was she merely a cog in the wheel of its cycle, there to provide the material information? And how much of this then was destiny? and how much related to Jessie and her sudden, odd behaviour?

"You said Je......"

Dot's hand on her arm stopped the flow of words. Mrs Castle's concentration was centred on the top row of photos from the past, the grey eyes intensely studying each image. For long moments she poured over the prints, finally selecting several after much deep deliberations and placing them on top of others.

"As I said, they are entwined," she almost whispered, topping another with one of a more recent time. "This family has a tragic past, so tragic it will be difficult for it to ever recover. Its members keep returning, reliving their lives over and over, yet for what reason I cannot tell."

Her frown deepening, she picked up one group of stacked portraits. "Jessica ... according to these, has been back at least three times ... as this person…" She laid down a photo which

Leesa recognised as Jessie's grandmother. "And this one ..."

It was a woman Leesa had never seen before.

"According to the photo, she was American," Mrs Castle read the lack of recognition on her face. "About the 1850s I'd lay a good guess."

Dean's whisper caused Leesa's concentration to divert sideways, taking with it the old lady's attention.

"How does she know all that?" he enquired softly of Dot.

For her age, Mrs Castle's hearing was acute, or was it her insight? Leesa couldn't tell. Her explanation was forthcoming before either PSI woman could elaborate.

"My psyche shows me," she said openly. The photos here are mere windows to the images appearing around and behind those captured on the negative. In this one, for instance ..." She pushed across the table the one she foretold of being an American woman. "... I see the American flag in the background, here, and a maple grove there, and an Amish-type barn," she waved her finger across the background.

"This one here ..." She tapped a finger on Jessie's grandmother's skirts.

"... is Jessie's grandmother," Leesa filled in. "The resemblance to Jessie is striking. I remember Mrs Kendall always did say Jessie was her mother all over again, that they could have been one in the same."

"She died the day Jessie was born," Mrs Castle revealed. Leesa hadn't heard that before, not from Jessie, nor from Mrs Kendall. But it did spark a similarity Leesa was aware of.

"Like John died the day Jade was born."

Mrs Castle looked slightly pale. She sat for a long moment staring down at the photo of the tiny child that was Jessie's son.

"You said it was Martha's voice warning you to save the others."

"Definitely! I'd know her voice anywhere," Leesa said.

"And she said *He* had taken her mother, father and son ..." Her knuckles rapped softly against the tabletop, her expression not revealing her thoughts. She blinked sharply a few quick times; her jaw fairly set hard when deciphering the events. Finally, she swallowed, and looked up. "What if He took Martha's mother so Jessica could return? and her son so Jessica's son could be in reach? ... The child has been back before too, you know. But Martha's father ... ...

"Who was Martha's father? ..."

Shrugging, Leesa looked equally confused.

"There are no photos of him, are there?" she asked hopefully.

Leesa shook her head.

"Why did He take her father? ..." Her withered fingers pressed firmly to her lips as she forced her mind to conjure an answer.

"Who is *He*?" Marion's tawny eyes were intense with questions. "We must find out who *He* is!"

"I don't know who He is," Mrs Castle said glumly. "He's not in here." She cast her hand to encompass the table. "I feel He was before this time, yet is drawn to stay for some reason."

She looked up as if a sudden revelation had taken hold. "He's waiting for someone. And He has structured the events He wants so He can have that someone."

She let out a deep sigh. "I feel the time has come. It is a time I feared would come regardless."

"Regardless of what?" Dean asked pointedly.

"The warnings. She didn't listen to the warnings."

"You said you knew Mrs Kendall before, didn't you?" Leesa remembered, piecing the past together; the visit, the plea for Jessie to call.

"We were very close friends ... close like you and Jessica." The woman's eyes dulled as if past memories caused her pain. "We used to go everywhere together, do everything together. She was a wonderful woman, was Martha."

Her grief washed over Leesa, maybe touched where her own remorse was sheltering.

"What happened?" she asked her gently. "I've known Jessie's family for most of my life, but have never seen or heard of you mentioned before."

"Martha and I parted ways when Jessica was a small child. And I fear now that it is Jessica who is in danger. The past has reached the present and what happened back then has been able to find her now."

"What happened back then?" Leesa clutched the lady's arm in desperation. "Please, tell me..."

The old lady's fingers entwined in nervous reflection, the grey of her eyes going smoky as the past filled her mind.

"It was nearly twenty-five years ago now," she said sadly. "We had taken a day trip up to her father's farm – he wouldn't leave it you know. He always said he was close to Elizabeth there. I had actually gone along with Martha because she wanted to spend some time with her father: I was to keep an eye on Jessica. She was only four at the time, and Martha didn't want her wandering off while she tried to assess her father's mental state. He'd been acting very strange since her mother's death, and Martha was worried that he was heading for a breakdown.

"Her mother had died on the farm after being involved in a car accident down at the Oberon crossing, but Mr Raybourne kept saying she had returned to the farm. He could feel her presence there. Then, as if in replacement, he suddenly turned his attention to Jessica. He doted over her. How he loved that child!"

Looking directly at Leesa, she nodded, affirming the strength of that love further.

"We were having a cup of tea with her father when I realised I hadn't seen Jessica for a while and went outside to check on her. She had been playing in the garden, sitting on the makeshift swing Mr Raybourne had made her. It must have been her first encounter with the souls of past lives, yet I didn't know then exactly what I was looking at. The swing was being gently rocked by the wind. The tree that held it was an old twisted oak that used to sit on the slope just above the cottage."

"It's still there," Leesa told her.

She nodded as if she suspected so and went on. "Jessie was laughing and talking and looking up as the breeze swirled around her. It was the strangest sight, I can assure you, one I will never forget. I called her. Asked her who she was talking to. Well, that wind just gusted upward and blew away ... it seemed to retreat back to the top of the hill, back to the trees there, if that was possible. She called after it ... and you know what she said?" Her eyes panned those at the table.

"She said ... 'Come back, Sailor. Come back. I love you too.' That's what that little girl said. That's what a four-year-old child who wouldn't know what a sailor was, said." The woman sighed deeply.

"As I stood there watching that wind hover above the treetops, I had the strangest feeling it was watching me, that it was wanting me to go. I did the only thing I could ... I gathered Jessica up and told Martha we had to leave. She thought I must have been on a time schedule or something, so it wasn't hard getting away. I told her on the way home what I had felt, and I told her that she must protect Jessica, and to do so, Jessica must never go to the farm again. Jessica would never be safe on the farm. There was something there waiting for her."

"She never did let her go there," Leesa confirmed, but the woman let the words pass over her.

"Martha hated me after that," she said dismally. "She told me I was touched thinking the way I did. She told me she didn't want me anywhere near her or her daughter again. I tried to contact her many times, but Bert ... Jessica's father ... wouldn't allow any contact."

The woman looked rueful. "I feel a little guilty of the next events," she said, "because more suffered for what I had sensed. Martha, as you say, did refuse to take Jessica back to the farm. She told her father it was because of what I had seen, that it had something to do with the trees. The old man was devastated at her decision, for the child meant everything to him.

"In his anger, he went out to cut the trees down, starting with the one in which the swing hung. He didn't get one bite of the axe into the trunk before he was struck dead. They found him weeks later laying beneath that tree, the axe still gripped in his hand ..."

Leesa looked to Dean, whose eyes were fixed on the old woman in sheer astonishment. Mrs Castle's gaze was still fixed to the past.

"In an effort to help Martha," she went on, "I started doing some research. I found the sensations I was feeling wasn't limited to myself. I found others who had experienced similar things and had used those messages to help others. That is how I came to be doing what I do, hoping that one day ..." Her voice trailed off and a long pause ensued.

Then, her thoughts restructured, she looked up. "I never saw Martha again, but I wrote to her often. I needed to constantly remind her that Jessica would never be safe at the farm."

"It's uncanny," she verbalised her thoughts. "It was John who the farm was unsafe for. He was killed climbing over the gate."

"In Martha's own words," Dot cut in, "he was taken."

"Yes, I must agree with you," Mrs Castle nodded. "John was taken so Jessica's baby would inherit his soul."

"What? But why? And who was John then?"

The lady smoothed the tablecloth absently, her deliberation concreting further. "I don't know. Other than the baby, there are no signs of his previous lives here. Perhaps he was out of reach, too far away to be of consequence – souls can surface in any country, you know, sometimes too far away to rejoin the family group. That happens sometimes when the lessons have been learnt but the soul is needed to help others learn their lessons … Or John may have been a new soul. Souls don't always have a past. Sometimes they are just beginning. I don't know what John was, but I suspect he had been around seeing he was taken. He was taken for a reason."

"Yes, but what reason?" To Leesa, they were going around in circles, getting nowhere.

Looking tired, Mrs Castle shook her head. "I don't rightly know," she heaved a sigh. "Tell me, Leesa, how has Jessica been since she has been visiting the farm?"

"Much better than she's been for a long time," she answered without hesitation. "Her mother's death upset her greatly, which was actually rather strange seeing they had never really gotten on together."

"And how is she now?"

Reflecting back to her most recent visit, Leesa shuddered. "Different. Very, very different! She's not the same at all anymore, and it seems the farm means everything to her. No one else is of any consequence."

"It is as I suspected then. The rest of your answers are at the farm. Without actually speaking with the host person – and I'm sure Jessica will refuse to speak of the matter with me or anyone else – I can help you no more than I have. But I will warn you …" She looked up sternly. "… if you do choose to go there, remember this … she called him Sailor, whoever *He* is. And He rides on the wind. Remember too, Martha said you have to save the others. I strongly suspect Jessica and her baby are the 'others' she spoke of."

It was only then Leesa realised all those years of conflict between Jessie and her mother, particularly those bitter arguments since John's death, was simply a mother trying to protect her own flesh and blood, just as she was still trying to protect her.

"You are right, Leesa." The woman apparently read her thoughts. "I also believe Martha knew the events that were going to happen. Somehow, she found out what was intended but could do nothing to stop it."

"Your name was written on the last entry of her journal," Leesa told her.

The woman looked sad. "She was tempted to ring; I could feel that. But she never did." A deep sigh emitted with the words.

Silently, Leesa apologised for all the malicious thoughts she'd ever had of Martha Kendall. All Jessie's life, the woman had strived to avoid this situation and suffered her daughter's hatred because of it. And now, her death had made those bitter years futile.

"Beware too …" The old grey eyes did a slow sweep around the table. "… He comes from the past. Well back from the past. From these …" Her hand gestured over the photos. "… I see He has not returned for a long, long time. He certainly is not amongst this century of the family, and therefore, I suspect He is waiting, just watching and waiting. Unfortunately, too, that much time on the Plane has given him much power. He can steer the lives of others, so much so that he can even end the lives of others. So please, please, do not take unnecessary chances. You cannot stop him."

Dean looked grave as he asked the next question. "If this thing, this man, whatever *He* is … if He really wanted Jessie, why doesn't he just go and get her? What's stopping him from taking her like He took the others? And what's the farm got to do with it?"

"The farm appears to be the central link to everything," Dot calculated aloud. "Nothing changed until Jessica started going there ... is that right?" she asked Leesa, her eyebrow rising with the question.

Leesa nodded.

"And her brother John ... her grandparents ... all died there."

Again, Leesa nodded.

"Then whatever set this chain rolling in the first place," Mrs Castle proffered solemnly, "it must have happened at the farm. Maybe, too, that is the limit of his realm."

"Is that possible?" Leesa asked hopefully.

"Yes, it is possible. Spirits generally remain close to their origin of death, but that doesn't mean it is always the case."

"Well, if it is so in this case, does that mean then that if Jessie doesn't go to the farm she will be safe?"

"If what we have predicted so far is true, then yes. But it is only so if he has fixed himself to a place, if he has surrounded himself with protection." She looked thoughtful. "They feel very insecure at first, you know, and are reluctant to leave their place. Only when they have a grasp on their purpose in life do they let go of that shielded security."

The old lady's gaze went across the table. "Marion, I feel the next stage of this situation is your task. You must make contact with Him and find out what He wants."

Blinking long, heavy lashes, the medium accepted the role without question.

And there the meeting ended, that little extra insight taking them forward to another journey, thrusting them further into an area unknown. It was then Leesa regretted ever stealing those damn papers.

Chapter Thirteen

Even though it was late in the day, they decided to head straight up to Amberlay. Jessie always made a point of arriving at the farm early on Fridays, and whatever Dot and Marion had to do, it was better to be done without Jessie being there. So, after changing into more appropriate bush wear, the group left Sydney's outskirts. Dean drove, following Leesa's navigation directions, which she felt proud was better than Ryan's first attempt to find the farm – but then again, she had to admit, the track was much more worn than it had been several weeks ago.

With Dot and Marion sitting in the back seat, their discussion on the old woman's health finally exhausted, they arrived at the farm gate. Clear, bright skies predominated and the early summer heat showed noticeably on the yellowing brush around the gate posts as they alighted in the breezeless, sheltered grove that had become the farm's parking lot.

Standing outside the rusted gateway, their hands on the red-brown metal, the PSI women gazed at each other in awe, their wide eyes drifting upward over the tall, stately gums that shielded the farm from view. Motionless, they stared for long minutes, their breathing seemingly diminished in their wonder.

"Oh dear!" Marion said, her voice sympathetic. "The souls are here. Many of them are here."

Dot's eyes were lightly closed, her hand clasped in the other woman's. "Yes. Yes, I feel them too."

Marion simply nodded.

The wire on the gate was now broken and pulled back from regular use, making it easier to climb through than over. The ladies took that option. Dean, on the other hand, showed his masculine dexterity and scaled it in a one-handed leap, landing lightly on his feet on the other side.

"Go quietly," Leesa heard Marion's soft whisper. "I need to hear them speak." Her face had taken on a deeply studious countenance as she concentrated intensely.

Complying, Leesa led the way down through the thick belt of gums, following the track that wended its way into the valley. The umbrageous gloom was more apparent than usual and Leesa shuddered uncontrollably, Dean's hand closing over hers doing little to allay her rising fears. It was the longest walk Leesa had ever taken down along that path, the embedding feeling that she was intruding growing stronger and stronger as they neared the light.

"The family still resides," Marion whispered to Dot as she panned the treetops above and behind her as she walked. "They have left this world, but never gone."

Sunlight filtering in through the branches and the thickening underbrush told of the nearness of the open pastures. The smell of eucalyptus, the moist, dank air of rotting leaves mingling with it, was not at all unpleasant, yet it was not as appealing as the sight of the tiny cottage nestling on the side of the hill, its walls graced by white climbing roses and shaded by immense fronds of tree ferns. Stepping out into the vast clearing, Dot's breathy "Ah," denoted her pleasure at the sight that lay before her.

"Jessie's worked very hard to restore all this," Leesa told them proudly. "You should have seen it a month ago."

"It is beautiful ...," she nodded, "... truly beautiful."

They started down the gradual slope towards the cottage, the sun warming their faces and putting them at ease. Dean's green eyes took a long slow appraisal of the surrounding countryside, much the same as Ryan's had on his first visit. Then they flicked down to Leesa.

"It's nice," he agreed softly. "A nice sort of place to retire."

"Oh, Professor Morrison," she teased him, "I didn't think you were old enough to consider retirement yet."

His smile broadened at her theatrics, then instantly diminished again as a sudden breeze whipped up from the valley floor. It reached them quickly, tossed wildly about, tousling their hair roughly before it gusted upward into the trees behind them. There it increased in strength until its force whipped loudly through the branches, a constant whistling emitting from the leaves.

"I can see why they call this place *Whistling Gums*," Dean commented drily, pressing his fingers to his ears.

"He is angry," Marion said shortly. "We mean you no harm." She directed the last words loudly tree-ward.

For a long moment, the wind seemed to linger. Then, diminishing in strength, it wafted away further down the belt, tickling the treetops as it took security elsewhere.

"He is confused," Marion sympathised. "He worries at our intrusion."

Rooted to the spot by her own concerns, Leesa wondered if Dean or the others were feeling the need to leave now while they still could. Dot's hand on her arm allayed those thoughts minimally.

"It'll be alright," she said calmly. "We pose no threat."

Not exactly convinced, Leesa started moving again towards the cottage.

"No ... Wait!" Marion's attention had swung downward into the valley. "I can hear the voices."

Turning, as if collecting the wind-borne signals around her, she centred her focus on the fork in the trail and stared upward at the trees beyond. Hesitant, her head snapped left, sweeping her vision downward to a point just beyond the house, then to a point deeper into the valley ... about where Jessie had exited the trees in a panic on Leesa's first visit.

"What do they say?" Dean asked in undertones.

"Nothing really. But they cry." Her eyes cast back to the cottage. "They all cry."

After long, slow deliberation, Marion signalled for them to go on, so they continued down towards the cottage. Before they reached the newly planted garden Jessie had toiled over, she deviated from the path and Leesa realised as she watched her walk that she was guided more than decided, her steps more floating, as if she were entranced.

Dot nodded affirmation at her silent assessment. Climbing a little way up the slope, the shadows of the ancient oak tree loomed over the medium as she went forward to its broad trunk. Caressing it with elegant fingers, she softly said, "This ... is Jarvis."

The tree seemed to bend gently over her, its branches dipping in the slight breeze floating down over it. For long moments she just stood there, then, without another word, she turned and marched away down the slope towards the river. Dumbstruck, they all followed, Dean drawing Leesa closer as they entered the cold, dark shadows of the damp grove.

"Ryan said to be very careful in here," Leesa relayed the warning. "He said the trees were dangerous."

Dot nodded her acknowledgment and cast a wary glance up and around, then quickly put her attention back to the ground that Marion had already covered. The sudden crack of old timber snapped overhead and a vehement hiss shot between them, chilling Leesa's skin, and she remembered the look of fear that had paled Jessie's features that day weeks ago. The sound's equally sudden demise was the only thing that stopped her from fleeing as swiftly as her friend had.

Edging closer to Dean, she looked forward again, to where Marion had stopped, her form bathed by golden fingers which forced their way through the tangle of overhead branches, the sun's limited penetration undoubtedly the cause of the stunted growth of the single tree that battled to survive the crowding. It was a tree like the one by the cottage, its oaken form equalled only in age, its height and glory crippled by its smothered position.

"This ...," Marion breathed, "... is Sarah. She cries the loudest." Her hand brushed the trunk in a warming gesture. "Come," she told them. "She would rather be alone."

Backtracking to the brighter daylight, Marion seemed to return to normal, the trance-like state dissipating. She let her gold eyes scan deeply across the top of the trees, perusing the slopes with careful consideration before letting them rest on a point directly above them. Leesa knew what she was sensing.

"There is another tree up there," she said, "... the same as the others."

Wordlessly they trudged back up to the top of the rise along which they had arrived. The clearing appeared a short way from the fork, within the belt of ghostly gums, its unencumbered ground giving instant view to the spreading arms of the third oak, its stature indicating a likeness in species.

"American oak," Dean noted wisely, his expression one of subtle interest.

"It too is Sarah," Marion said, looking somewhat puzzled. The name, this time, stirred her conscience, and Leesa also frowned, trying to force a recollection. Where had she heard Sarah mentioned before? Where in the Kendall charts had that name appeared? Her confusion deepened, for she was reasonably sure that it hadn't.

"Why would American oaks be growing here in Australia?" Dean stated his inner quandary.

"They have a reason for being here," Marion said, her voice a strange mixture of acceptance and understanding. "And yes …" She looked at Leesa. "They are all the same ... yet they are all different."

Suddenly the wind was back around them, not fierce this time, but insistent in its dominance, its circling current surrounding them as if in slow assessment. Then it ebbed again, withdrew to the gums and seemed to linger there in the low shrubbery. Dot's hand went to Marion's shoulder, bewilderedly.

"Do you see him?" she murmured.

"Yes, I see him."

"This is unbelievable," she breathed the words again.

"What's happening?" Leesa could see nothing but the gentle breeze toying in the brush.

"He's materialising," Dot whispered. "He is actually materialising."

Staring harder at the bushes, Leesa could just make out a slight density forming from the breeze. It rose and massed, the vapours slowly lifting higher and deepening in hue, strengthening in substance, forming human shape and colour, and though, still rather faint in its image, a man emerged from the shrouding mist and stopped beneath the trees.

Tall, tanned and broadly structured, he had the coldest grey eyes Leesa had ever seen, yet even though they were quite noticeable, they were softened somewhat by his insolent stance as he propped his shoulder against the white of a ghostly tree trunk. As his image strengthened, Leesa noticed the smoothness of his bronzed skin and the deep cleft in his strong, square chin. His features were, to say the least, rugged, the shock of black hair that topped his height was tousled, as if ruffled by strong wind or hard work.

"Jesus Christ!" Dean hissed sharply beside her as she studied the white flouncy shirt and tightly fitted trousers that heralded centuries past. She wondered if Dean's words might not have been in prayer. And if they weren't, then maybe they should have been. She looked to Dot, the woman's own amazement apparent in the keenness of her eyes.

"He looks so young," she whispered across the gap.

"Time here is ageless," Marion informed them wisely before stepping slowly forward, her hands held out and open to show no threat. "Sailor?"

"Why do you come here? Why do you interfere?!" He straightened away from the gum's trunk and shifted a kink by idly rolling his shoulders, that motion increasing his breadth further. It didn't appear to be meant to intimidate, but his physical power was evident in the rigid stance. He would not have been a man easily defeated, and the reports of his power over the others did not surprise Leesa at all. Still, she sensed a gentleness that was possible if he wished to show it, its presence detected by the mellow tone of his voice.

Marion answered his question with one of her own. "Why have you not passed over, Sailor? Your time here is long past."

"I am not ready." He heaved a breath out defiantly. "I will go only when they will come with me."

"But you have no need to stay. They will pass over when their time comes."

"No!" A stiff gust lashed the grass around them. "I have waited far too long already!" His voice echoed resonantly in the grove, his stance undeniably seditious. "I will have them, and have them soon. Then it will end. Then, we will all pass over."

As inconspicuously as the mist had formed a definite shape, it just as quickly began to vaporise again. Becoming transparent, it drifted back into the trees.

Marion took a few courageous steps forward to follow him. "Who is it that you want?!" she demanded to know.

His words were but a mere whisper in the leaves above them.

"I want my son ... and I want my Sarah."

Then both the wind, the whisper and the man were gone.

"He means business, doesn't he?" Dean's pert remark made them all turn. It pulled their gaze away from the endless circle of trees that girded the farm. Dean's eyes remained on the waving tips of branches down the valley.

"That he does," Dot said, then she exhaled loudly, a breath of relief that at least this part was over. "And that will be a big problem."

"Sssh. Say no more," Marion warned sibilantly. "Come, we had better go while things are in our favour."

Obliging without argument, they retreated to the safety beyond the boundary fence, there to look back and ponder over what had been in the past, and what was in the future.

"Can we stop it?" Leesa asked, her fears evident for her friend.

Marion's answer was one meagre word. "Maybe."

Chapter Fourteen

The drive back to Sydney was filled with possibilities ... possibilities of solutions, the ifs and buts pouring out fluently from one woman to the next. Leesa's involvement was lost in the first ten miles. However involved she was or wasn't now mattered little, just as long as someone was able to help Jessie.

A concrete plan of attack had been formed by the time they boarded the light plane back to Brisbane. First, they had to locate this 'Sailor' in the Kendall tree and link him to Sarah and his son. That apparently was the easy part, Dot advised, for the combined research of her charts and Mrs Castle's linking of the reincarnated to their previous lives would uncover the time periods. From there, it would become harder. They would have to follow the history of the family, find a date that could be determined as the day Sailor had in mind to take what was 'his' and pass over, then somehow prevent it from happening.

Leesa sensed it was going to be harder than it sounded.

The originally sceptical professor unwittingly made that task more elementary by advising that their search should start back in the mid to late 1700s, the mode of dress the entity had worn being from that distinct period.

And so they returned to campus, their 'field trip' successful to a point yet not gracious enough to have provided the full solution. At least they now knew what they were dealing with.

Retiring early to facilitate an early morning start, Leesa lay awake for hours, the name 'Sarah' nagging deeply in her brain. By the time she fell asleep, she knew the morrow would bring nothing but disappointment.

At ten o'clock, three of them stooped over the conference table in the PSI Wing. Dean had fallen by the wayside, opting for more academic duties such as lecturing and supervising Tutorials, though he had made them promise to keep him fully informed.

The pedigree charts Leesa had prepared on those first days of opening the Kendall files held the majority of interest for both PSI ladies. They were convinced the answers lay on those pages.

"There is no Sarah," Leesa told them adamantly. "I have checked and rechecked all the listings, all the certificates, all the births."

"There must be," they insisted, finger-tracing the carefully written print across the pages.

"There's not! And I've gone back as far as I can, back to the mid-1700s like Dean said. That was when William Kenton Fintish Sanderson arrived in Australia. There are no Sarah's from that point in time, nor after."

"What if it goes further back than that?" Dot supposed.

"It wouldn't!" Marion was adamant about that. "If William ... whatsit whatsit ... Sanderson arrived on our shore, then it would start there, or be after. Remember, the farm is the key link. If the events start before that time, then it wouldn't be happening here. It would be happening wherever the family originated."

"America."

The ladies looked up querulously.

"Will Sanderson came from America."

"Oh."

Apparently, it wasn't all that important for that was all they replied before going back to the papers strewn over the desk. "Somewhere here there must be a Sarah."

"And his son," the other added.

Marion suggested, "Define first who He is," and then we can centre on her and the child.

"Start at the beginning, Leesa," Marion sanctioned, pulling a chair out and sitting down. She held a pen ready to jot notes to look back on. "We will try to piece the returning lives to the periods Joy Castle suggested."

Pulling the charts down to the edge of the large rectangular table, she signalled for Leesa to start.

"Well, the family records started here with Will Kenton Fintish Sanderson. He was born in America on May 10, 1766. He supposedly arrived in Australia on the 'Bellona' in 1793, though I haven't been able to locate his name on any of the Charters."

"Maybe he was a sailor ...," Dot suggested thoughtfully.

"No, I don't think so," Leesa countered her point. "As soon as he arrived, he took an option on a land grant which was the location now known as 'Whistling Gums' though it was vastly larger than it is now."

Marion nodded in confirmation. "And that would be correct then. Sailors of the Fleet weren't entitled to land grants. They were forced to work alongside the convicts when they finished service. To get land, they had to be an officer or what they called 'gentry'."

Dot accepted the logic with a nod.

"In 1801, he married Rebecca Morton," Leesa went on. "They had a child in 1803, a daughter, which they named Jane. William Sanderson died that same year, aged 37, yet no place of burial has ever been recorded."

The ladies nodded that the first member had been eliminated.

"Rebecca was born in England in 1774. She came over as a child with her mother, a grazier's wife. She died in 1820, aged 46. Had no other children but Jane."

"What's Jane's full name?" Marion just beat Dot in getting

the words out.

Leesa scanned the page and flicked through Mrs Kendall's other paperwork. "I can't quite read the entry. Something's been spilt on the certificate and smeared it."

Tilting the page, she directed its written surface towards both women. Dot redirected the paper towards better light; she looked at her counterpart with brightening eyes.

"A ... R ..." she spelt, pointing to the middle of the word.

Marion nodded that she, too, had detected the letters; she closed her eyes and let her fingers run along the word. Her eyes opened again.

"It's Mary," she said without emotion.

Taking the page back, Leesa also studied the flourishing scrawl. Barely discernible but faintly resembling what could have been an 'M', Leesa languidly agreed. It was more 'Mary' than Sarah.

"Okay, Jane Mary Sanderson was born June 23rd, 1803; she married Ken Wentworth in 1823, had one child, a son, John William Wentworth in 1836."

"That's a long time to be married without having children," Dot commented wryly, "... especially in those days."

"Maybe he was one of the exploring Wentworths," Leesa smiled pertly. "He might have been off on a long excursion."

Marion's scowl put them straight back to business, Leesa's humour instantly quelled. "Jane died in childbirth." She cleared her throat and shot a quick glance at her insubordinate friend. "Now, John William Wentworth married Joyce Lillian Richards in 1856. They had three children ... uh ... two daughters ... Rose Ingrid and Eliza Jane ... and a son ... Philip Kenton Wentworth.

Birth years were 1857, 1860, 1876 respectively."

"The last one an accident ..." Dot couldn't resist it this time, and nor could Leesa withhold her childish titter, Marion's staid demeanour making it harder for them to keep serious. Her loud sigh again forced them on.

Leesa rattled off the deaths and marriages of that clan, the era beyond that which they were looking for and therefore shining little hope on their search.

"Then we come back to Philip who married Rosalie Moore in 1899. They had one daughter, Elizabeth Rose Wentworth in 1900 ... Jessie's grandmother. Philip died in 1927 and Rosalie in 1937. In 1919, Elizabeth married Jonathan Raybourne. She had two children, a son Albert in 1922, and a daughter Martha in 1926. She died in 1963, aged 63. Her husband died four years later: he was found dead beneath the oak tree by the farmhouse."

Marion nodded that she remembered the allegation that he had been 'taken'.

"Martha Raybourne married Bertram Kendall in 1950, had John Edward on October 24th, 1953, then after a large gap, Jessie was born, in 1963. Jessie's father died first, in 1985. He died of cancer. Then John was killed in 1990, struck by lightning entering the farm." Leesa felt it necessary to add that fact. "Mrs Kendall died July 30th, 1991. Jessica is the sole survivor of the family, excepting now for Jade, who was born December 20th, 1990."

"What was Martha's middle name?" Marion questioned without looking up, her pen continuing to jot notes.

"Umm ... Rose," Leesa told her.

"And Jessica's?"

"Linda."

Another loud sigh emitted from the older woman. "No Sarahs."

"As I said ... no Sarahs!"

Marion leaned back on her chair, her tiredness and concern showing as she scanned the pen lines. A stifled yawn further indicated that she'd probably had a night similar to Leesa's. Then she suddenly tipped forward again, a new thought evolving.

"Go back to the beginning," she instructed, pointing her pen at Leesa, a hint of rising interest returning to her voice. "Go back to Rebecca Morton. What was her middle name?"

Leesa looked for the missing information, shuffled a few more papers around in search of the original documents. "She didn't have one," Leesa soon verified.

"Okay then, what was the exact date of her birth?"

Leesa looked. "July 3rd, 1774."

Marion wrote it down. "Now, give me Jessica's birth date."

That one Leesa knew from memory. "July 11, 1963."

"Rose and Eliza's births and deaths …"

"Rose: born December 15; died February 12. Ingrid: born September 25; died June 5th."

Marion struck a line through both names. "Rebecca Morton's date of death …?"

"October 12."

A line flicked across that name as well. "Give me Elizabeth Wentworth's."

"Born July 22, 1900. Died July 11."

"What year?"

"1963."

"1963?!" Marion paused and looked up at the former entries. "She died the day Jessie was born?"

Leesa nodded ruefully. "If you remember what Mrs Castle said, she was injured in a car accident at the Oberon crossing and later died at home. Apparently, the other driver walked away without a scratch."

Marion looked thoughtful. "Taken," she said pointedly, "as John was taken for Jade."

Dot's affirming nod showed she had also pieced it together. "The returning souls," she said with conviction. "Sarah was Elizabeth, as she is Jessica."

"… as she was possibly Jane – all the same Star sign."

"And Jade?" Leesa sought verification.

Marion looked back to her list. "Jade was definitely John, having been born at the precise time of his death. On the other dates listed though, I can't see any other sign of his return either. The Star signs are all different."

"Maybe he did spend a time too far away," Dot considered aloud.

"Just as Sarah may have been out of the immediate family range between 1836 and 1886," Marion consulted her page. "Joy did say they could branch into other parts of the family, didn't she?!"

They all nodded in agreement.

"But there is still no Sarah," Leesa deigned to remind them.

Dot's expression didn't gloom at the reflection. "It is quite possible that, if a soul could be out of reach in later time ..." She looked directly at Leesa, her finger pointing out the facts, "then maybe it was out of reach before then, before Rebecca even."

The room hummed with their silent thoughts, their eyes roving over the table to the cases at the far end.

"What else is in there?" Dot asked warily.

"All sorts of things," Leesa ratified. "Portraits, Bibles, journals ..."

"Let's see."

Going around the other side of the table, Dot pushed the brown case and her black one across to where they sat. "Is there anything in particular you've noticed?"

"Not really," Leesa answered. "I haven't really had a great deal of time to delve very deeply. Most of what I have been working on came straight from the material Mrs Kendall gathered ... apart, of course, from the photos we took to Sydney."

The sigh Marion heaved was, this time, filled with hope. She let her hands rove slowly through the cases, her gaze directed at the wall as if a sounding board to whatever her mind would pick up. Shuffling fingers worked their way through the aged parchments, receded for a second then delved deeper. Finally, she withdrew a tome from the bottom-most depths of the receptacle.

Setting it down on the tabletop, she let it lay a moment while she stared at its time-worn cover. Then her eyes lifted to take them into her vision. She flipped open the pages and flicked through several more until the volume's centre was revealed. There, in coloured print, was a photograph Leesa had not seen before. Marion lifted it from where it had been slotted, studied it briefly, and passed it over. Dot received it in her hand and shared its glossy image.

"I think I can safely say that is Jessica?!" The medium's words were soft but certain.

The child who sat upon the homemade swing dangling from the strong arms of an old oak tree was indeed Leesa's best friend, her wonderful friend with whom she'd grown up. Even though the child on film was very young, Leesa knew it was Jessie for she had shown her others of herself in preschool years and she recognised her instantly. The man who rocked the swing though forced her jaw to drop. And she stared, horrified. HE who rocked the cradle-like seat was none other than 'Sailor' himself.

Chilling, she looked closer, felt a subtle warmth rise from deep within. There was something in that image that had caused the cold shiver to dissipate; it was the absence of fear. Or was it the appearance of caring on that man's gentle face? Touched, Leesa could read the love in his eyes as he gazed down on the tiny girl with the locks of spun-gold hair, on the girl who was centuries removed from his own time.

"It is," she confirmed.

"See. He waits for her even then."

Dot looked earnestly at their worried faces. "It will not be easy to stop him ... He has waited so long."

"Dwelling on the difficulty is no way to waste our time," Marion chided. "We must find the beginning of both these lives so we can calculate what He has in mind."

Idly, she flicked back through the fragile pages of the old manuscript. "Where did you get these?" she looked up critically.

"From Jessie's," Leesa half admitted.

"I feel there is something not right with these papers." Her eyes narrowed as she peered at the writing.

"Could it be that I took them without asking?" Leesa asked guiltily, hoping her aura portrayed the same stigma.

The surface of Marion's nose wrinkled with her deliberation. "Well, maybe, but I think it goes further than that." Her brow knotted deeper. "I don't know why, but I have this strange feeling that there's been a lot of falsification in this family. If not that, then there have been many secrets."

"The biggest one," Leesa huffed with frustration, "is who the Hell is Sarah!"

"... was Sarah," came Dot's correction as she took her turn poking through the folders.

Marion, on the other hand, had headed for the kettle which resided on the room's corner cupboard. Setting down the cups, she turned inquisitively. "How did you know that Will Sanderson arrived on the *Bellona* if his name wasn't on the Charter lists?"

Her question threw Leesa for a little while, her mind trying to resurrect from where the information had come.

"Oh," she suddenly remembered, "it was written in the front of one of the journals." Fossicking quickly, she found what she was looking for: "This one." She held up the leather-bound book – "only I couldn't get too much information because most of the pages are stuck together."

A warm feeling flowed back over her as she remembered that elegant style of writing, that hopeful inscription of finding a new life. Will Sanderson had been an adventurous man, and she loved that trait in a man.

Bringing with her the steaming cups that heralded a break in their work, Marion took the volume into her hands and resumed her seat. Wordlessly, she laid it flat in front of her, the cover still closed. Her all-seeing hands spread wide across the blue. Then her eyes closed, ensuring no interference broke through her concentration.

Her words when they came were quiet yet firm with accuracy and slow in their delivery as she mind-read the contents.

"This is the first journal of William Kenton Fintish Sanderson, born May 10, 1766," she began. "He began his journey to the colonies aboard the American ship *The Philadelphia* in 1786, destined for England. It was intended for him to collect younger members of his father's family there and accompany them to the new world where his father would later join them. It appears they were disillusioned by the unrest in the country and sought hope of a peaceful life elsewhere."

There Marion paused for a moment as if taking time to glean the more important data. Sipping their coffees, Dot and Leesa waited with obvious impatience, the room's silence becoming unbearable.

Drawing a long breath, the narrative went on. "He writes that the journey was long and tedious, one on which his boredom made him offer himself to ship's duty ... He took work on the ship," she clarified. "He arrived on English soil, only to find those members who had expressed their wish to join him had long since changed their minds and now wished neither to exile themselves to a penal settlement, nor finance one to go there. This unexpected turn of events left him penniless and he had to work for several long months to raise more fare. Having done this, he put himself aboard another ship for the new coast, longing for the day he could return to, or be joined by, his own family."

Leesa sighed with calculation. He would have been only twenty. Twenty years old and all on his own, thwarted at every turn for his good deeds. It was a damn shame one so young should suffer so much. Her jaw tightened as she turned her thoughts back to Marion who was speaking again.

"But that too proved a long and hard sea journey," she went on. "Heavy gales and turbulent seas did much damage to the ship and made it necessary to lay over at the Cape of Good Hope.

"It was there a fight broke out between the marines and officers on the British transport. Will gave aid to the captain who was unarmed when set upon by a large contingent of mariners. The captain escaped serious injury while Will Sanderson was wounded and put nearly to death. His recovery was slow, so slow the ship put to sea without him, though a land grant was offered him for his heroic service should he survive his wounds.

"Well, he did survive ... naturally," she added her own point, "though it took many more months before he was able to travel." She looked up, her eyes lighting with revelation. "In that time, he befriended the surgeon's daughter who expressed her desire to also make a life in the new world. Her name, my friends, was Sarah ... Sarah Thornton."

Dot's eyes met Leesa's, their jaws simultaneously slackening. Neither of them smiled though. It seemed so inappropriate under the circumstances.

"... He writes that he took employment to raise passage on the next available ship and had barely enough when the *Bellona* reached the Cape. By this time, he was feeling much affection for Sarah and felt remorse at the thought of disappointing her by leaving her behind. So they married. But still, he had only fare for one, so he bought passage for his new wife and offered his service to the ship to work for his own. By the grace of God, the captain deemed him 'muscularly framed as to be well calculated to hard work'." Marion's smile was pert. "My, didn't they talk funny in those days?!"

"Good Lord, the shock they'd have if they heard the kids of today," Dot added wryly.

And Leesa? Well, she smiled too, but minimally, for she could see this poor young man sent on a journey from his family, finding it a worthless task on his arrival in a strange land, making his way as best he could in an effort to regain his place at his father's side only to be further hampered for his bravery. She felt sorry for him, though she was glad he had found a friend. Remembering his handsome features and those steel-grey eyes, she didn't wonder that Sarah had accepted to marry him.

"And so the ship set sail, bound for Australia," their seer continued. She paused once more to delve deeper into the closed pages, then, after a long while, looked up. "The rest is just his entries on how the voyage was; the harsh conditions; the atrocious treatment suffered on the female prisoners by the men; how he had to protect his wife at all costs. This journal ends two months into the sea voyage."

Her hands lifted from the blue leather surface. "So," she sighed, "... we have found Sarah." Dot's eyebrows rose as much as her lips pursed. "And we have found 'Sailor'. All we have to do now is find the time he lost her, or some significant date at which he may reclaim her as his own."

"Don't forget his son!" Leesa remembered suddenly. "Wouldn't the date relate to both of them?"

These words further touched a soft spot in Leesa's heart. How much this poor man had endured. So much had gone against him. She didn't wonder now that he felt some sort of justice was owed him; that he had a right. A cold chill crept over her as she considered what they had just heard, and that it wasn't the end of the trials he had suffered.

"What else is in there?" Marion flicked an index finger at the cases. She looked tired now, her energies drained from intense concentration. Dot took an investigative perusal through the satchels, heaving a deep sigh at her own studious relief.

"There's something here. It may be another journal … its wrapped in brown paper."

"Open it," came the simultaneous instruction.

She did, the edges of a brown hard-backed diary being revealed. Passing it across, Marion didn't even bother to open it. Holding it was apparently enough. "It's the third journal," she said dully, "… dated 1800. It tells of his marriage to Rebecca Morton and the birth of his daughter … He makes mention of his infatuation with the child; the only mention of Sarah is a brief entry in which he reflects that for the first time since her death and that of his son, he has felt some sort of emotion. … He regards the revival of his heart is due to his daughter's arrival. The entries end in December, 1803. His daughter was barely six months old." She laid this volume down. "Are there any others? It's the second journal we need."

Again, Dot dug deep into the layers of papers, and ended up lifting the contents fully and systematically examining the folders before slipping them back into their original place. Repeating the process with the second container, she lifted her gaze to take them into her vision. "Nothing," she said. "There's no second journal here."

"Damn!" came the medium's annoyed response. "What we need is obviously in that second volume – his life in the interim. Leesa, were there any other books where you got these?"

Reflecting back, Leesa knew the ceiling cavity in Jessie's house was empty and, while the loft still held plenty of family treasures, she knew no book similar to those they had just infiltrated existed there either. Marion huffed a sigh, which Leesa sensed was from a mixture of tiredness and frustration simply because it mirrored her own.

"It hasn't been with these items for a long, long time," Dot predicted deliberately. Turning back, her hands closed over both cases, her grip tightly securing visions from her inner senses. "It has been hidden ... well hidden."

Marion blinked heavily with deep understanding. "It's part of the secret," she prophesied. "His life He wanted kept that way."

"He had something to hide!"

Marion and Dot now seemed to be on the same wavelength, Leesa's existence seemingly forgotten.

"Yes, but He hides it from others as much as from himself."

"... and it has to do with the trees. I sense that very strongly." It was the medium, her other talents rising to meet the situation.

"Yes. I feel that too."

"Didn't He say something about Mrs Kendall's father had touched his trees?"

Leesa's thoughts flew back to Jessie, to Ryan and the problem that had grown out of all proportion. "Jessie has shunned Ryan because he wanted to cut down some of the trees. She won't let him near the place anymore."

"Well, that's just as well," came Marion's reply. "He will kill whoever harms them."

Leesa remembered another fact, remembered their walk around the farm. He named the trees ... the oak trees in particular ... Sarah, Sarah and Jarvis. I wonder if the gums were called anything. And then ..." She frowned. "...why two Sarahs?"

"Well, this doesn't bring us any closer to a solution," Dot broke her thoughts. "We need to know more about this Sarah."

"Well, now that we have a name, I can go back through the State Archives and dig a bit deeper. There's another set of records altogether for those that served on the ships ..."

And that was where they left it. Leesa would set about doing research far deeper than Mrs Kendall's had ever gone to pick up on leads she had obviously overlooked. It was late afternoon when she finally found the sunshine again, more pieces of the puzzle having been revealed yet bringing them only slightly closer to helping her friend.

Chapter Fifteen

For the next three working days, Leesa plagued the clerk at the State Archives Building. She waded her way through file after precious file, meticulously kept listing after meticulously kept listing. She delved and dug at names, dates, and eras until her eyes were sore, and for the first time ever, she hated genealogy. The only facts revealed were that Will Sanderson had indeed arrived on the *Bellona* as a sailor and that a land grant promised him by a grateful ship's captain was honoured.

No entry existed for Sarah Thornton, but that was to be expected, seeing she was born and married elsewhere. Sarah Sanderson was listed as a passenger on the migrant ship, though her death and burial were never recorded.

The Archivist seemed to think this was due to the remoteness of the area where the land was granted, immigrants being encouraged to open new areas further and further away from the settlement. Leesa saw his point, but it didn't help much.

Dismally, at the end of the third day, she returned to her flat for a long hot bath and a stiff drink to try to clear her head. She wanted to dwell on other things just for a while because, frankly, this course of events was producing the biggest headache she could possibly ever imagine.

Laying back in the luxury of a deep tub, the hot steam encouraging her eyes to close and her thoughts to flitter, she let her head rest back on the hard enamel surround. *Life could be so languid if one just let themselves go ...*

Then she remembered: that thought was the same she'd had the last time she'd taken such a luxuriant soak. It had been at Jessie's, the end of the day they had first gone to the farm. She had so needed to rest her feet and her aching back. Doing that same thing right now, she wondered what Jessie was doing, what Ryan was doing, and if he would phone her when Jessie told him of her intended move to the farm.

Reading the blank, hazy ceiling in careful calculation, she realised the date was soon ... two days away. The thirteenth of December. She wondered when Jesse would tell Ryan. *Surely it will be tonight, or tomorrow.*

Sighing, Leesa felt a heaviness touch her heart and realised she was waiting for Ryan to call. *Yes. It will be tonight ... or tomorrow. No matter how much Jessie resents his accusations or threats, she would never go without telling him.* She knew her that well.

Idly mooching around her flat, her nerves steeled for the call, she practised what she would say to her friend's husband, to her friend – for he was indeed her friend too – but no call came ... not early in the evening, not late at night. She retired at the midnight hour.

The next day was Thursday. Leesa stayed by the phone, whether in her flat or in her office. Surely Ryan would need to talk! He would be devastated by Jessie's plans to take Jade ... his son ... away to a place he was forbidden to go. She shuddered at the prospects, for what if he chose to follow her?

The thought sent chills all over her flesh. Needless to say, she was in a terrible state when the phone stayed silent another night.

The morning of the thirteenth she walked through the empty campus gardens, deliberating as to whether she should call Ryan herself. Maybe he was too upset to talk just yet. Maybe he and Jessie had been up late discussing ... or even arguing ... over their hopeless situation. *Or maybe I should just butt out and let whatever is going to happen, happen. Isn't that how fate works?! And wouldn't that be the easiest way out?!*

Her head throbbing, she unlocked her office door and succumbed to the need and immediately dialled Jessie's number. There was no answer. Five minutes later, it gave the same response.

Releasing the tightness in her throat with a long, slow breath, she looked up as a shadow continued to loom across her doorway. Dorothy stood there.

"I've had strong vibes from you all night, Leesa. What's the matter?" she frowned from the opening.

Rubbing the tension in her brow, Leesa held back a sob, the emotion becoming so great that it surprised even her. "Jessie ... she ... she's going to leave Ryan."

"You've sensed the conflict is starting?!" Dot queried sharply. "You have the date?!"

"I think she is leaving today ... going to live at the farm!"

"How do you know that?"

"A date she circled on the calendar. At first, I thought it was an event I must have forgotten, but in light of what's been happening between her and Ryan, and after what she said the other day ... she's going to take Jade and go."

"This date has been on your mind for a while, hasn't it?"

"Well yes, I guess so. But I thought it was an anniversary or something I'd forgotten."

"Then Jessica knew from the beginning this day would mean something special." Dot frowned again.

"But ... she had the date circled before she and Ryan had ever argued!"

"About the time she first visited the farm?"

Leesa nodded slowly, her throat tightening further at her error. "Oh no! Oh God, no!" Her eyes widened in horror. "Don't tell me He will take her today!! It can't be today!!"

Snatching up the phone, Dot thrust it at her. "Ring her husband. Tell him she must not go to the farm. Tell him he must stop her at all costs!"

Punching out the number, Leesa listened intensely, the buzzing of urgency distorting her hearing and adding to the burring at the other end of the line. *No answer. Still no bloody answer!* From the recesses of her top drawer, she found Ryan's office number and clumsily tapped it out on the touchpads. Again, the annoying burr of a number unattended. It was still too early for the office to be open; he was probably en route.

But where is Jessie?!! Has she maybe already left? Has something happened and she is already staying at the farm?

Shoving Ryan's number into her purse, her head in turmoil, she left Dot standing. As she hurried down the corridor and up the jarrah stairway, several students gave her a querulous look. She cared little about how she must have looked. In her room, she tossed a few items into a small overnight bag then headed back downstairs to the car. Within minutes, she was on her way to the airport, though it seemed like hours had flitted away, and she prayed there would be a cancellation, prayed she could get an immediate flight.

For a Friday morning, the Terminal was chaotically busy and she cringed that all flights would be fully booked. Further hampering her exit from Brisbane was a long delay in organising her car in the security compound, that giving her less chance of being available if a seat became so. Joyously to her favour, there had been a cancellation on the flight that was just boarding, and her hopes soared, only to be dashed again on finding it had already been promised to a gentleman who had rung through a short while before.

Why didn't I ring?!! she cursed her haste. *Why didn't I take a few minutes to arrange things properly?!!*

Turning around, she saw a man hurrying towards the Baggage counter. He was fat and red-faced from effort, his huge size unenhanced further by the creased grey suit that encased him. *It has to be him.* She had but one chance. Just one chance of persuading him to let her take his place. Totally out of character, she stepped across his path and begged him to let her have his seat on the waiting plane – it was a matter of life and death, she insisted as he tried to duck by her. "I have to get to Sydney for my friend's sake. She is in serious danger and I have to get there urgently. Please, please ...," she pleaded, any repugnant thoughts of subservience completely diminished in light of the situation.

The man just looked at her with piggy blue eyes. "Cut the theatrics, lady!" he grunted as he rubbed the end of his rather bulbous snout on the edge of his sleeve. "I have an important business deal that can't wait."

"I have a friend who might die if I don't get there!!" she yelled after him as he brushed her aside. Heads turned and looked her way as people's interest rose. Scanning their faces, she tried to forget how stupidly she was behaving, and how idiotic she must have looked. The fat man was the least affected by her plight.

"We all have our problems ..." he jeered and kept going. He reached the desk and the ticket was in his hand. He disappeared through the doorway, and her chance was gone.

Catching sight of the phone booths in the corner, she hastily tried Jessie's number again. No answer. She tried Ryan's office: he hadn't come in yet. The girl at the ticket counter seemed sympathetic to her problem, though her sideways glance showed she thought Leesa was probably more than slightly cracked. She promised her the next available seat.

The next flight was in another two hours. By this time, her nerves were knotted, and her heart thudded noisily. She called Dot and told her of the delay. Dot sounded concerned.

"If Jessie gets to the farm, there's nothing you can do. Do you understand that? Once she has reached his realm of power it will be very dangerous for you to even speak of this to her."

Leesa's words were taken by silent imaginings.

"Do you understand me, Leesa? The only hope you have is to stop Jessie getting to the farm!"

"I know. But it'll be hours yet before I can get there."

"We will pray you will make it," she promised.

Leesa sighed heavily, "So will I."

Using her waiting time wisely, she rang ahead and booked a car for her arrival and tried Ryan again and again. She tried Jessie, then tried to read a magazine but could only see the horrendous outcome of her stupidity. Not remembering that damn date, which had been so blatantly written on the wall, was unforgivable.

At last, a seat became available, and she was able to pay for it and secure her place to avoid any further scenes with pugnacious – or should she say pignacious – ugly men. Not soon enough, she was in her seat and the plane was taxiing, her heart and mind pounding in unison with the screaming engines, her voice wanting to match them in sound. But it didn't. She had to stay in control. She had to rectify the idiotic mistake that had let things get this far; maybe too far.

The prearranged hire car was ready and waiting when she landed in Sydney. From the airport, she tried Jessie again to let her know she was coming and hopefully keep her at home. Then she would ring Ryan to let him know what was about to happen and get him to stop her from going anywhere.

As Murphy's Law predicted, 'If anything can possibly go wrong, it will', and it did. The long bank of phone booths was occupied when she got there, every single one of them. The only one that wasn't was Out of Order. Pacing back and forward along the row, she dived in and snatched up the first one vacated.

There was still no answer at Jessie's, but she'd really come to expect that now. Ryan's office answered, but her relief was immediately quashed again when the receptionist reminded her that this was Friday, and Ryan always had every second Friday off. This was the second Friday.

Damn! Damn!! Damn!!!

She wondered if maybe He had structured this set of circumstances deliberately to have his own way. Was it possible his power was that great? Or was she just looking for excuses for her own bad luck?

The little car she hired proved rather zippy as she headed out along the Great Western Freeway, her eyes peeled for any sign of Jessie's blue Cortina. She saw none, the drive becoming tedious in her constant search, her eyes becoming strained in the mid-afternoon glare. Oberon was quiet when she passed through, and so was Amberlay where she made the turn-off to the farm. She had hoped maybe Jessie would have been in town somewhere, but knew by her luck to date exactly where she was. She could only hope she was wrong.

The main gravel track heading up into the hills was lined with tyre tracks. *Fresh tyre tracks. From a small car.* Her hopes dashed dismally. *I'm too late. Jessie is already at the farm; she's already under his power.*

Indicating to turn onto the lesser track, she heard an incessant barping of a car horn. The only vehicle in sight apart from hers was coming down the track towards her. The white utility looked about as aged as its driver, and about as rough in appearance. She braked and peered closer through the windshield. The driver was male and was obviously pleased she had stopped. His head poked out through the driver's open window.

"I wouldn't be goin' down there today, Missie," he called out, his stubbled jaw seeming hard to control ... jawing, she found the right word for it. "Today is not the day to go onto that place."

"Why?" she asked, stepping from the car to hear him better.

"This day, every year, He wails and whines and gets pretty wild. Been doin' it every year since I been here. The wife says He's grievin'."

Leesa sensed he was studying her for a reaction, but she didn't give him one.

"He's already tossin' about in there. The wind looked mighty fierce when I drove by the upper pasture a while back. I'd go back to town if I was you. Annie says it'll be calmer tomorrer, and Annie is always right on these things."

"Who's Annie?" Leesa questioned wryly.

"My wife ... Annie Carter. The old girl knows all about these things."

Leesa gathered she'd be an old girl seeing he looked about eighty-not-out. "Heed her words, lass. No good can come of goin' there today."

He had started the car moving again and rolled it slowly past her hire car. Leesa watched as it continued to roll on down the gradual slope, watched until it rounded the bend and disappeared from view. Her eyes turned back to the side track, to Jessie's tyre tracks. Steeling her nerves with a deep breath, she returned to the driver's seat and continued along her intended route.

Jessie's car soon appeared in the treeless sward. It was empty. Stepping out again, Leesa noticed what the old man had said: the trees within the boundary were whipped by a storm, their tops bending violently, the wind whistling a piercing scream of anguish through their leaves. And she shuddered coldly, for outside the fence line where she stood was breezeless, a pure summer day, warm and mellow and completely still.

The cold chill remained as she climbed through the gate, noting that an attempt had been made to repair the gaping hole. Instantly the wind was around her, chilling her skin further with its obvious annoyance at her intrusion. Quivering visibly, she followed Marion's lead.

"I mean you no harm," she said shakily, hoping the words had emitted audibly through the tension in her jaw.

This time though, it made little difference to the force of His insistence. The wind continued to bluster. The whistling in the leaves became louder. Determinedly, yet cringing inwardly at the possibilities, Leesa started to walk the downward path to find Jessie, ignoring his battering protests. She would not let him stop her. And she would not let him take her. She was her friend first! Her best friend! And regardless of the recent flaw in their relationship, she was not going to let her go without a fight!

Halfway down the slope's narrow trail, she spotted Jessie. She was sitting beneath the oak tree above the cottage, her legs drawn up beside her, her form hunched like hers against the force of the rainless gale. Harsh, cold wind continued to bluster about her, tearing at her clothing and whipping her hair into a stinging, painful lash. Leesa called to her, though much of the sound was whipped away down the paddock. Even so, Jesse turned and looked up, her eyes wide and pleading. Tears stained her cheeks, her anguish and fear obvious. What steeled her harder than her grief was the dark red stream of blood running from a deep cut on Jessie's forehead.

"Jessie, what happened to you?!" Leesa reached her side and crouched down to her level.

"Oh please, help me! He's gone down there."

Leesa's arms wrapped around her, the consoling hug issuing warmth as it never had before, hers just as vitally returning the gesture. "Come on, we'd better leave here. I'll get you away from this place."

Jesse started to rise to her coaxing; she started to respond to her suggestion. Then suddenly her arms became repelling, her hands pushing Leesa's away.

"No! I cannot leave here. He needs me. He needs me," she yelled above the storm.

"But look at what he's done to you!!" Leesa shot back at her.

Her face took on a look of horror. "No! He'd never hurt me .... NEVER!" Her blue eyes widened further.

From down in the valley Leesa heard a voice, a woman's voice. It was filled with fear and pleading.

"No, Will. No! Please no!! Will ..." The last word was a fading scream that made her blood run colder.

"Jessie, please ... we must leave here ... NOW! ... before he comes for you." Leesa realised she was shaking her. "COME ON!!"

Jessie prised Leesa's hand from her arm with angry fingers and looked incensed. "He would never hurt me."

Then, looking down the valley, her eyes went soft again. "He loves me, Leesa. He truly loves me."

"He's going to kill you and Jade. He's going to hurt you both!"

"NO!! He'd never hurt me ..."

Looking up, Leesa saw a movement in the valley below, a movement of white. It was Sailor, a visible-to-the-eye Sailor. He was exiting the trees in the glade below, and looking somewhat stunned. More frightening than the sudden appearance of him, was the bright red blood dripping from his hands, a rifle gripped in one of them.

Leesa had had enough; she'd seen enough. Hauling Jessie up by the jumper, she dragged her a few steps further up the slope. "Come on, Jess. Come on!"

Jesse stumbled a few slow, absent-minded steps as if entranced, caught between two worlds.

"NO, SARAH!!"

The voice from the valley boomed. The subsided wind, which until now had gone unnoticed, resumed with all its force and hit with such strength it almost knocked them both off their feet.

"Please ... NO!!"

Jessie turned back. "Sailor," she called back to him, then she screamed as Leesa continued to pull her after her, "Sailor ... help me!"

Another glimpse of those blood-soaked hands gave Leesa greater strength. There would be no hope for Jessie if he reached her. Her teeth gritted with effort and her next words hissed vehemently at her. "Jessie, he'll kill you."

Jesse was crying now, large tears as if believing what she'd said but not wanting to believe it. "He'd never hurt me. He'd never hurt me or Jarvis."

"Well, he has already, hasn't he?!" Leesa tried to bring her back to reality. "Look what he's done already."

Jessie's hand slowly went to her forehead, her fingers leaving little marks in the red trickle oozing down her face. Blank-faced, she looked back at Leesa. "He didn't do this," she admonished coolly. "Sarah did. Sarah hates me! She's always hated me!"

Will was now halfway up the slope, the anger on his face making her release her hold on Jessie's jumper. Leesa backed away. *He's going to take Jessie and Jade and maybe also me.* The blood already on his hands looked brighter and fresher the closer he came, yet even so, Jessie retook those few steps back towards him.

Being about her size and strength, Leesa knew she could do nothing to stop her, to save her. But she could save Jade. She would never let him take the child. But there was no sign of Jade around.

Making a grab for Jessie, she swung her abruptly around. "Jessie, where's Jade?!" The blood-soaked hands brought terror to her eyes. "Where the Hell is Jade?!!"

Without haste, she huffed deeply then frowned, bored with her insistence. "With Ryan," she said dully.

Oh God no!! ... No ... Her heart stopped beating.

Leesa looked back to Will, to the place in the valley where he had exited, her thoughts running wild at the reasons why Ryan had not answered her calls, at the origin of the blood. *He followed Jessie! He'd suspected her of having an affair and followed her!* Her tears started to flow profusely.

"JESSIE ... WHERE IS RYAN?" she screamed her anguish above the rising wind. "WHY DID YOU LET HIM TAKE HIM?"

"I couldn't bring Jade today," she said absently, her eyes still on Will. "It's not a good day for Sailor. Not a good day for either of us ... too sad ... so I had Ryan take Jade to Penrose." She sounded so matter-of-fact.

Will had almost reached them, his anger obvious in the coldness of his eyes. Leesa knew better than to stand there any longer, the woman's scream returning to her mind, the blood on his hands making her tremble. For her life's sake, she turned and bolted, sprinted away up the hill, and left Jessie standing beneath the tree as Will came up behind her.

Turning back only once, Leesa stared through tear-misted eyes as Will's arms locked around Jessie, and her head buried into the curve of his shoulder.

Leesa's jaw gaped in her astonishment as Jessie's arms enfolded around him, his body solid to her touch. Then his head lifted, his eyes glaring upward to where Leesa stood on the top of the rise. Then a wind blew up, fanning the grass flat on its swift approach. Instantly Leesa's feet started moving again, and she disappeared in amongst the tall, dark trees, the eerie wind following just moments behind her. Her throat burning for air, she reached the gate and scrambled over, the wind hitting with a sharp blast against her back as she did, lashing her hair forward to whip her face and blur her vision.

As she touched safe earth on the other side, she felt its instant retreat, felt too the tear in her skin where a loose wire had penetrated her slacks and torn both flesh and fabric. Its smarting sting warned her of her luck, the blood on her hand much less than the blood on his. And she stood and cried, and prayed for Jessie.

Then she heard a voice drift from the trees, a quiet, dismal plea ... "Don't go. Please don't go."

It was Martha Kendall's voice.

And Leesa knew they had both lost.

Chapter Sixteen

It was a good hour before her hands stopped shaking long enough for her to drive. She made Oberon and stopped at the small roadside cafe. At the phone box on the roadside, she rang Dot, under the curious eye of the bowser attendant who manned a row of petrol pumps nearby. Her tears had subsided somewhat, though she could feel her eyes were red, and she struggled to hold back a new flow as she related to Dot all she had seen.

"I had to leave her …" Her sobs started again, her chin quivering and dimpling at the ramifications the words brought. She pressed her lips together to hold the tears back, letting only a few words out at a time. "She wouldn't come …" A tear glistened.

"You did all you could, Leesa. You did all you could. But it's alright. Jessie will be fine for now."

"But He …"

"She will be fine for now. Believe me. As long as the baby is not with her, she is safe. Remember, He wants them both. If he takes Jessie, there will be no way Jade will ever be taken to the farm. And he's smart enough to know that."

Swallowing thickly, Leesa let Dot's words take hold, her head throbbing painfully from all that had happened, her thigh stinging from the long scratch in the flesh. *Hell, I must look a sight,* she thought as she shot the curious young man an inquisitive look of her own. He turned and walked back inside the roadhouse.

"What are you going to do now?" Dot's voice came again down the wire. "Are you coming straight back to Brisbane?"

Hesitating, Leesa considered her options. "No ... I think I will stay in Sydney a while. I need to talk to Ryan." She heaved a sigh, her nerves coming back to a level near normality with the forced necessity to think. More decisions helped further. "I'll book into that motel we stayed at the other night, if you need to contact me. And can you let Dean know? I didn't get a chance to tell him I was leaving."

Dot promised she would.

"And ... can you keep praying? Something has to be helping us somewhere."

"Sure," Dot said warmly. "And you look after yourself, and remember what I told you ... you cannot help Jessie once she is on the farm."

"I'll remember," Leesa promised. "I'm going to stay here till Monday and see how things go. Maybe I can talk reason with Jessie when she comes home."

They rang off, the empty void of the receiver making Leesa realise now just how lonely she was.

Night had prevailed without warning, and she drove back to Sydney in the dim yellow beams of her headlights. The motel, thankfully, had a vacancy and she booked in, taking the same room Dean had used the time before. The emptiness was so complete, the darkness so incredibly potent as she lay there staring at a black spot on the ceiling, the last few nights and days flitting in and out of her mind, replaying the events of what was starting to seem like a very real horror movie.

What a world I've become engrossed in! Psychics. Mediums. Clairvoyants. Regressionists. Souls from the past. Even strange old ladies who know all about the goings on, she scoffed that she apparently was the only one who didn't know anything about it. *I'm so blind to what everyone else is seeing so clearly. Except that really isn't true anymore, is it? For I have seen Him in the flesh, and Jessie in his solid embrace.*

The thought made her cold again. She would really rather not have been witness to that, and she wondered what they were doing right then. Could Ryan really have been right and she was indeed having an affair? She tried to force a laugh. *An illicit love affair with a ghost?!! This is getting just too weird!*

And what of the old man and his warning? She dwelt back a little further. *He knew what was going on on the farm!! – he said his wife knew of these things. She'd said He was grieving. Jessie confirmed those very words when she'd said it wasn't a good day for Him, or her. But who is he grieving for? And how much more does this Annie Carter know?!*

Leesa now knew what her next course of action would be the next morning.

Then another issue rammed its point home: Jessie had said Sarah had been the one who'd hurt her. *But ... isn't she Sarah?!* That small reflection kept her awake longer than anything else. And when she did finally succumb to sleep, it was broken, traumatised by spine-chilling dreams in which no one could win. She awoke to the cold grey of an early dawn bathed in clammy sweat and gasping for air. Yet, even so, the morning was a blessed relief.

Chapter Seventeen

She was back on the road to Oberon by ten o'clock, having first stopped at a teller-machine to replenish her dwindling reserves of cash. She'd tried to phone Ryan again, but there had been no answer so she made it her last try. Maybe he had stayed over in Penrose seeing Jessie was probably staying at the farm with her 'other man'. She wondered what Ryan's reaction would be if he really knew, and wondered if he would even believe it if he was told.

Shelving that problem for the moment, for there was another one more pressing, she mingled back amongst the north-west traffic. How would she find this 'Annie Carter' when she reached Oberon? How did anyone go about finding a stranger they were looking for?

Her frown deepened with the thought. *Well, there was always the local Police Station* ... but Oberon didn't have one. Then there was the Electoral roll, but that was back in Sydney and she doubted the little Postal agency would have one ... even if it did open on a Saturday. *I could probably ask someone ...*

Then she remembered Mr Bateman at the corner store in Amberlay. He seemed to know everyone in and out of town. He knew Jessie even though she only went to the farm on weekends. Leesa crossed her fingers for him to know the Carters.

He did, and put her on the road past *Whistling Gums*.

"Take the main track for another three mile," he'd said, "then turn right where the road curves sharply. The driveway is long and pretty rugged so be careful."

Hoping she wouldn't run into Jessie as she passed, she travelled the long red gravel track Mr Bateman had put her on, keeping the speed to a minimum for the rocks were loose and the tyre tracks deep and rutted. It was well obvious this wider track was the more often used, and she was careful not to lose concentration for fear of damaging the hire-car.

Carter's gateway was easy enough to find though she braked in the gateway and stared for long seconds when she saw the length and condition of its entry. If she had driven carefully till now, her wits had to be doubly prepped to avoid panel injury on this stretch, and she didn't wonder that the old man's utility was as battered as it was: it was now so totally understandable.

Creeping at a snail's pace around gaping chasms in the fragmented road, some which were unavoidable to transverse, Leesa made slow progress down the beaten track. At the lower junction of two rises, water coursed beneath the wheels and though she tried by speed, or lack of it, to avoid splashing, it was to no avail – the car was splattered in red dust and mud by the time she came in sight of the house. It would definitely need to go through a car wash before its return.

The Carter's was a ramshackle old place, a very good likeness for Ma and Pa Kettle's, and about as rough and decrepit as the old man himself had appeared. Piles of rusted rubbish were strewn about the yard and surrounds, yet almost organised in its careful manner of deposit. One of wire, one of tin, another of machinery, old posts at yet another, and so on. About the piles and along and under the rickety verandah, a multitude of hounds stirred from their indolent postures. (She called them hounds because none of them was defined enough to be a dog, being bits of this and that. A couple even looked as if they'd been trading off parts ... certainly not a pedigree amongst the lot.) Their inbred barking became a deafening cacophony of yapping and baying as they bailed up the intrusive vehicle and its occupant, while Leesa remained safely confined within.

In just a short while, movement appeared at the door and the wire screen door opened. A woman, white-haired with age and bean-pole thin, stepped out to the verandah, her hands drying on the crumpled apron that protected her floral day frock. Shading her eyes with her hand, she peered down the yard to where Leesa had parked, then mouthed something that Leesa couldn't hear above the noise.

Coming forward, she clapped her hands twice, which gained the hounds' attention; then one sharp word sent them all skittering to places unseen.

Heaving a sigh of relief, Leesa warily stepped from her safety zone. "Mrs Carter?" she presumed.

The lady's cloudy eyes regarded her dubiously as she nodded a slow ratification.

"My name is Leesa Bradden. Your husband told me yesterday that you know things about what happens on the farm next door ..."

Her expression darkened.

"I was wondering if you could tell me more about it."

"Why would you want to know about that old place?" she hedged, not coming any closer.

"Mrs Carter, my friend is Jessica Robinson. She recently inherited the farm from her mother ... and I'm afraid things aren't going too well over there."

"Oh dear," she exclaimed deeply. She stopped wiping her hands and smoothed the apron down over her dress. The deep look turned to concern. "I told Syd things would start brewing again. I told him that when he said he'd seen Jessica Kendall over there. It's not good."

She seemed not to have noticed Leesa's reference to Jessie's married name, yet now viewed her with a more careful scrutiny.

"You say you are her friend ...?"

Leesa nodded. "... and I'm very worried about her."

"Come inside, dear," the lady said warmly, "and I'll tell you what I can. And please," she added as she ushered her forward, "call me Annie. Everybody does."

Walking into Annie's household was like walking into a world far removed from the outside. Annie seemed to sense her surprise as she went forward and switched on the kettle.

"The inside is my responsibility," she said proudly, her eyes fleetingly encompassing the bright walls and airy atmosphere the rooms exuded. The house was immaculately neat and clean, cosy and well-maintained. The furniture, though old and restored, enhanced the setting perfectly. "Syd's domain is outside that door." She set down two cups and saucers.

"We made a deal a long time ago," she smiled pertly. "He doesn't mess my house, and I don't tidy his stock piles."

Leesa smiled with her.

She was a likeable old lady, young for her appearance, even if maybe it was just at heart. She didn't touch on the subject Leesa had come to discuss until the teas were poured and placed on the table before them. Then she sat down, perfectly suited to the floral curtained room and the very feminine pink wallpaper, and, although strangers, the warmth of the room seemed to drift between them, making the subject more approachable.

Leesa sipped the steaming brew and wondered where to start, wondered just how much Annie really knew.

"So, you want to know what I know about the Raybourne place," she mused tautly, peering over the rim of her cup.

"Yes. It's very important."

Putting down the vessel, Annie looked up and took a long, hard scrutiny of her as she sat there, then she blinked slowly, as if in hesitation. Her lips pursed. "Well, you'd better tell me just what you know about the place so far then."

"I know it's haunted," Leesa said, using Ryan's words.

Annie smiled wryly and picked up her cup again. "And how do you know that?!" she scoffed with a widening smile, her eyes brightening at her observation.

"Because I saw him."

With a sudden wobble of shocked hands, Annie's cup fell, clattering against the saucer and tipping its contents across the tablecloth. It almost rolled off the table edge to the floor had Leesa not intercepted its drop just in time.

The old woman didn't move, just stared at her, her face ashen. "How do you know it's a he?!" she snapped, her hand going to her breast.

There's something wrong here. Leesa knew it instinctively. *I've struck a raw nerve.*

"It's Will Sanderson." Leesa fed a little further information to gauge her next reaction. "I saw him."

The woman's eyes cooled a little and she moistened her lips, then heaved a long sigh. "How do you know it was him?" she asked a little suspiciously as she rose to tend the widening pool of brown liquid on the table.

"My friends and I have been involved with this for only a short while," Leesa told her honestly, without elaborating on the ladies from PSI. "I myself trace family histories ... and I was at the farm yesterday, contrary to your husband's warning. I saw Will then ... for the second time."

Leaning forward, Leesa studied Annie a little harder, trying to read her face and, therefore, her response. There was much going on behind the eyes that did not reveal on the surface features. Annie continued mopping the spill in silence, then gathering both cups, she refilled them at the bench and came back to the table.

Putting Leesa's back before her, she again sat down, her fingers interlacing as she recomposed herself. Her head tipped back against the high-backed chair and she looked at Leesa, blankly at first, then another sigh emitted as if a giant weight had been lifted from her.

"At first, I thought you were here to cause more trouble," she said. "You see, I'm known around these parts as Mad Annie." She leant forward again. "You are the first person to ever admit to seeing him, you know – the first person to know who he was. Everyone else doesn't believe it. They think I'm crazy."

"What about your husband? It was he who told me you knew all about the happenings on *Whistling Gums*."

"Syd is a good man. And he knows alright. But he has to suffer the ridicule of others around here too, just because of what I know. They make jokes about us, and it makes him angry. So he says I shouldn't talk about it no more. He says if we stop talking about it, people will forget. But we can't forget. We've seen the turbulence that goes on in there. We know our stock won't go onto that place. And we've heard Him wailing in the night, like he did last night."

"Your husband told me you said He was grieving. And I know you were right! But what is He grieving over?"

"The past. All the things that pained him in his life, and that one day in particular. Some days when He's just tossing about, He isn't grieving …" Her sparse white eyebrows rose with the ensuing revelation. "Sometimes He is just angry … sometimes, like today, He is happy. I can read his moods by the treetops. Yesterday, He grieved … today He is content though He will grieve again soon."

Leesa sensed she knew Will well, and shuddered at the implication, and she prayed that Jessie was still alright. Reaching out, she put her hand on the old woman's. "Annie, I need to know as much as you can tell me. I need to know about Will, and about Sarah."

"Sarah died," came the droll response, her eyes gone starry with incoming memories. "... and He still grieves."

"Annie ... how do you know all this? And when did Sarah die? ... For that matter, how did she die?"

The woman's eyes refocused on Leesa and became clearer. "You don't know the full story?" She frowned deeply.

"I've managed to fathom Will came from America, and that he married her on the way over, yet there are no records other than her arrival. And I can find no record whatsoever of Jarvis, their son."

"It is obvious there is a lot you don't know then," she said cynically. "Though I don't know if I should be telling you the story. Some things are just better left in the past."

Leesa heart dropped to her stomach. *She's going to withhold the vital information I have come for!* "Annie, please! My friend's life may depend on what you know." Her hand involuntarily clamped over Annie's harder to impress the point. "You see, we believe that Will is going to harm her. He thinks Jessica is Sarah!"

"She has a child?" was Annie's worried response.

"Yes. A baby boy."

"Oh dear."

Her cup lifted again, slowly, and she sipped deliberately at its contents, her thoughts flowing in the gap of silence that resulted. Then she looked up and sighed. "You really do need my help, don't you?"

Leesa nodded firmly, noting at the same time the sudden beam of sunlight travelling around the room.

Annie noticed it too, and her eyes blinked quickly. Leesa felt her sudden agitation even though she tried to conceal it.

"It's Syd," she said tightly, following the sun's reflection from his windshield as it swept past her. "We'd better not talk of this no more. Not today!"

"But I need to know ... Annie, I need for you to tell me."

Rising from her seat, she picked up the cups and replaced them on the bench. "Syd won't like me talking about this. You can come again on Tuesday when he goes to market. I will have something then that might help you."

She hustled Leesa out to the verandah as her husband slammed the car door and crossed the veldt of weeds to the house. Passing him midway between the cars, Leesa smiled and said 'Good day', hoping her presence wouldn't get Annie into trouble. He looked not a mean man, and she prayed this impromptu delay would not bring a solution too late for Jessie.

The drive back to Sydney was long and tiring, and Leesa cursed that she would have to do it again in a few days' time. In the interim, she decided to visit Ryan. It was time he knew the story. It was time he knew just what was happening to his wife and the risks to her and his son.

It was Sunday afternoon before she finally made contact with him. He'd stayed on at Penrose for the company since Jessie offered him none of late, and it was a good time for his folks to catch up on their time with Jade. He also said he was pleased to see her, and asked if she'd been to see Jessie. Leesa nodded that she had, muttering that she'd been up to the farm. They went into the lounge, a place where Jade could play happily in his toy-filled corner while they talked.

Ryan looked drawn from the whole ordeal, the worry of his marital problems starting to take its toll. He reached over and laid his hand on Leesa's.

"She's found someone else, Lees. I've had my suspicions for a while now, and I know she's found someone else." He heaved a remorseful sigh and turned his beautiful blue eyes her way. "I don't suppose she's told you anything."

His question didn't surprise her. He knew Jessie told her everything. Yet for once, she knew the situation without Jessie having said one word. Her own regret was obvious in the look that went back to him.

"I do have something to tell you, Ryan, and it's something I don't know how you are going to take." Further than that, the words just wouldn't structure ... not to come out sounding sane anyway. *I mean, how do you tell a person that his wife is in love with a ghost?! A real live ghost?! And how can she be having an affair with something that doesn't exist?! It's just so far from reality Ryan is going to laugh himself silly - or else get angry with me for being funny under such serious circumstances.*

She had no idea which way it would go, but knew he wasn't going to just accept it. Ryan didn't believe in ghosts: she remembered that from the jokes at the farm.

He looked at her now with hard eyes, her long silence a verification to his intuition, his anger not needing her words to make it rise.

Leesa huffed a frustrated breath and glanced at the tray of bottles on the side cupboard. "Hell, I can't say this without a drink!"

His hand fell from hers as she rose and headed over to pour two glasses of whatever was in the bottles. *Ryan's certainly going to need one too.* They weren't big drinkers, he and Jess, so there wasn't a great selection, and plenty of whatever was available. Leesa chose the Scotch: it seemed so appropriate. A good stiff belt of that, she'd heard, could cure anything.

Ryan had turned on the chair to follow her movements. "What the hell is it, Leesa?! I know you well enough to know that something isn't right."

He stood, and Leesa drew a breath in readiness.

"She is having an affair, isn't she?!" he surmised quickly.

"Well ... yes ... maybe ... and no." Leesa recapped the bottle.

Ryan came forward, his eyes turning callous. "Either she is, or she isn't! Just what has she told you?"

"She hasn't told me anything! What I know is what I saw."

"Well, what is it then?! Don't tell me it's someone we know!"

"No! ... but you're just not going to believe ..."

"Good God! It's not another woman!" His face went pale.

"Ryan, don't be so bloody ridiculous!"

"Well, what else am I supposed to think? All this damn secrecy and stalling!!"

For a brief instant, Leesa wanted to laugh. It was just so comical that what he thought was the absolute horror of horrors was not a patch on what he was about to hear. "Jessie isn't really Jessie, for starters!" she told him, taking a fair gulp from the glass, and noting that he hadn't touched his. She took another shot of her own. "She's Sarah!" she said, "and if she is having an affair, it's as Sarah, not as Jessie!"

She coughed, the drink hitting hot in the back of her throat, the words not coming out as structured as she'd wished.

"Giving herself another name doesn't make it any more acceptable ..."

"No, you don't understand! Jessie isn't Jessie ... not at the farm anyway. She's Sarah!"

Ryan quickly knocked back half the contents of his own glass, his brow tight with annoyance at her incomprehensible information.

"Jessie's lover is a ghost!" she blurted out. "Only Jessie isn't Jessie."

Ryan wiped a hand firmly over his face and laughed, loudly, his Scotch spilling with his humour. "You look so serious, Lees."

The laughter died and he steadied his glass again. Leesa didn't feel the least bit jovial.

"You can laugh, Ryan Robinson," she challenged him sharply, tears threatening that he wasn't going to believe her, "but your wife is in love with a man from the past, and your son isn't your son either ..." She spied Jade playing in the corner. "He's that man's son!" The tightness growing in her throat was all the fears forming into words. It made it harder to get them out. She tried to wash that tension away with another large swallow from the glass.

"And if you're not very careful," she warned him further, "you'll lose them both!"

Ryan's face sobered with anger. "She'll never take my son from me!!" He shook his head decisively.

"No, of course she wouldn't deliberately take Jade from you ... but He will! He'll take them both, and you won't be able to stop Him!"

"But you said he's a ghost!" Ryan reiterated, casting her a derogatory glance.

"He is, but He's more than just a ghost! And he wants Jessie back."

Ryan leant down and put his glass on the low table, his sombre expression indicating things were passing through his mind. Straightening, he turned back to her.

"You really believe all this shit, don't you?!" he said sharply.

Leesa nodded slowly, her throat burning again. "I saw him, Ryan. I saw him and Jessie together." A breath heaved out at the memory. "He does mean to take them."

Ryan shook his head again as if shaking away the possibility that what Leesa said might be true. "Nah! I don't believe any of this! You're dreaming into your glass!!"

Admittedly, Leesa felt a little woozy, having almost sculled a full glass of Scotch, but Ryan knew her better than that! She was capable of more sense on twice the quantity. Leesa quickly emptied the contents and put the glass down.

"Don't try to tell me you haven't seen Jessie changing before your eyes! Or that Jade hasn't turned into the most perfect baby since she started going to the farm. I've seen both sides of Jessie. I've taken the time to notice she's changed, and she changes more each time she goes there. Haven't you seen it? She becomes more Sarah and less herself."

Then she grew angry with him. "But you're wallowing so deep in your own self-pity you haven't noticed anything, have you?! No ... you don't even know the half of it!!" Her blood boiled. "You're so antiquated in your ways, Ryan Robinson, and so pig-headed at times, I think you would probably sacrifice your wife and child just so you don't have to believe in something as far-out as ghosts and ghoulies."

Suddenly she felt giddy, nauseous. Maybe the drink had a quicker response than usual. Hell, she couldn't remember the last time she'd put something solid in her stomach. But it didn't matter, she had to convince Ryan. She had to have help from someone.

"You'd probably let her and Jade end up like her grandfather and John and ..." Her hand waved about to encompass whoever else Will may have taken, the action starting up a sway.

Ryan looked taken back. "What's John got to do with this?" he asked, coming forward.

A tear fell and rolled down Leesa's cheek as she stared back at him. "Jade is John ... or John is Jade, or whatever ..." Her hand waved the meaning about. "... both of them are Jarvis anyway."

Ryan's arm encircled her and drew her into him. Whether it was for his own comfort or to steady her stance mattered little. It was his words that were important. "You really do mean what you're saying, don't you?" he suddenly realised.

Leesa nodded, the motion of her head falling against his shoulder. "He'll kill them both." Her tears fell again. "He intends to kill them both."

Ryan's arms folded around her, tightened, the embrace more secure and she warmed as she usually did when he did that. She knew then that everything would be alright.

"Come on," he said, easing her away again and pushing her down onto the sofa to sit beside him. "You'd better tell me everything ... the whole story, starting with who Jarvis is."

Jessie arrived home several hours later and found them sitting in the kitchen drinking coffee. Giving Leesa a studious look, she went forward and picked up Jade, cuddled him affectionately and whispered words in his ear. Then she put him back down in the corner and went through to where they were sitting.

"Hi," she said, her tone rather cheery in light of the state Leesa had seen her in the day before.

"My God, what have you done to your head?!" Ryan gasped, reaching out to touch the padded plaster that now covered the wound Leesa had seen and told him about.

Jessie pulled back from his reach, her hand slowly going to touch the dressing on her forehead. "I can't remember," she said dazedly. "I must have hit it on something. It's nothing ... really."

"It doesn't look like nothing to me," Ryan challenged her. "Maybe you should go and see a doctor."

"It's fine, really," she impressed as she crossed to the bench to pour herself a coffee. Leesa noted she was a long time at the percolator and looked up as she moved back to stand against the sink. There was another date now on the calendar on the wall. The 18th of December, a Wednesday. She never went to the farm on a Wednesday, so Leesa wondered what the relevance of that day was. It was a date she was keen to check on, to see if it coincided with anything in the past. She noted, too, that Ryan seemed more tolerant now he knew the situation and allowed her to keep her distance.

He soon slipped out of the room and left the two of them alone. Their conversation was very amiable yet nothing personal – that annoying aura of being with a stranger back again.

For their own privacy, Leesa didn't stay for tea. Her duty was done, and it was up to Ryan now to be the watchdog while she delved further. That new date irritated her to the point where she couldn't wait to find its importance.

Cursing that she'd brought no paperwork with her, she rang Dot and set her to dig through the Kendall journals and search out what she was looking for. And then, she rested. At least Monday promised to be uneventful, and she knew Jessie wouldn't be going anywhere!

Mid-morning on the 16th of December, Dot got back to her. The date she'd given her held no significant point in the family history that she could find. But she was still checking. "I'd make sure Jessie doesn't go to the farm on that day just to be sure," she warned Leesa pointedly.

"It's okay," she sighed with the added knowledge. "Jessie won't be going anywhere for the time being. Ryan's fixed her car so it won't start. She's going to be staying home for quite a while, I'd say."

"Well just to be safe, you make sure she does!"

The only way Leesa could keep an eye on Jessie on Tuesday was from the road to Oberon as she headed for her scheduled meeting with Annie Carter, though she doubted now she could be of any great help. The date Jessie had scribbled on the calendar was a blatant indication of the day Will intended to take her, so anything Annie Carter had to say now would be secondary information. And in light of the situation, she felt rather safe seeing she would never make it to Amberlay without her car.

It was still reasonably early when she turned in at the Carter's farm and prepared to navigate the rugged terrain of their uninviting driveway. Her foot instantly went to the brake as a white utility drove across the top of the far slope and arced downward to the valley. Syd Carter obviously hadn't yet gone to market, and grimacing, she backed out again and continued on up the track. When several more miles brought the road to a very scrubby end, she realised he would have to go back past *Whistling Gums* to get to the main road. Backing up, she drove quietly down to Jessie's narrow track, took it to its end and turned around. Returning to a point where she could see all traffic passing while staying well concealed, she sat and waited. Syd Carter would have to go by sooner or later.

Hours passed before he did, her eyes just starting to close from the sheer ennui of wasted time. She checked her wristwatch. It was two o'clock; half the day had dwindled away in wait. Giving him several long minutes to be sure of his continued journey, she pulled out and took the road back to Annie's.

The lady seemed glad to see her, and must have seen her approach down the long, winding driveway for the kettle had boiled and a pot of tea was already brewed for her arrival.

"I don't get many visitors," she explained as Leesa settled on the same chair she'd used before. "It's nice to have someone to talk to, you know."

Leesa nodded, acknowledging her loneliness, yet wanting to get straight to her reason for being there – the brew, though, was definitely welcomed in view of the long, dry delay.

"I was wondering just how you came to be involved with the happenings at *Whistling Gums*," she said as she picked up her cup. It was something she'd been dwelling on for days ... Just where did Mad Annie fit in?

The lady smiled – a little grimly if Leesa detected it right – as the cup reached her lips. "Oh, our involvement goes way back," she answered before sipping. "My family has lived in this area since the pioneer days, just like the Raybournes next door. My great-great-great-grandmother, Alice Carpenter, settled here. Not on this very farm, but on one further over. She knew all the goings on around here, including what went on over there."

The smile touched her lips again and she blinked heavily. "My grandmother told me once that her great-grandma Alice had fallen deeply in love with William Sanderson. She said he was a fine figure of a man ... educated, and very handsome."

"She was right on that," Leesa smiled back. "I've seen him."

Again, Annie's eyes lit warmly. "He never had an easy time of it, you know. It seemed his life was destined to be plagued with disaster and trauma from the moment he arrived. Nothing ever went well for him. And then, when the other settlers eventually turned against him, he planted that full ring of trees, just so they could be left in peace. He wanted to protect what life he had left; he wanted to make sure no one could ever ruin things for him again."

"Why did the settlers turn against him?" Leesa frowned with the question.

"It was after his wife's death." Annie took a moment to study Leesa over the top of her cup. "She died under mysterious circumstances, you know. Everyone blamed Will for it. They said he'd shot her because of what was going on over there ... Then to make things worse, he went and planted a tree on the spot where he did it. They said that was to mark the spot, that he was slightly touched by the sun ... or the devil."

Leesa's rising eyebrow caused Annie's eyes to sparkle. She had Leesa enthralled.

"He wasn't ... though he did become quite irrational for many years after Sarah's death. On that same day of each year after it happened, he used to go crazy, used to rant that he couldn't get her blood off his hands."

She paused to gather her thoughts, or her strength, then went on. "My Grandma Alice was the only one he spoke to for many a long year, though that wasn't too often. He went reclusive from the world. Just hid inside that wide rim of trees and never came out."

"But you said he spoke ..."

"Yes, and he did. Grandma Alice was a fine fettle of a woman, I was told. When she realised her feelings for the gentleman farmer, and knowing he no longer had a woman to keep him company, she rode boldly across his land and made her affections known. He wasn't too impressed from what has been told, but he admired her spirit, and took her to his friendship. He had no want to marry again, so Grandma Alice eventually met and married my grandfather some years later, only to find heartache when Will too met and married a few years after that. I think she would have been good for him, for she had fine spirit and so did he."

Annie's wrinkled fingers interlaced as the story unfolded, her smile gone tight with rueful reminiscence. "Even after his marriage, he entrusted my gran with his best kept secrets, things he wanted no-one else to dwell on. And she kept them well."

"How do you know all this, Annie? Surely stories change as they are passed down from family to family."

Reaching across to a cupboard beside her, Annie opened its door. "I told you I would have something for you today," she reminded as she drew out a large thin cardboard package. "I guess it is time this is returned to the rightful family for I cannot see Syd keeping it safe as each member of my family has done in the past. I had no children, you see. No children who would carry on the keeping of the story, nor the secret this book contains."

Leesa's hands suddenly trembled, and a cold shiver tingled at her fingertips and worked its way up and over her shoulders. "It's the second journal?" Leesa breathed unbelievably.

"I don't know. It's just a diary of the events in Will Sanderson's life. In it he admits to his indiscretions, if that's what you'd choose to call them."

She handed the journal across the table, its packaging firmly intact and wrapped in gold ribbon. "I trust you will return this to its place when you get the chance?"

The parcel felt icy in her hand, so much so that Leesa wondered if the secrets she spoke of caused it to be so, or whether it was just her grasp on what might be the final solution. She wanted to take the book and run, wanted to find a place and immediately delve into its pages. But she couldn't do that when the old lady had been so generous. So she sat, had one more cup of tea with her, just to give her company, and succumbed to her wishes not to ask about the contents of the book. It was something Leesa would have to read, she said, by which she could form her own opinion of the man who had committed such sins to mankind as to stay and plague the living with his presence.

Annie saw her off, keeping the hungry hounds at bay as Leesa thanked her for the visit. She warned Leesa as she waved to watch the roads as there was a change in weather coming, and the changes in the mountains were sudden and severe.

The clouds overhead were indeed gathering quickly and Annie predicted rain would soon fall, hopefully not as Leesa drove through the mountain passes. Looking up for long minutes she nodded at her assessment. "Tonight or tomorrow," she further forecast.

Leesa's nerves itched with impatience as she drove back down that interminably long driveway a short time later, the parcel seeming to glow in the late afternoon dusk as she made her way back to the city, its existence continually drawing her attention from the road ahead. In sudden determination to stay on the bitumen, she tossed it over onto the back seat, and kept going. The sooner she reached the privacy of her room though, the better she would like it.

There was a note from the Manager tucked under her door when she arrived stating there had been a phone call in her absence. It read:

PICK UP D. MORRISON FROM THE AIRPORT. ASAP.

The time printed on it was 2.00 p.m. Leesa looked at her watch. *Hell, he's been waiting for hours.* It was now just on half past five. Wondering whether he was still there, she tossed the book she carried in her folded-arm embrace onto the bed, backed out of the room again and locked the door.

It was easy finding Dean at the Airport Terminal. Find the coffee shop and you find Dean Morrison. He looked peeved when he saw her, the quick glance at the clock on the wall behind him signifying his annoyance. She shrugged a simple apology yet felt no real guilt for he had given no warning of his intentions, and therefore had made no prior arrangements. His long wait was no one's fault but his own.

"You had me worried," he said, rising to his feet as she reached him. "I thought something must have happened to delay you this long."

"Well, yes ... and no," she answered shortly, remembering Syd Carter's late departure dragging into the day. "Everything is okay now though," she assured him.

His arm linking through hers, he directed her out towards the main arrival hall. "What are you doing down in Sydney anyway?" she asked him pertly.

"Dot said she was getting very strong vibes through. She was worried something was going to happen." He looked down at her in a concerned sort of way. "Is everything okay down here?"

Leesa heaved a sigh, shrugged and nodded, then told him briefly about her meeting with Annie Carter. Getting to the part about the book as they reached the car in the crowded parking area, Dean's eyebrow rose.

"The second journal ..."

Leesa nodded. "It has to be. I would be reading it now if it wasn't for your message."

"Never mind," he consoled. "We'll go somewhere and get a bite to eat first, then we can put our attentions to your precious book. Personally, I don't think I could concentrate on a thing until I put something into this belly."

Personally, she had to agree with him as her own stomach rumbled its protest. They dined in style at a small restaurant near the Quay, sitting in a secluded corner and chatting comfortably until Leesa forgot she was even in Sydney. It was late when they left, her constant yawning making Dean excuse his dull personality. Leesa simply laughed and explained her tiredness – the day, the long driving and the worry had all taken its toll. He smiled and offered to drive her back to the motel.

Either she was indeed that tired, or else rather naive for her advanced years, but it didn't occur to her until they parked outside her room that Dean would have to stay somewhere. But where?

She looked at him with dry suspicion, her expression apparently enough.

"I'll sleep in the car," he smiled wryly, edging himself down below the wheel and turning up the collar of his jacket.

If he'd intended to make her feel mean, it worked as she felt her back was pushed up against a wall. *He has come so far to help me, how can I just turn my back on him? How can I leave him out in the cold,* for the weather had indeed changed for the worst since darkness had prevailed. *Has he deliberately planned it this way?* She gave him a terse look, then told him to come inside. *We will work something out.*

The bed and the book stood out glaringly as they entered. Seeing Dean give the larger item a long perusal, Leesa went over to the tray on the sideboard cupboard and put the kettle on, the little sachets of coffee and sugar emptying into the cups being her escape from the obvious thoughts in her friend's head. She wondered if it came to the push, did she really want to become more than just friends with Dean. And had she done anything that would make him think there was more to it than just that?! *No, ... we're good friends. It can never be more than that until I stop comparing him to Ryan.*

On turning back with the steaming cups, she found Dean comfortably settled in the big armchair, the book open and under scrutiny.

"It's the second journal alright," he confirmed, reaching up to take his cup. He put the cup down on the small table beside him. There being no other place to sit, Leesa moved across to the bed and put her cup on the bed-stand. "The date he starts it from is October 15th, 1792. He's still on the ship; the seas are turbulent, many are ill from travel, others have been injured in the gales. He helps where he can."

Leesa settled back against the pillows which she'd banked up against the headboard.

"The prisoners are still held below deck; the holds are wet, miserable places but there is no hope of them coming on deck until the weather improves. He hears coughing through the night. Many of them are not well from the cold. Sarah too has a slight cold and spends much of her time in the cabin. It is fine because it keeps her from the eyes of other men. They watch her constantly."

Dean turned the page, read a few lines silently then went on. "He is concerned about the talk amongst the sailors. Some of them have been taking liberties with the women prisoners below deck. He has heard of a cabin which they have put aside for their pleasure. He must watch Sarah more closely: the men are hungry for women."

Another page flipped over. "The weather has improved, though still the prisoners are held below. The task of emptying water from the bowels of the ship has been left to them. Their clothing is sodden. The food they receive is poor, a vast difference from the migrating families who sleep above them. It is a cruel punishment regardless of their crime. The ocean voyage is a torture of its own."

Dean yawned, sipped his coffee, and turned another page. Leesa also yawned, widely, her eyelids feeling very heavy.

"It is ... 1st ... December... no sight of land ... not been for what seems ... Rarely ... see a bird ... ."

It was quite a long while before Leesa realised the voice had stopped, and her eyes opened slowly, the surroundings taking a longer while to sink in. It was extremely cold, which is what had woken her. Dean was still on the chair, the book open on his lap, his head fallen back against the side of the chair. He looked rather cute, the shaggy haircut making her wonder how his barber ever got employed, though it contributed to making him look even cuter, like a helpless little boy. The gold-rimmed glasses which made him look so academically sophisticated were now discarded to the table. Feeling very safe, she pulled a blanket from the bed and went forward.

The book closed, she laid it beside the cup and intellectual specs, draped the rug over him then dimmed the light. The clock on the wall said it was three a.m. The wind outside said it wasn't a very calm three a.m. Feeling chilled, she pulled back the covers, flipped off her shoes and snuggled down for a few decent hours of sleep. The book would have to wait till morning as she was far too tired to take up the challenge alone. The darkness, Dean's gentle breathing and the sound of the tossing wind outside let sleep come quickly. The bed seemed doubly warm.

It seemed no time at all had passed before she was jostled back to consciousness, the insistence of the voice doing little to undo her reluctance to be so.

"Leesa ... I think we have it! Come on, wake up!"

Grousing, she muttered a complaint. "Too tired ... It can wait."

"No. Come on!"

Leesa felt the edge of the bed dip as Dean's weight was added to that side.

"Come on, sleepy-head. Your coffee's going cold."

At that, Leesa stirred, but slowly, the awareness of Dean's position forcing more consciousness. "And listen to this ...," he said. "The female prisoners have been spending more time on deck now the weather is better. They receive little respect from any of the passengers, nor from the officers or crew. They are a surly lot, except maybe for one, a young fair-haired woman of slender build. She seems different from the rest, and I have seen her forgo on the promise of extra rations if she gives her pleasures to the men. Indeed, she showed her dignity by swiping the second mate with a stout rope. I fear she will reap much wrath before this journey's end."

Stirring further, Leesa sat up, and Dean edged further down the bed to give her room, his eyes not leaving the pages. "I can't see that being of help," she retorted, yawning.

"Sssh. I haven't got to it yet. He goes on in this next entry ... I have caught the young woman watching me from a distance. Her smile is warm, when not tested by persistence. Her golden hair attracts the men's interest and I do not blame them. She is more than fair to look at. Today I took her water. She called me 'Sailor'. ... Isn't that what he was known as?" Dean looked up with interest.

"Yes. But that was what he was, wasn't it?! You can't make any conclusions on that! And besides, it was Sarah who called him Sailor."

"Okay ... but keep listening. ... Today two barrels of ale were broken. The men had fine reverie while the seas becalmed us. Many fell in a stupor by evening, others lusted. My Sarah is safe below deck, her cabin well locked from their ungentlemanly ways. I keep a check on the female prisoners lest they suffer ill at the hands of the men. Most are willing for the benefits they receive. One in particular is not.'

"Next entry: I find much affection for the young lass with the golden hair and smile. Today I caught her watching me as I worked about the ship.'

Next entry, gleaning a lot out, but listen to this ..." Dean sounded excited. "Today I spoke with the young woman. She asked my name. I told her, yet still she calls me Sailor. I am anguished that my Sarah spends so little time above the decks, feel more than cautious that my feelings are swaying towards the woman. Why should she now wish to spend her time below in the holds. Why does the inside of that cabin there hold her interest so? I worry at the thoughts that stir.'

"Sounds like men back then had the same problem as men do now," he mused with a teasing glance her way.

Leesa cast a derisive glance back at him "Stop drifting," she quipped tautly. "Just stay on the subject."

"What's the matter?" he smirked. "Getting engrossed in this tawdry little sex thriller, are we?"

She tossed him a look of determination, yet couldn't help feeling a little vulnerable sitting there in bed with him so very close, and thanked God she had stayed fully clothed. "Go on."

Tipping his head in defeat, he flipped the page and read on. "I cannot stand the thought of the young woman being taken against her will. It is what I overheard in the galley. The men feel it is their right as free men – the prisoners have no right to choice. I find I leave Sarah more often now, spend much more time on duty where I can keep an eye on the holds.

"Next: the 26th of December. We spoke today. Her voice is mellow and warm. It lights a fire deep within. I sleep not now, wondering what is to become of this poor girl on our arrival.

"January 1st. Land was sighted. We have reached the coast of the new lands. The seas are rough and progress is slow. The men are making keen for the final days aboard. I was reprimanded for fighting with Jimmy Doogan. He is determined to take the lass against her will. I must save her from this unfortunate life she has been thrust into. I fear for her daily.

"Then this: With the days so soon to landing on the shore, I spoke to Sarah. She is sympathetic to my fears for the girl. She has agreed to help me smuggle her ashore. It is a great risk we both take. What our punishment if caught, I hate to think.

"And this ... 15th of January. We will be docked tomorrow. Sarah is willing to take the chance. My Sarah has put aside a dress for her so she might get to shore unnoticed. Then she will follow on the morrow."

Leesa scowled with confusion. "Read that again?"

Dean did, his own ears having detected a flaw in the account. "Sarah is willing to take the chance ..."

He repeated it a third time.

"He said that in the last entry too. Then 'My Sarah'..." Her brow knitted deeper. "I can't quite get what he means in that entry."

"I'll read on a bit further," Dean offered. "Sarah and I, with the help of Sarah's bonnet, made shore without detection. I stowed her in a small hut at the edge of the settlement. It is dangerous but we must remain in the settlement until Sarah can join us. Our only hope is that the shift will change tonight and Sarah's presence on board is not questioned. I return to the ship to duty."

Dean's smile was slow, his comprehension shining a light in his eye as much as Leesa envisaged her own gleaming.

"There were two Sarahs! My God, there were two Sarahs!"

"Your friend has to be this new one," Dean reflected. "She calls him Sailor."

Her throat tightening, Leesa nodded. "Now we just have to find a date that he intends to take her back."

"Well read on, McDuff."

Dean threw her a slight smile, and Leesa sensed he knew her deep despair. His eyes returned to the book. Scanning quickly, he picked out another entry.

"This one ... Feeling ill with worry, we made it to land, yet the first mate watches us suspiciously. I feel he does not believe her story. Nevertheless, we find the hut where Sarah is waiting. My Sarah questions my plans. What do I intend for the female prisoner? For the first time, I wonder too. My chest goes hollow at the thought of sending her to fend for herself. In truth, I do not wish her to be separated from me.

"Oh-oh!" Dean gave a suspicious look of his own. "Something's developing."

He flipped another few pages while Leesa rose to rebrew hot drinks. The weather outside the window was overcast, the air nippy against her skin. She noted Dean, too, looked a little hunched, yet his interest in the diary caused him not to make note of it.

"Here ... My Sarah has agreed that it is in our best interest to take the woman along. Our land has been granted, and we will need much help to get established. I have warned her of the isolation that others speak of. Sarah will be good company for her."

A number of pages were quickly screened before more information emerged. "They have made their way through the mountains, have found and staked their land. Will has pitched tents for them to sleep in but Sarah is ill-at-ease. She dislikes the hardship."

"Which one?" Leesa asked Dean.

"He doesn't say ... just Sarah."

"Next entry, dated several weeks later: I have found need to hide this journal for fear Sarah will find it and learn of my feelings towards her companion. I can now only write occasionally. Maybe when the cabin is completed, I will find a place closer where my entries will be more regular."

More pages turned. "The cabin is progressing well, a room on one end Sarah has promised for our bedroom. The other Sarah will sleep in the loft above. Still my Sarah is unhappy. She helps little. I am fearful of her thoughts and her manners towards her companion. I wonder if she has seen my feelings towards Sarah; they grow stronger every day – she works beside me in the field, helps fetch the timbers I need for the house. Toil has become enjoyable.

"Today I had to write for I have such pleasurable news. Today Sarah spoke of her love for me. My feelings are not one-sided. Still she calls me Sailor. It is a name I find pleasant from her. She even sings my shanties; they sound so much better in her voice."

Dean slowly calculated dates on his fingers. "Weeks pass: Sarah and I quarrelled today. She has found my journal, has read my accounts. She has ordered Sarah Aintree from the house. I will not let her go. What do I do? I love both women and cannot suffer to see them hurt. What have I done to them both?"

Leesa breathed a sigh of remorse for the situation the poor man had suffered. Two women, in love with both, and still trying to provide for them in a wild, cruel land. And she thought of Jessie, the second Sarah, for she always called him Sailor. He had saved her from an uncertain future, uncertain except that she had been destined to a life of servility.

"Here's something. Things are starting to sort themselves out. This entry is six months later: The second cabin is complete. It sits on the hill above, where Sarah can see the valley. She loves the top of the hill. It is doubly fine for I can see both cabins from most points of the land. I will now spend time with both my Sarahs, and though it was my dear wife's suggestion, I sense she is not happy with the solution. She has done this for my happiness, not hers. I am sorrowed that I cannot put her with child in return." Dean looked up over the top of his glasses and smiled, catching Leesa blush as his eyes roved over her face.

"Keep your mind on the facts," she reprimanded him severely, hoping he would get the hint. She just couldn't imagine the thought of her and Dean that close together. He just seemed too sedate, too academic, too ...

He pushed his glasses back up with a forefinger, then returned to the paper. "This is it, I think," he sounded somewhat excited by the words before him. "Listen ... My wife is much distressed. The news she has not taken well in light of the fact that she cannot conceive. She expresses her failure and the fear that I will turn all my attentions to Sarah. I assured her that the fact she is with child will make no difference to our situation. My love is equal. My greatest fear is that word has reached others of our arrangement. Men nearby who are without women are protesting. I can only hope that my obligation to my legal wife will hold stead there, as will the responsibility I must maintain to the child that is coming.

"To protect our life from this situation, I will plant a ring of trees around the boundary of our home location. Hopefully, this will let us live our lives in peace. I must still plant the seeds I carry from my homeland. There has been no word from my father since I left the Americas. Should he arrive, I wish his trees to be strong and thriving. The soil here is good for raising stock and plants and children.

"Sarah has laboured to put in a new vegetable patch, placing it on the slope between the two cottages as a peace offering to Sarah below. That woman peeves her so. She holds malice now that a child is to be born to the other. I know not how to remedy this unhealthy behaviour. She believes in my love no longer. I am wearying of the conflict.

"Next one, dated the 13th of December, 1794," Dean said without looking up. "It has been sometime since I have written. Much has happened in that time. My emotions are mixed with elation and grief. This very night at the height of the storm, the child arrived. My need to tend Sarah in her hour was overshadowed by my wife's insistence that I stay with her. Indeed, it was her night to be companied yet there is no midwife to deliver the child. I could not, for the safety of mother and child, leave them unattended.

"To those who might one day read this admission, I state that whatever is said of the events that occurred here this night, and whatever charges might be laid against me, what is written here is the whole truth. And still I grieve.

"This night, after I had left the lower cabin to tend the labouring Sarah, my wife lifted down my rifle from its niche upon the wall. She took herself down to the river and there, amongst the trees, ended her life. I knew not of her intentions and neither was aware of just how badly she grieved her barren state. She could not bear to see a child born to me through another.

"I have a son, a dear innocent son, and yet I cry."

Dean drew a deep breath and let it loudly out. Then drew another, recomposing whatever he was feeling. For a long while he just sat staring at the book, then he slowly turned another page. The grey gloom outside the window matched the air of discontent inside. Leesa realised what Annie had meant by 'his indiscretions', and making up her own mind.

"The 14th of December:" Dean went on, "Today, I buried Sarah. I buried her down where she chose to die, and planted an oak beside her, forever to her memory.

"Sarah grieves deeply for our loss. She will not move down to the lower cottage. I will eventually join her on the hill. But not yet."

The book was part-way through, the entries now screened before Dean spoke. Leesa rose and made another round of coffees, noting he had taken a moment to remove his glasses and pinch the bridge of his nose. *He couldn't have got much sleep in that chair,* she realised, then, looking at the clock, took shock at the time. It was noon. The whole morning had gone by in print.

Dean was back into reading. "We have made our home in the top house now. Jarvis – that's what they called the baby –" Dean clarified, "... has almost made his first year and is growing well; Sarah is a good mother. We are very happy. When a priest comes by this way, we will marry. There has been no rain for many months; the land is dry and yellow, but the creek still flows freely. If it ceases, we will be in dire need. I visit my wife sometimes when I fetch water from the creek. Sarah has not been able to go down there for a long time.

"Clouds are now on the horizon and we pray for rain."

The pages flipped over, two ... three entries lost before Dean picked up on other points.

"It is the saddest days of my life. I feel it is better over. I have lost my Sarah. The storm we prayed so strongly for has robbed me of her life. The lightning preceding the rain sparked the grass, the breeze fanned the fire towards the cabin while I was on the furthermost slopes. By the time I had made it down and up the other side, the cabin was in flames. Sarah and Jarvis were trapped inside. I tore open the door, could see them both huddled in the corner. Sarah thrust Jarvis at me. A beam had fallen and she screamed she could not walk. I rushed my son outside and turned back to get her, but the roof came down in a fiery blaze before I could get back in. My life is empty, my grief the most complete emotion I could ever feel. Jarvis pines as much as I do."

Dean turned his eyes to the next page. "My son is ill with chills ... This is a few days later," he explained, looking up briefly. "I have nursed him through the night but his breathing still labours. There are no doctors within reach and the neighbours suffer their own injury from the fires the storm winds spread."

The page turned. Dean heaved a sigh. "This is another few weeks on. "I buried my son today. The pneumonias took him from me while he slept. He never recovered from the sufferance the fire caused. I feel so helpless. So lost. I will plant a tree outside the cottage where lies his grave. And one for Sarah where she rests.

"I pray to God to give them back to me, or join me with them. I suffer my guilt for bringing them both to this place, for letting this come to pass. Nothing can ever come of such happiness that I had. My pain overrides me. I can only live for the day we are reunited.

"I can write no more. My life ended today."

The tightness in Leesa's throat made swallowing difficult, the tears hid just below the surface of her lids, burning to escape. They both sat in silence, their initial intention momentarily overridden. Dean closed the book and sat staring down at it.

"That's all he wrote," he said shortly.

Leesa nodded that she'd heard, the blackness outside reflecting the remorse she felt inside. She went to the window and looked out. The darkness was unusual for the early hour: it was only one o'clock.

"Life really stinks!"

"I know," Dean replied, his position on the side of the bed unchanged. "But his life didn't end there, remember."

He turned to look at her. "He remarried some years later."

"Only after his guilt had driven him crazy."

"Life drives everyone slightly crazy sooner or later," Dean

philosophised. "Think what all this is doing to your friend's husband!"

Leesa did think of Ryan. And yes, this whole damn affair had really destroyed everything. The perfect marriage – it had made them both very bitter. Her friendship with Jessie, which was on the borderline of ruin. And it wasn't fair. Ryan and she had done nothing to deserve it. Yet somehow, deep down, she felt a little happy for Jessie ... as Sarah ... and for Will Sanderson. They had finally found each other again.

Looking at Dean, she read the doubts that shadowed his face, too.

"Well, what do you want to do now?"

Leesa shrugged and sighed. "Ring Dot, I suppose." Her old escape from rational thinking. She went back to the bed and picked up the phone, dialled the PSI Department. It was quickly answered, Dot's voice coming clearly over the line.

"We found the book," she told her. "The second journal."

"Did Dean find you?" Dot disregarded her words.

"Yes. He's here now."

"Good. Have you read the book?"

"Yes. There were two Sarahs."

"Marion said last night she expected there might be. Both trees were the same, yet different."

The rest of the grim tale of Will Sanderson's past was related and Leesa heard Dot's groans and oh dears! She sounded as glum as they were at its final words. A long moment passed before she spoke again.

"We read through the third journal more thoroughly," she came back slowly. "The final entry there was written by his wife. Hang on a minute and I'll get it and read it to you."

The sound of paper flicking filled the receiver. "Have you seen Jessie since we last spoke," she asked, still turning the pages.

"Just briefly the other night. She seemed okay."

Dot sighed deeply from whatever it was she had to tell them. "Here it is ..." she said. "I quote: This is the last entry in the diary of William Kenton Fintish Sanderson. I scribe this on Will's behalf for he is no longer with us. The fires of the past two days have taken another in its wake, yet we are safe from harm. Caught unawares by the wind change, the blaze swept up the hill and attacked the house with sudden fury, the flames carried on the wind igniting the roof. In no time at all, the walls and ceilings were ablaze. I had been sleeping, the crackling flames waking me. Thick smoke filled the room, and I could barely see, let alone breathe.

"It was daytime yet darkness was all around. I had to find Jane and get her out, but I couldn't find the doorway. I was choking, slowly suffocating, the flames all around me when Will grabbed me from behind. He pulled me out, tossed me across the ground clear of the house, then dashed back inside to save our child. The flames rose up and covered the opening, blocking all ways out. I feared I had lost them both.

"Then the glass in the side window broke, shattered outward. I could see Will behind the smoke and flames. Jane was in his arms. He saw me and threw her through the gap, her fragile body landing in my arms. And then the wall collapsed. Will was still standing within its reach.

"The child coughed, then screamed with a recognition far beyond her tender years. The flames rose higher, flared more brightly and I swear I heard Will's voice above the trees behind us. He said, 'Sarah, I will find thee. We shall all be together as it was supposed to be.'

"Jane stopped screaming then. I feel she heard his voice too but can't be sure. Then it rained. Out of nowhere came the rain. It was a miracle.

"I buried my husband in the wilderness he had tried to conquer; he sleeps forever beneath the soil he loved so much.

"We will not rebuild the top cottage again. It seems ill-omened and it has caused Will much pain. Instead, we will move down to the old cabin on the slope below, to Sarah's home.

"I know the story of Will's two Sarahs, though he never knew I did. I knew too that he didn't really love me ... not like he did them. But I truly did love him. Will was a good man, whatever anyone might think. He would do no man harm. He gave his life for me and for Jane. I hope one day He will find his Sarah again.' Unquote."

Dot gave another sigh, and Leesa did likewise.

"That's why he never came back," she apprised. "He corrected his error in life by saving his wife and daughter where he had failed to save Sarah and Jarvis."

A cold chill crossed Leesa's soul, deeper than the weather could be blamed for. Deep within her head visions played a vivid picture as all the pieces came together. "When did Jane die?" she asked Dot sceptically.

The answer was a while coming.

"July 18, 1836."

"Have you got my other stuff there?"

"Yes."

"Give me John's date of death again."

Her hand over the mouthpiece, she looked to Dean. "What was the date of Sarah's death and Jarvis's?"

Papers flitted noisily in both ears as Leesa kept the phone pressed hard to her ear. Dot came back first.

"20th December, 1990."

Then Dean. "His wife Sarah died December 13, 1794; Sarah Aintree on December 18, a year later." He flipped more pages. "His son a month later: January 18th."

"What date did Will die?" she asked Dot drily.

More time was lost to silence before she came back.

"There was no date given in the journal here, but Marion just found something in the front of one of the Bibles. It's very smudged like the other pieces were, but she's having a go at deciphering the dates."

There was another pause, then her voice came again. "The ... 18th? ... It's the 18th ... of December, 1803."

"That's it!" Leesa stared blank-faced out the window, the dates correlating in her head. "That's got to be it! The 18th. Can't you see? Everything happened on the 18th. Sarah's death. Will's death. Jarvis died on the 18th a month later. And it's the date Jessie put up on the calendar! The 18th of December!"

"But ... that's today," Dot rasped. "Today is the 18th!"

"Oh God! Oh God no!!" Leesa's hand went to her mouth. *Today's the 18th, and I'm too late.* The wall clock pointed to two o'clock. She slumped onto the bed, beaten.

Taking the handpiece from her, Dean spoke briefly into it then hung up. He looked anxious. "Are you sure you're right?"

Leesa nodded. "It all fits. The dates all coincide along the years. They all died in summer, in fire, then the rain. Look outside, Dean. Look at the weather! Today is the 18th and a summer storm is about to break, and I'll bet you when it does, Jessie and Jade won't be around any longer."

Dean's face straightened. "Ring Jessie's husband ... make sure of your facts before we leave."

Leesa did as told, chilling when there was no answer at the other end. She tried the other number.

Ryan was at work. He didn't sound too impressed to hear that Jessie wasn't in; he said he would ring her himself and asked for the motel's number so he could get back to her. Ten minutes passed before the phone rang. Ten incredibly long minutes. Leesa snatched it up, her nerves as taut as a tight wire.

Ryan sounded distraught. Jessie had indeed gone from home. There being no answer, he had rung his neighbour to ask if

Jessie's car was in the driveway. It was, she had told him, but Jessie had gone out by other means. A taxi had collected them early that morning ... collected her and Jade. Leesa could understand why he was distraught, for she felt the same. Ryan said would meet her at the farm, the disconnecting buzzing instant across the line.

Grabbing her coat, she headed for the door, but Dean's hand on her arm pulled her back sharply.

"And where do you think you're going now?!"

"The farm! I can't just sit here and do nothing."

"Just hang on a minute," he said firmly. "Let's not all waste our time driving up." He picked up the phone again, quickly punched in a number. The guy he asked for was Bert, from whom he requested the loan of a plane. "Close friends in good places," he smiled tightly at the reply. "There'll be an old two-seater waiting for us at a private field not far from here. It'll cut the time down once we're in the air."

They were out the door in a moment and heading south to a private field Dean knew of, his driving both daring and aggressive to say the least as another side of Dean Morrison emerged.

Chapter Eighteen

True to his word, a small red and white plane was parked at the end of a narrow runway, at the end of which was a gap cut between the rows of yellowy-green poplars. Dean skidded the car to a stop and scrambled out, his friend turning to watch their hurried approach as he readied the last few details inside the cockpit. Leesa had never been airborne so fast, Dean skimming wordlessly through the usually lengthy pre-flight check. He said little until they were well above the trees and had banked to fly a line south. Then he smiled, the plane's engine having dulled to a constant low drone. The sky all around was dark with ominous black clouds. The white fluffy balls that usually made her so happy were as absent as that mood, and her hopes dampened dismally.

Why did I take so long to decipher the facts? Why did I dally over the information? Hell, I should have gone straight back to the motel from collecting Dean and read the damn book then. I am now fully responsible for the seriousness of the outcome, for Jessie could have been stopped from going to the farm in time. If only I had seen things with more clarity!

Dean's voice cut through her thoughts, his hands trying to hold the plane steady against the turbulence. The map he had been studying was now discarded to his lap. "I think I've found us a safe place to land," he rasped with effort, the plane taxing his strength. "There's a level strip of ground above *Whistling Gums*. I should be able to put it down there."

Diligently, he passed the map over, turned it and pointed to a spot. "There. There's the roadway up to Amberlay; there's Jessie's track. Here is where we might land. Do you know that area at all?"

Leesa shook her head. She'd never been off the farm in any direction other than the front gateway.

"We can make it down to the cottage by descending here where it's not too steep and climbing up again there." He pointed to a lot of squiggly brown lines which meant very little to her. "But we'll circle around first, just to have a quick look at the situation."

Nodding, Leesa definitely decided there was another side to Dean, a side she hadn't previously taken the time to notice.

Mountains loomed on either side of them, the wind lifting then suddenly dropping the aircraft with a stomach-churning thud as they reached the other side. There, Dean started a gradual descent, his eyes on the ground, then the trees, then the sky. They were almost directly above *Whistling Gums* when the first spear of lightning split the sky, its potency and closeness tipping the plane almost side-on. Leesa almost screamed; Dean swore.

Then another streak of silver snapped. It ran across the top of the hills to their right, the sliver not stabbing downward like normal lightning, but dividing, like a long thread unravelling; it ran parallel to the ground. Despite the danger, its beauty was awesome, and Leesa stared in wonder. Dean immediately righted the plane and pulled its nose up, quickly finding safety at a higher altitude. The craft shuddered against the wind's resistance as he did. He shouted above the noise, the violent shaking of his arms under the strain of the air pressure further confirming his words.

"The turbulence is unbelievable. We'd better not pass directly over the farm. I'd hate to think what the result might be."

Banking to the right, he looked down again to sight the ground. "There's the strip we can use. See it?"

Leesa nodded, then cringed as another streak of electric blue split the air beside them, its intensity whitening the cockpit for long seconds and jolting what nerves touched metal. It had been far too close for comfort. A thunderous boom pealed across the sky, rolling long and loud around them, hurting their ears.

"I'M PUTTING HER DOWN ..." Dean hollered again, "BEFORE WE GET PUT DOWN."

The plane's nose suddenly dipped groundward. Leesa could see all the land ahead yet her eyes centred on just one place. *Whistling Gums*. It was on her left, smoke rising from the ground slightly east of the cabin. The grass had ignited with the last lightning strike. The flames, as yet, were suppressed by overgrowth, the wafting smoke being the only evident sign that the sequence of events had started. As red and gold appeared through wisps of black, she shouted a warning to Dean.

The plane suddenly jolted as its wheels touched down on rugged earth, the rocky ground causing it to buck and shudder violently. Dean put all his effort into holding it steady as he tried to break its run towards the distant trees. They were approaching far too fast, rising far too quickly from the ground. They weren't going to make it, the yellow fields and gravel beneath them ending in the towering green border directly ahead. White trunks filled the windshield and Leesa drew breath and prepared for impact. She heard Dean curse through clenched teeth. Then the plane arced sharply, bumped, then took a smoother run along another line, a line running parallel to *Whistling Gum's* top boundary. And there it rolled to a slow halt.

Dean leaned across and pushed open her door. "Go get Jessie out of there!" he said. "I'll turn this baby around ready for a quick run out of here. Go on, I'll catch you up!"

Within seconds, Leesa was climbing through the decrepit fence that was *Whistling Gum's* limits. The trees inside the line tossed wildly in the blustering, angry wind. It moaned low and deep through the branches as she scuttled down the steep incline, her hands on the broad trunks to restrict her downward speed. The drop seemed endless, gravel and rocks following her down as treacherously soft landslides beneath her feet. Below, she could see the creek, gentle in its flowing, and narrow enough to cross. Without slowing down, she leapt from rock to rock, caring little when a step missed and soaked a shoe.

The incline on the other side was harder to bear. It rose steeply upward, the slippery, unforgiving ground taxing her energy, the hard, pushing strides more draining than the down trip. She was halfway to the top when a whoosh of air came thundering down the valley towards her, its sudden and vibrant appearance making her freeze instantly. Unwilling to look back and watch its pounding punishment as it hit against her back, she buried her head against the rocks and shuddered at its onslaught as Will vented his wrath at her intervention.

Or was it just the storm building further, its power increased by the unusual lay of the land? She never found out for it deviated up a shallow gully a short way over and blew quickly to the top of the rise.

Silently praying, Leesa pressed on, a quick glance back checking to see if Dean was following. If he was, she never saw him.

As the hill reached its height, the trees thinned, creating less and less handholds near the top. There, the gradient became less severe and she came to stand at the edge of pasture, the smell of smoke acrid in her nose as she looked around horrified.

Further down the valley the grass was well alight, rising tongues of red, gold and yellow licking the earth hungrily on its path towards the cabin. Smoke of grey and black clung low to the ground, wafting in rolling swirls across the untouched span between the fire and the wooden structure above her. Yet even so, flames already tapped about the walls of its base, wanting to get in. A sudden burst of adrenalin pushed Leesa stronger than ever before, and she sprinted towards the cabin, screaming.

Jessie has to be inside. She has to hear me!

The closer the cottage loomed, the higher the flames rose around it, vermilion and orange digits rapping at the walls, places blackening where they touched, where they still harboured their heat. The wind fanned another layer of embers towards her, the lay of the grass starting to flatten towards the cabin while a constant gust fuelled the fire's direction.

The cottage door was closed, tight, its resistance doing little to deter Leesa's need.

"JESSIE! JESSIE! LET ME IN!!" The words came with tears as she put her shoulder hard to the barrier. Pounding force against force, the resultant bruising became sadly noticeable, and she prayed for Dean to come. Or Ryan.

Oh, where the hell is Ryan?

There was nothing but silence from within, and nothing but smoke and crackling and her insistent pounding from without, the solidness of the door holding the line of difference. Another thrust of power rammed the wood, almost snapped her collarbone, but the pain was almost worth it for the barrier yielded and Leesa fell into the room. The heavy thud of her hitting the floor bruised more than just her shoulder.

Her head smashed against the floor with emphasis and for a long moment, blackness reigned in her eyes; then it faded as a haze of silver swirled across her mind, lingering for a second before her vision cleared again.

Forcing her eyes to focus, she looked up.

Jessie sat in the middle of the room, reading. Jade played quietly at her feet. Behind her, a red glow reflected and yellow fingers flickered and crackled under the eaves, reaching for the thatching on the inner ceiling. The plastic that had previously sealed the windows was molten, the quaint checked curtains redder in their flaming demise. The fire was insatiable. The crackling of flames became louder as the wind fed them generously. Tiny cinders drifted downward, filling the room with speckles of glittering red. Jessie looked up, her face briefly purporting surprise.

She smiled warmly, the old Jessie back. "What are you doing here?" she asked. "I didn't know you were still in Sydney." Her mood seemed genuine, her calmness daunting. "Can I make you a cup of tea?"

Leesa's violent entrance and heavy fall simply hadn't registered. She was in another dimension, a time not relevant to the dangers in this one.

"Jessie, we've got to get out of here! The house is on fire!!"

She might as well have stayed silent.

"Are you staying down long?" Jessie put the book down.

"JESSIE! COME ON!!" Leesa grabbed her arm and pulled her from the chair to a position where she could grab Jade. Her action only surprised Jessie further. "COME ON, JESS!!"

Wrenching her arm sharply away, Jessie looked annoyed. "What's the matter with you? Don't you want to stay and have a drink with Sailor? He'll be in shortly."

All Leesa could see was the red glitters increasing in their fall, the boards below their feet starting to speak as their age gave up to embers. The far side of the house was a high wall of flame, the roof overhead a pattern of glowing brilliance. The heat intensified, singeing, yet Jessie saw nothing.

Brushing away the falling chips of glowing straw drifting downward, Leesa made a grab for Jade. *Jessie will never let anything happen to the child,* she thought, ... yet already his playsuit was darkened across the shoulders by falling debris. He cooed as Leesa lifted him into her arms, then she quickly ducked back out the door, Jessie's angry voice shrieking behind her to bring him back. Leesa would never take him back! She would run as far as she could. Then Jessie would have to follow her. She would follow her off *Whistling Gums*, and therefore to safety.

Leesa didn't get very far at all, her run stopped short as she crashed into a solid wall that blocked her way just outside the door. It almost knocked her off her feet in its unexpected appearance. Gasping, she looked up, and saw Dean, his face full of concern, and maybe, if she'd taken the time to analyse it then, a little fear as his eyes quickly scanned the roof above them. His arms encircled her, the action steadying her and the child. He held them till their balance stabilised.

Smoke now billowed thickly skyward, meeting and mingling to obscure the black of the overhead sky, yet even so, a glow surrounded the cottage and haloed it with an aura of shining gold.

"Jessie's still inside," Leesa cried. "She doesn't understand."

His jaw tightening, Dean moved them aside then ducked and disappeared through the smoke-filled doorway. Black haze started a slow swirl around the wooden structure, the other walls burning profusely. She heard Jessie screaming, her words difficult to decipher above the snapping din of weakened timber; but she heard her. She cried for her child. She begged to be left alone.

Dean soon appeared back in the doorway, stooping again to stay below the portal flames, her friend locked hard against his chest in a tight embrace. She struggled violently and writhed in his arms, but Dean held on and shunted her forward into the smoke-hazed daylight, his skin looking red from the blistering heat. Leesa, too, backed away from its fiery intensity.

Dragging her with him, Dean retreated further from the raging flames.

On seeing his mother, Jade started to cry and Leesa soothed him gently, rocking him on her hip. They had saved them, saved them from the horrid fate the others had suffered. Leesa looked to Jessie; her face was streaked with tears, her blue eyes wide as she stared at the cabin she had made her home.

"What ... What's happening?" Her hand went to her mouth in shocked horror. "Oh, my God, what's ...."

Her words trailed off as sanity locked them in her throat. Bewildered, she looked at Leesa. "Jade! Oh, Jade!"

"He's fine. He's okay," Leesa assured her. "You're both going to be fine."

"Oh, my baby. My poor, poor baby," she swooned, reaching out to take him. Relieved, Leesa handed him over and stepped back a little further from the blazing walls. Jessie sighed her own relief as Jade turned and clung to her. Her head shook slowly as her eyes gazed blankly at the house-engulfing flames, then she looked to Leesa.

"What have you done?!" she hissed the accusation. "What the hell have you done!"

She charged forward, a sudden dash back towards the doorway and, with the child, ducked beneath those fire tendrils of death.

"JESSIE, NO!! OH, DEAR GOD, NO!!" Leesa screamed after her, too shocked to respond otherwise, her anguish doubling her over. They were both gone into the fire. Then Dean was gone too. The flames doubled in intensity, the pinnacle reaching high above the roof. And history repeated itself as walls started to topple, first from one side of the cottage, then the other. Smoke poured out of what was once the doorway, and with it came a bundle that was hurled her way. Leesa heard a voice, Dean's voice. He said, "Take him and run."

Barely catching Jade before he hit the ground, she scooped him up and tucked him hard against her. A sharp wind blew up from the valley, its aggression rising in its swift approach. Leesa thought she heard it more than felt it yet she obeyed Dean's command – she started to run, as fearful of the wind as she was of the racing fire streaking towards the trees to her right like a raging torrent. It was trying to cut off her line of flight.

For a long while Leesa was unsure of exactly where she was going; she was just running for their lives. It seemed longer still before she became aware that the track she was on led to the farm's front gate. She continued on determinably, for now she did know where she was going, and she knew that rusty gateway meant safety for her and for Jade. She couldn't be sure for Jessie or Dean, if there was indeed still an option for them.

The wind blew fiercely around her as she ran, its sudden onslaught almost knocking her down with its powerful blustering as it tried to hold her back. All the while behind her, the flames closed in, helped by steady gusts to speed its deathly reach. The dry grass was an easy avenue for its fiery feast. She reached the trees, the moaning overhead provoking a clammy sweat to match that caused by her exhaustion. She cursed her lack of fitness, cursed the burning pain in her side as a stitch bit harshly at her determination. The fire made the trees, needing no wind now to touch the underbrush with flame, its rapid demise already filled with roaring, snapping and whistling.

If I can only reach the gateway. Just the gateway. I have to reach the gateway. The words became a chant, rapping in rhythm with her footfalls. Breathing was limited as the air filled with stifling heat, filled with stuffy smoke. Her eyes burned then watered as her mouth dried, choking her. The fire soared above her, raced across the treetops, bombarding her with missiles of falling bark and flaming leaves which hissed on contact with the ground. The ground succumbed to its ardour and rustled with ignition, leaving everything around her red and glowing. Only a small patch of green directly ahead showed the way to go.

The fence line was that way, just a short way ahead, just a short way at the end of that tunnel of glorious green. She was going to make it. She was going to get Jade away from the fiery death for which he'd been fated. And if Jade could survive, then Jessie could too – if it wasn't already too late.

Tears replaced the sting of smoke, tears incited by fear and the thought of loss, and of Dean and how she had sadly misjudged him. How odd that she could think of such things in such dire moments; how strange that she should even think of Dean when Jessie was so much more important. Yet Dean's face shone through the pain of her loss. He had been so brilliant, so wonderfully controlling. She wished he was beside her then, to help further as her exhaustion became complete, as her feet started lagging under the weight of the child. She could feel herself starting to stumble.

But I'm nearly there. Just another few yards, another few steps.

Red flickered just behind the passage of green, taunting her. It flickered at the end of her tunnel of safety. Her feet stopped their mindless motion. Stopped all forward movement. The child in her arms abruptly ceased crying, the jolting of her run no longer shaking him violently. Leesa paled. And looked back to see how close the fire was behind her, how near the falling branches dropped to where she stood. She dared not move, for before her stood Will Sanderson. And she swallowed, thickly.

He stood rigidly in her path, his handsomeness startling, his austere look turning his grey eyes darker. He looked capable of malice, and she visibly shuddered.

"Leave the child and you may go," he said coolly, his voice absent of the anger apparent in his face. "He is mine. He belongs with me."

Locking Jade closer to her, Leesa shook her head. "NO!"

Will stepped closer, the power of his intentions evident, the malevolence in those steel-grey eyes potent. "I mean no harm to no man, but I will have what is mine."

The gap closed even further, the flames around them holding

place, burning only what was immediately beneath them. Leesa looked for an escape route, but there was none bar the way he blocked. She could see the gate behind him through the flames. And there was no way she could pass him. No way to make that short distance without evoking the wrath of the man and the fire.

"Don't harm Jade," she begged, her tears flowing as Will drew closer, his grey eyes focused on the child.

"Give me my son!" he demanded, his strong arms reaching out, reaching for Jade.

Leesa had no other option. She cried her despair to God, and whimpered at her loss. "No. Please, God, no! ..."

Will closed the gap to almost nothing, and Leesa turned about in a futile effort to keep something between him and Jade. Suddenly a flash of white brilliance struck downwards, hitting the earth ahead of her. A white, blinding knife of violence struck from the sky, its potency cracking sharply, ear-splittingly. Then another snap equal to its velocity echoed through the scrub, followed by the mightiest creak of splintering wood as a tall gum over the boundary line received the lightning spear's full brunt. The storm-shattered tree swayed for long moments, teetering on its base, then down it went, crashing through the belt of gums encircling *Whistling Gums*, forcing aside those trees that stood in its hell-bent path groundward.

Awed, Leesa watched motionless as it pounded against the earth slightly to her left. Flinching as pieces of breaking branches rebounded into the air in all directions, she ducked, and shielded Jade further with her back, shuddering that he and she would be taken from this world one way or another.

The tree beside her slowly settled, the shaking ground stilling. It lay idle a short way from where they stood, her eyes still wide at its angry descent. Its recumbent height spanned the gap to the boundary line in total, flattening the rusty wire fence in its terrible wake. Will Sanderson's scrutiny of the narrow trunk was brief. Then he turned back to his first priority, his eyes the coldest of greys as his arms stretched out again to take his child.

"GO! RUN! TAKE THE ROUTE I GAVE YOU. SAVE HIM!!"

Martha Kendall's voice rang out loud and clear. The reclining white trunk stretching like a road before her was now obvious in its purpose. Cold with sweat, Leesa shinnied up onto its top, awkwardly with the weight of Jade hampering the use of her arms; she scurried along the smooth white line, cautious not to lose her footing. Jade became heavier in her arms.

Ahead the flames rose suddenly higher, torched by a sharp and sudden gust of air. A channel of flames flared up on either side of the log.

"GO!" the voice insisted again as Leesa neared the outer limits. "SAVE THEM BOTH!!"

Leesa's goal was in sight, and she saw Will's look of anguish as she made it safely past him, his horror growing as she lessened the distance to the safe, outer world.

"MARTHA, NO!!" he bellowed, his hands going to his head in despair. "MARTHA, NO!! I NEED THEM! I NEED THEM!"

Then she heard him cry, a pitiful wail of grieving for all he had lost. And she remembered how much He had suffered, and wondered as she stood there poised above the crumpled fence-line if she really had the right to ruin all he had strived for.

He turned, his eyes almost pleading. And she remembered Jessie and how she loved this man, and just how alive she had become in his presence. She had never seen her happier, not even with Ryan. And she wondered if she could really do it. She had the power, but did she have the right!

And who was to say Jessie belonged in this world at all? Maybe she really did belong back in the past ... Leesa steeled at the thought. *What am I to do? What choice is the right one to make?*

She looked at Jade perched on her hip, that tiny young life that had been so tortured in its first year, that little boy who had become so happy in the past months; she knew it was because he had found his place – as Jessie had. Then she looked to Will Sanderson, the man who had suffered so much when all he wanted was to regain those he loved the most.

"I need them both," his voice pleaded softly, morosely.

Leesa's eyes misted at his situation. He had been a good man, so the tale told; maybe he deserved to be let go in peace.

She fought with decisions, torn between reality and the past. *How can I decide, and whose lives will be affected by that decision?*

She looked at Will, deeply sympathetic as his eyes implored her to understand. He needed no words. Even the flames around her had calmed as a persuader. And she hovered between the worlds of life and death, dithering with the uncertainties.

To her right, a movement caught her eye and she glanced quickly down at the gravel track. A car was hurtling up through the bushes, racing in a cloud of dust to the area where they parked the cars. It was a station wagon: *Ryan's car*. Glancing back to Will, she saw he had closed the gap between them, his hands reaching up, almost grasping Jade's leg.

Hearing again Mrs Castle's words to 'save their souls', she leapt from the log and landed on her feet just outside the fence line, the weight of the baby toppling her onto her knees. Rolling onto her shoulders to protect the child in her arms, she groaned at the painful tearing of her skin, at the jolting of hitting the ground so hard. And she heard him groan deeply at his loss.

Then he wailed, "NO! GIVE BACK MY CHILD. SARAH! I NEED MY SARAH. JARVIS ... I NEED MY SON. I NEED ..."

There was no Will in the flesh any more, just a rising opaque mist, flaming gum trees, and swirling smoke, then a howling wind whipping the naked trees with a vengeance. Then there was

Ryan, his hands lifting her to her feet, his arms folding around her and gathering his son into the security of his embrace. The look on his face as he stared out above their heads was one of horror, the sight of the fire contained within the boundary telling a macabre tale. His strength engulfed Leesa further as her tears loosed, unrestricted at his question.

"Where's Jessie? ... Leesa, where the hell is Jessie!!"

The words barely escaped the hard, choking lump in her throat. "In there. They're both in there."

Ryan's eyes fell on the raging fires within the now jumbled fence line; his face blank at the horror growing within. She saw his jaw tighten, his grief building at his loss. But she was grieving too. He had lost Jessie. But she had lost Jessie and Dean. She sank to the ground and wept bitterly; the tears uncontrollable. And she cried for Will Sanderson and his loss. Nobody had won.

For a long hour, they just sat there, shedding their remorse, watching the fires burn themselves out till all that was left was black ground and smoking sticks where once had been a perfect stand of ghostly trunks and shimmering green leaves, and a pleasant narrow path down into the valley. An acrid layer of smouldering haze now hung low to the ground, further marring their view. Ahead of her, Ryan stood looking down that defunct trail, muttering, his hands gripped tightly to the warm, mangled red metal of the gate.

"Oh God, Jessie. My poor, poor Jessie."

"Ryan! Ryan!!"

The words fell on her ears as much as they did his. Even Jade blinked and looked up from where he had been sitting in a sort of limbo, unaffected by his unlearned years.

"Ryan!"

Climbing to her feet, Leesa saw movement through the darkness, a subtle rolling of the eerie greyness as a figure emerged from the destruction.

"Jessie!"

Ryan was over the gate and running towards her and she soon reached the haven of his arms. Rising to her feet, Leesa peered deeper into the gloom as another shadow loomed, taller and more solid.

"Dean!" she shouted, her joy. "Oh, thank God. Dean!" The tears of the past six weeks erupted again, and she let them flow. Never before had her emotions been so erratic. She cried with joy and pain. She stood and cried, but she didn't climb back over that gate as Ryan had just done. That had been very dangerous.

As the others neared the metal barrier, Ryan and Jessie locked arm in arm, Dean walking a little further behind them, a sudden gush of wind came thundering up the valley. Leesa's eyes widened as she heard it, as smoke rolled grey and swirling towards her, pushed forcefully by the turbulence of His power. Grabbing Jade into her arms, she tried to shout a warning, but it was too late. The violence of his wrath was directly behind them.

High overhead a voice hissed harshly. "Get out!! YOU MUST NEVER COME HERE!!"

Gathering Jessie into his arms, Ryan hoisted her up and dropped her over the gate, the wild wind whipping the saplings directly behind him as he did. Then he too landed, yet more heavily, beside her. Dean was last to scramble over, the crop of shaggy brown hair blown stingingly forward to his face as he released his hold on the metal. He shot a look back over his shoulder as he found his feet, and toppled solidly against Ryan.

Then the rain began, at first just a few spots, then a slow misting drizzle that fell and touched the ground, making it hiss as it snuffed out the last of the flames.

Ryan's arm went around Jessie's waist as she told how Dean had saved her, how they had escaped the cottage and taken shelter down in the creek below, dousing themselves with water when the wind tossed flames their way. By the sheer mercy of God, they had survived.

"And by your mother's determination," Leesa reminded her. Now maybe, she would see her mother in a different light. Now maybe she would understand why she had been forbidden.

They were almost at the station wagon, Dean at her side as they guided Jessie forward. The sooner she was away from this place, the better.

There was no reluctance in her step as they approached the car. In fact, she seemed perfectly normal, the Jessie Leesa used to know. The spell He had held her under was gone, gone as completely as the beautiful trees rimming the property. No more would He hamper their lives with his insistence. He'd had his chance ... And he had lost.

As Jessie reached the car and opened the door, Jade deposited in first to shield him from the increasing weather. A gentle breeze fanned around the hilltop, played around the fence line, and then drifted upward to the top of the trees again. It circled there, building to a whistling wind, stirring greater and toying with the hissing skeletal trees that were now charred and dingy. Leesa heard a gentle sound emit from the leafless tips.

Jessie turned, her eyes dreamy blue, for the word He had sighed was 'Sarah'.

Chapter Nineteen

"Jess? ... Honey? ... Are you okay?"

Jessie's attention swung back from the storm outside the window. "Mmm. I'm fine," she said, turning around and resting a hand on Ryan's shoulder, then she sighed, deeply. He returned her a tight smile.

They were back in Mosman, sitting in Jessie's lounge room. Leesa was across the room waiting for a call to connect to Brisbane. Dean made the foursome complete, having taxied back from returning the plane he had borrowed. He sat beside Leesa at the dining table, as keen for the call to connect as she was. That John Denver look was now drawn, blackened streaks of ash marring the cuteness of his face. Leesa noted, too, the large red marks on his hands and arms; they looked as sore as the burns covering her skin. She looked to Jade, and smiled, if not somewhat grimly. He had escaped the wrath of the flames. Apart from a little singeing of his beautiful golden hair, he had come out of it almost unscathed. They had all been very lucky.

Another flash of lightning fingered white streaks through the blackening sky outside and took Jessie's attention again. If not for it being so deadly, it could be so beautiful to watch. But that was usually the way it was: the most wondrous things in life could be so lethal.

Ryan's hand found Jessie's, which was now on the back of the lounge, and covered it. She looked down again, and heaved another sigh, her exhaustion fully apparent. But there was something else in the look, something Leesa couldn't quite decipher, and she didn't have time to pursue the thought as the continuous bring-bringing was replaced by a voice.

Dot was happy to hear they were safe, and her comments were pleasing. She couldn't wait to relay the news to Ryan and Jessie and, therefore, didn't dally with idle conversation. Dot and she would get together as soon as she returned to Brisbane.

Crossing back across the L-shaped room to the lounge, Leesa noticed Jessie cast a quick glance at Jade before looking up again. She drew another deep breath, preparing herself for the outcome of the phone call; it was then Leesa tagged the look in her eyes with a name. Uncertainty. Jessie looked confused, her blue eyes showing none of the glint of life she would have expected having just survived against such terrible odds. But then, how alive would one look after such a terrifying experience? It would take a long time before any of them would truly return to normal.

Dean moved beside Leesa as she settled onto the long lounge opposite Ryan. Jessie kept her place at the window, unwilling, it seemed, to take her eyes off the cruel sky overhead. Leesa looked to Ryan who seemed oblivious to what she was seeing, oblivious to the tell-tale sighs from Jessie. Another escaped her without him looking up, and Leesa wondered if, indeed, they were the perfect match. *Maybe, just maybe, Ryan and I would have been the better choice of couple.* She looked back to Jessie, her back to the room, and chastised herself for the thought. It would do no good to anyone! Ryan and Jessie would sort out any problems they had once all this was over. *And me? ...*

I will go back to Brisbane, and maybe be with Dean – maybe not. I'll put myself back to work and sort out my own feelings.

She caught the look in Ryan's eyes as he glanced from Jessie, then back to her, his blue eyes also holding uncertainties. She wondered if the Three-men-in-tub would survive. *Could it survive if Dean makes a fourth? Would we sink, or would we just get a bigger boat?* She quelled a sigh of her own and structured how to best relay the important points of the phone call. Ryan leant forward and interlaced his fingers in front of him.

"Dot seems to think it's over," she said, nodding. "The fire destroyed everything on the farm: the cottage, the oaks, the majority of the boundary trees. Dean flew a couple of wide circles around to see the extent of the damage before he left."

Beside her, Dean nodded, and she felt a hollowness develop inside as Jessie kept watching the rain on the window pane. The trickles were constant and wide, the ground outside getting a thorough soaking, and she knew from this time on, summer storms would bring new meaning. She watched as Jessie's spread fingers relished the rain on the glass.

"And what do you think?" Ryan asked, another quick glance checking Jessie's reaction.

"I don't really know," Leesa shrugged. "It's not my field of study ... but if what Dot says is true, then maybe she is right and it is over. You see, it all stems on the spirit's origin ..."

Jessie turned back from the window, briefly checked Jade who was still sitting quietly in the corner, then she let her gaze rove around the group. Her eyes held an interest now that had not been there before.

"... According to Dot," Leesa went on, her eyes fixed on Ryan, "the spirits have a place they stay very close to. Sarah Thornton's spirit – Will's wife – remained all the time at the oak tree down in the grove. It's possible she wouldn't pass over because Will was so remorsed by her death; she was waiting for him. The oak tree there is gone now, so she would be too."

"What about the one by the house?" Ryan asked.

Bending down, Jessie picked up Jade, shuffled him around to her hip and clutched him possessively. Her eyes returned immediately to Leesa.

"That tree was Jarvis," she told them, her soft focus attending Jessie. "But it is of no real concern because the spirit never remained there after death anyway. He was too young to know real attachment, so he passed on and on, and kept returning."

She looked to Jade, who was now yawning and looking rather tired from his ordeal. Leesa was glad he was still too young to ever remember much about what had happened in this lifetime. Jessie muttered something about putting him to bed before he fell asleep on the floor, and moved towards the stairs, Ryan's gaze following her, though Leesa sensed his attention was more on his son, and wondered how he would cope with the fact that his son, deep down inside, was somebody else's. His face revealed nothing, just remained intently concerned.

"... so did Sarah, the other oak tree on the hill," Leesa went on.

Dean's blue eyes also followed Jessie's path, his action causing Ryan to pull his gaze away and reach for the cup of coffee that had been sitting empty on the low table. He examined it studiously as Jessie stopped at the base of the steps.

"What about Him?" Ryan put down the empty cup again, his eyes going hard with the question.

"Well ..." – Leesa shot a glance to Jessie who was still standing there, her back to them, waiting – "... going again on what Dot said, the diffusion of spirits would have been all round. The oaks are gone, which is what Will stayed to protect. The gums are gone ..."

"And thank God for that!" Ryan cut in. "I hated those goddamned trees!"

"... and seeing they were His protection, probably even his origin, then I guess it is safe to say that Will Sanderson is also gone, or at least so restricted in his realm that He has been made powerless by the destruction."

Without a word, Jessie started walking again, her slow, heavy-footed climb up the staircase rhythmically patterned.

"The trees aided him in life," Leesa continued a little softer as Jessie disappeared onto the upper floor, "and they aided him in death. And if the trees are no more, then maybe He is too!"

Ryan let out a loud sigh and said, "Thank God."

Silently, they all did.

Epilogue

12th January, 1992

Leesa returned to Sydney several weeks later, her thesis completed and delivered, its reception gaining good response from faculty heads. As far as the PSI Department's delivery had gone, much of what had been proved as fact had been thoroughly pooh-poohed. They were a group included but obviously never to be accepted regardless of their findings. Supernatural occurrences were nothing but a fabricated fantasy of warped minds: they could never infiltrate the real world of sane-minded Academics.

The ladies from the bowels of the basement seemed to have expected the derogatory remarks and had warned Leesa to keep fairly low-key on just where some of her research had come from. 'For the sake of Genealogy's reputation,' Dot had said. And she'd smiled. And so, Leesa had been commended on the depth of her research, and assured of another year's tutoring.

The semester ended, and Leesa returned to be with her friends. Dean had promised to join her later when he finalised his moral obligations to his students. Leesa had heard it was to be a great end-of-year party to honour the Professor.

It was a beautiful sunny day in Sydney. Mild blue skies and gentle breezes wafting from the coast made the day even more perfect now that the weight of worry had finally lifted from her mind. Leesa's high mood, however, did little to dispel Ryan's annoyed look when he opened the front door. Obviously, something wasn't right on Raglan Street.

Things indeed were not right, he confided to her quickly. Things hadn't been right ever since the fire.

Immediately, Leesa looked for Jessie, for Jade.

"Oh, they're here alright," Ryan assured her. "It's just that we don't seem to connect anymore. Jessie seems a stranger, and Jade can't seem to stand me touching him."

Leesa studied the look on Ryan's face. He had changed.

"And how do you treat them?" she asked him bluntly. "Can you honestly say you see them the same?"

He paused a moment, battling with his answer. "Well, no, I guess I don't. But who could blame me, Leesa? Hell, it's not like she's only ever been mine before. She's had this other bloke. And her son isn't really my creation, he's somebody else's! How the hell do you expect me to feel? Sure, I treat them differently!"

"And how does Jessie feel?"

"How should I know? She spends all her time sitting out in the garden. We hardly even speak let alone stay in the same room together."

Her anger started to rise. Not towards Ryan. And not towards Jessie. Just simply for the fact that when they should have been drawn even closer, the whole horrid episode had hammered a deep wedge between them. She sighed deeply and let out a loud breath.

"Put yourself in Jessie's place, Ryan. Don't you think she'd be distant? First, you accuse her of having an affair, and now you're treating her as though she's soiled goods. It happened over a hundred years ago, for Christ's sake."

Ryan's jaw set, and his gaze lowered to the floor.

"Maybe I don't blame Jessie. Maybe the person who needs the help is you, not her!"

She left him standing, his eyes downcast and went in search of Jessie. She found her in the garden, sitting on the child's swing, gently rocking with Jade on her lap. She looked serene in light of the conflict within the house. Leesa felt sure she could talk her into seeing how Ryan felt. She was, after all, a very forgiving person. And she loved Ryan so. She always had. It was so, so cruel that lives of the past could destroy the ones of the present.

Well, it's over now. Both just have to let it go and put it from their minds, pretend it never existed. Jessie will see reason. She was always realistic.

Leesa watched her friend snuggle her chin into the side of Jade's neck, the child chuckling gleefully as a light breeze fanned her long hair across his cheek. Jessie looked up at the tall trees surrounding the yard next door and looked at the gentle sway of their tips in the caressing zephyr overhead. She smiled as the gusts started a slow, dancing circle in the trees in other neighbouring yards.

Then Leesa froze mid-step as Jessie rose to meet its slow descent, as it blew around her skirts and ruffled her hair, as Jade chuckled deep in his belly. She called Jessie's name as the wind called her … 'Sarah.'

Other Adult books by Helen Iles:

Adult/Young Adult Fiction:

- Bitter Comes the Storm
- Fire in the Heartland (YA)
- The Horse Keepers
- Dark Secrets
- Indelible Ink - Award-winning stories, poetry, and articles

Poetry

- Writing Poetry – Simplified (Textbook)
- Of Bushmen and Brumbies

About the Author

Helen Iles (born 1954) is a Western Australian author who writes in various genres, including crime, romance, suspense, and mystery. While primarily a novelist, she also writes poetry, short stories, and non-fiction, saying 'the genre is whatever falls out of my pen.' Many of her short stories have been published in collections or won awards.

In 2015, Helen was awarded life membership to The Society of Women Writers WA for her service to The Society. She is an Editor and Creative Writing coach and guides new authors through to their goal of being published. All this while penning her next novel or illustrating the next children's book.